SUSPICION

ROBERT McCRUM

SUSPICION

W. W. NORTON & COMPANY
New York • London

Library of Congress Cataloging-in-Publication Data
McCrum, Robert.
        Suspicion / Robert McCrum. — 1st American ed.
        p.   cm.
        ISBN 0-393-04046-1
    I.   Title.
PR6063.A1658S87   1997
823' .914—dc21   96-39013 CIP

W.W. Norton & Company, Inc., 500 Fifth Avenue, New York, NY 10110
http://www.wwnorton.com
W.W. Norton & Company Ltd., 10 Coptic Street, London WC1A 1PU

1 2 3 4 5 6 7 8 9 0

For my Grandparents

In Memoriam

SPRING

[1]

I have always lived alone. My parents are dead and I have lost touch with their families. I've attended the weddings of friends, but have never found myself in a honeymoon suite shaking rice or confetti out of my hair. I prefer the bachelor state. In the obituary columns of the newspapers, a special interest of mine, such a phrase is often code for homosexuality, but in my case that would be a misreading. As my neighbours will confirm, I have, from time to time, shared my house, its sloping garden and unrestricted view of the Downs, with a girlfriend, but it's an experiment that never seems to work out. I am no stranger to the suitcase open on the bed, or the box of books in the hall. Sometimes I feel as though there's an invisible wall around me that no one can penetrate.

In this personal summary I have omitted to mention my brother, Raymond, who doesn't, I'm afraid, feature much in my life any more. Perhaps I should not become too emotional about this. The fact of the matter is that, from the start, Raymond was always something of an absentee. Fifteen years my senior, he was born into another generation and became a committed communist at an early age. He had moved abroad when I was still a teenager. During my adult life, we had met but rarely, and he had, I believe, become a stranger even to our parents.

So it was something of a shock when one day, just before last Christmas, I received in place of a dutiful greetings card, a long, almost confidential letter in which Raymond announced he was planning to retire to

3

England with his wife and children. Would I find him a place to live?

I discovered, as I read on, that his intention was to come and settle in my neighbourhood. Indeed, if this did not seem excessively 'ruhrselig', a word my dictionary defined as 'sentimental', and depending on what was available, etc., he would be only too delighted to join me in the village itself. From the way he expressed it, the move seemed to be a matter of some significance.

I read the letter three times. I think I was pleased and more than a trifle apprehensive. Raymond's handwriting – large and untidy with maverick punctuation – and his epistolary style, occasional foreign words, dashingly underlined, and out-of-date English slang – was a more than rough guide to his personality. We were always very different. Raymond had conducted his life in public; I would always prefer to do things discreetly, behind closed doors. Raymond had caused quite a bit of trouble over the years and I knew enough about myself to understand that my own life had been a response to his, a tactful reply to an outrageous statement.

He was, he told me, coming home to live out his days among his nearest and dearest, a typical exaggeration. 'I have every intention', he wrote, in a phrase that struck a chord with me, 'of dying in the bosom of la famiglia. I hope', he went on, 'that it will be some time before I'm pushing up the daisies.'

I remember smiling at this. In my line of work, I hear such euphemisms almost every day. I am a lawyer who chooses to live in the provinces where I serve my county, part-time, as the district coroner. So I meet Death on a regular basis and have become quite expert in the clues to his whereabouts: the widow's desolation, the suicide's despair, and the peculiar anguish of the cot-death parent. I am well versed in the bizarre secrets of the hearse. So often have I travelled the grim byways of mortality that there was a time when, against my will, I used to think of myself as the angel of death. I confess that in those days this made me feel powerful in the community. Now, I find myself disturbed by the proximity of oblivion.

Still, for relaxation at the end of the day, I will occasionally take a stroll in the cemetery of our Norman church and remind myself of the lives that have paraded before me on the bench. A passer-by might conjecture a solitary act of piety, but that is not my mood. I'll be rehearsing the particulars of each case, like a cricket enthusiast with a Wisden. I am forty-four now, and I have reached the age when a man begins to fear for his memory and his future.

Living alone, I am accustomed to talking to myself. I am not gregarious. Occasionally, I will joke, a shade defensively, that I may be the most interesting person I know. Unlike my brother, who accumulated friends in the way some tourists collect souvenirs, I keep my counsel and confine myself to a small circle of acquaintances, drawn from the vicinity.

At the office, where I draft contracts, issue writs, execute wills, prepare deeds, and monitor the due process of law in my clients' best interests, I believe I am known for my reserve and my sense of propriety. A lawyer's work is confidential, of course, but I feel it does not do for a senior partner to become too close to the staff. Many years ago I had an affair with one of the secretaries. In retrospect, this was an egregious miscalculation.

Now and then, for recreation, I will go to town, see a show, have dinner in Covent Garden, and catch the late train home. I suspect that those who recall my time at university are not surprised to find me mouldering in the shires, as my brother would put it. I do not repine. Village life suits me. I have my place here and I know, more or less, where I stand.

I suppose I have always been out of step with my contemporaries, preferring a *modus operandi* of my own devising. I attribute this to having had elderly parents and a brother who was already a rebellious teenager the day I was born. Mine was the upbringing of an only child, and I always had the pallor of the solitary. I told myself stories and lived with imaginary friends. I was the kind of adolescent who lolls on his bed reading the novels of Hardy and Dostoevsky. In those days I wore National Health glasses. Later, thanks to feminine influence, I graduated to contact lenses.

When I went up to Oxford, an awkward scholar, I left a world as regular as a ticking clock and found myself in the company of noisy high-achievers. I met young men and women who would go on demonstrations, produce agitprop dramas and stage outrageous parties. It was the Sixties. The atmosphere was sleepless and effete. I was fascinated yet alarmed, content to be a spectator. My brother had already exposed me to my fair share of extremism, and I was in no hurry to follow his example. I sat in the library with my historical periodicals, swotted for a First, and paid occasional visits to chapel to hear the *Messiah* or the *Missa Solemnis*.

I had to earn a living. I studied Law, passed my exams with ease, and elected to settle down here on the south coast, not twenty miles from my parents' home. In 1979 I voted, with some misgivings, for the Conservatives, though I did not admit it at the time. Like many of my generation, I had vague literary ambitions which I fulfilled by writing bad plays in the style of Harold Pinter. I am, in summary, square and straight and terribly English: Julian Whyte, son of Anthony Whyte, grandson of George Whyte, the undertaker. Death, you might say, runs in the family.

My brother, Raymond, who always had a taste for the flamboyant, styled himself Rowley-Whyte, a peculiar affectation for a communist. The fraudulent nature of his opinions had always been a bone of contention between us. At our last meeting, in 1982, we had argued throughout a week-end. Much of my annoyance came from my conviction that he was on my side, although he would not admit it. I was in my thirties then, no doubt prickly with the remnants of a larger ambition. We had ranged freely across time and space, hurling names and statistics at each other – Lenin, Trotsky, the kulaks, the six million Jews, Katyn, 1956, and so on. Each of us was argumentative in his own way: I, restrained and clinical; he, passionate and engaged. Not for the first time, it struck me then that I was more naturally the rigorous idealist while he was essentially a woolly-minded small-c conservative.

On that occasion, our ideological differences were sharpened by personal animus. Raymond had come over for Mother's funeral. His behaviour had caused her much sadness and disappointment, but he had always been her favourite. His grief was charged with resentment. He did not say it, but he blamed me for failing to get him to her bedside before she passed away. Estranged and miserable, we had buried her alongside Father, as she had wished, and hurried home through the rain to hand out tea, sherry and ham sandwiches to a party of almost total strangers.

Once we were alone with the debris of the wake,

Raymond could control himself no longer, and the tide of sorrow and misunderstanding tossed us this way and that, without restriction. I thought Raymond touchy, arrogant and predictable. He, I have no doubt, found me cold, bitter and aloof. As I look back, I can see that his defensiveness was understandable. Perhaps he sensed that the great commitment he had made was about to be exposed. The Soviet Union was a military dinosaur on the point of extinction. Within five years, all he had worked for would be destroyed. The Berlin Wall would be demolished by that extraordinary upheaval, swept aside in one long night of popular tumult.

When Raymond's letter arrived on the eve of 1991, all that was behind us. Assuming his communication could be taken at face value, he was coming home, contrite and defeated, looking for a reconciliation with me and with his country. I could not suppress a feeling of satisfaction. Mine would be the triumph of David over Goliath, the stay-at-home stripling over the worldly colossus.

He was returning to a country in shock. Mrs Thatcher had just been deposed. The heady, triumphant order of the Eighties was being dismantled. We were all having to make adjustments. This was not the England of his youth. On the edge of retirement, he was going to have to make a final accommodation in a life notable, as I saw it, for its absence of accommodation.

Since our last encounter, he told me that he'd married for the third time. This union had been blessed with two offspring, a boy and a girl. 'Strong Whyte seed', was his boisterous comment. The letter was accompanied by a single Kodachrome print, two blobby children standing in anoraks beside a snowman. Their mother was standing next to them in a red coat but Raymond, in his clumsy way, had cut her off chest-high. All I had to go on was his description – 'gorgeous blonde' – which was, I assumed, another of his exaggerations.

My life, in contrast, had been circumscribed by the constraints of village society. My Internationale was 'Jerusalem', my soviet was the parish council, my flag was the Union Jack, my army was the Territorials, and my cadres were to be found at the coffee morning and the whist drive. The grapevine to which we all subscribed was the gossip of the village shop and our local pub, The Royal Oak. It was this network that sprang into action for me once I had digested the news in my brother's letter.

Raymond said he wanted a house to buy or to rent, and he named a monthly figure that was within his modest means. He had some savings, he told me, and the promise of translation work. There was also his share of Mother's will, a few thousand pounds from the sale of her bungalow. So, one morning before Christmas, I spoke to Derek, our newsagent, as he delivered my weekly copies of the *Spectator* and *The Economist*. Derek spoke to Leslie, who runs the village shop, who chewed the whole matter over with Shirley, his sister, who spoke to Barbara, our publican's formidable wife, rumoured among her regulars to be a judo black belt.

Within a matter of hours, Raymond's homecoming was the talk of Mansfield. I have a position of some consequence in our little community, and I'm rather proud of the fact that, collectively, we rose to the occasion, despite the distractions of Christmas shopping and seasonal partygoing. My brother's letter arrived just before the winter solstice. By late January of the new year, a suitable property had been found, the paperwork completed by my office in record time, and the house made ready for Raymond's appearance in all our lives.

9

It so happened that he and his family were due to arrive in the village on 14 February, St Valentine's Day.

[2]

There are three ways to the village of Mansfield – the sharp descent from the Downs, the circuitous B road that leads from Brighton and the South Coast, and the short cut from the motorway – and, for me, each route suggests a different mood. Climb up the hill, catching the wind in your face, and you are scanning the horizon for the Armada, defending our island shore. Take the bend past The Royal Oak, bumping over potholes and dodging stray pheasants, and you have an agreeable ride in the shires. Nip up the High Street, past the museum, press the accelerator on the long, straight stretch to the by-pass, and you're off to the bright lights of the city. I think it was appropriate that Raymond made his entrance into our community from the London direction. After all the build-up, he was certainly an out-of-town attraction.

The house I'd found for him and his family was not, strictly speaking, part of the village. A gloomy Edwardian villa, Jericho Lodge was nearly a mile beyond the Mansfield sign, standing apart, on the edge of fields. For as long as most of us could remember, the place had belonged to Enid Nicholson, a reclusive spinster who had died at a great age, leaving the property to her nephew, a Mr Barker, a taciturn fellow from the Inland Revenue who showed little interest in his aunt's bequest. It was rumoured that he intended to postpone the sale of the house until the recession lifted. For the moment, it stood empty, forlorn and unloved.

When I approached Barker to rent the place for my brother I was confident of success. The truth was that he owed me a favour. He was well aware that in my capacity as coroner, I knew his aunt's overdose had almost certainly not been accidental. Barker was a stickler for propriety who had been anxious to have her buried without scandal. When the case had come before me, I'd agreed that there was enough uncertainty about the old lady's final hours to allow me to record an open verdict.

As I expected, Barker responded well to my proposition. He was glad to have a small but reliable rental and, drawing on my professional expertise, I offered a contract that did not impair the sale of the freehold once the market improved. With four bedrooms and a ragged garden for the children, Jericho Lodge was ideal. Raymond could feel part of the community, but he would also have a certain privacy, the quality of English life he claimed to crave. After so many years of indifference and even hostility, I must confess that I, too, wanted a decent space between us. It was going to be strange to share village life with my family.

On the morning of Valentine's Day, I got up early and went for a walk through the village, savouring the hour of solitude. I encounter accident and catastrophe every day, but I am not used to change in my personal life. I needed an opportunity for final reflection. I have often speculated about the workings of Fate, but rather in the abstract. I was apprehensive, but mildly optimistic. My brother was coming home on my terms. Mansfield was my territory. I would not be overwhelmed.

A milk float was purring down the twisting High Street. A flock of seagulls was pecking for worms by the village pond. Charles Stephenson, our local doctor, was exercising his collie. Our morning voices rang out in the mysterious dawn stillness. Despite the cold, there was a hint of spring. Somewhere, the ice floes were melting.

Raymond and his family arrived in Mansfield towards the end of morning, rather later than expected. They had driven from Germany in an overloaded Volkswagen van, sailing overnight from Hamburg to Harwich, a wretched crossing, my brother reported. Wan with sea-sickness and the strangeness of a new place, they had lost their way in London and found the route south with some difficulty. I had taken the day off to see them into their new home. When I heard the van pull up outside I was sitting in my front room, with house-warming presents next to me on the sofa, reading the *Daily Telegraph*. I hurried out to welcome them.

Raymond, of course, was a not-unfamiliar shambling, ebullient figure, all arms and legs and excited cries of greeting, an animated scarecrow. I find that as people age they become more like themselves. His hair, now white, was wilder than ever. Looking him over, I saw that his corduroy trousers were baggier, his jacket more patched and shapeless, and his lopsided smile more vulnerable, a question as much as a statement. He had been in a car crash many years before, somewhere in Africa, and his face was rather like a squashed fruit. Now, as I shook him by the hand, I could not decide if his stove-in look was the expression of victim or fighter. I sensed he was putting on a show that he did not entirely believe in any more. It was only later that I discovered the full extent of the facade he was presenting that day.

I took all this in at a glance, instinctively, for my mind was otherwise engaged. It was his wife, Kristina, who commanded my attention. Raymond had sent me that ludicrous photograph of his family in the snow. I had wondered about the features that might accompany the anonymous figure in the red coat. Kristina was tall and blonde with melancholy grey eyes and high Slavic cheekbones. She was wearing a white wool beret, and even the children dragging on her arms could not dispel the indefinable grace of her bearing, the aristocratic coolness. I knew from my brother's letter that she was a former government interpreter, but not much more. I suppose I had prepared myself for a proletarian hausfrau, not a woman of poise, even glamour. Kristina was perhaps not unaware of the impression she was making. When I looked into her face I found she was smiling, as if at a private joke.

I think I smiled back, but I do not remember for sure. There was something about her presence that flustered me and made me feel more than usually awkward. My confidence with women depends on the certainty of their affections and approval which, unlike my brother, is something I have never taken for granted. What I do recall is the formality of the occasion as my brother made the introductions. We shook hands, and when I said Hello to the children, Olga and Sasha, both mute from the journey, they turned away in shyness and spoke urgently to their mother in German, a language I did not then understand at all.

We came inside. My brother was talking non-stop, as he always did, complaining about the traffic and the road-works *en route*. Looking back, I see that he was as nervous of the step he was taking as I. To break the ice, I handed out my presents. The children tore into the wrappings with excitement. Olga, who was seven, had a T-shirt; Sasha, not yet six, a model train. I handed my brother and his wife glasses of champagne.

'Welcome home,' I said.

'Cheers,' said Raymond.

I saw Kristina's look of isolation. 'Welcome to England,' I said.

'Thank you, Julian,' she replied, with disconcerting hauteur.

I had prepared a light lunch, some hot soup and baked potatoes. I guessed they would soon want to see their new home.

Raymond had picked up my newspaper and was browsing through the pages of valentines. 'Listen to this. "Chimps. Sorry about the Hoover incident. Bumweed." What dark drama of domestic misunderstanding, or sexual experiment perhaps, do those lines conceal? Or this. "E17. 8.21 a.m. BR commuter. I reciprocate your gorgeous smile. RSVP. Mr Big." No homeward journey for him, eh? And look at these names. Snuggles, Chuff-chuff, Crystal Tits, Mollusc Mate, Wigglely Wildebeest.' He put the paper aside. 'I suppose I mustn't laugh. My first wife called me Pudding.'

'Your first wife called you many things,' said Kristina, with sudden and unexpected merriment, 'and so did your second.' Her English was quite good, with a strong but not unpleasing accent.

'Thank God I'm on good terms with my third,' said Raymond lightly.

'So you always claim,' said Kristina. 'I don't know why anyone should believe you.'

I watched my brother put his arm around his wife, and thought how oddly matched they were.

'Isn't she wonderful?' he said, appealing to me with that question-mark smile.

I smiled back. I was at a loss to know what to say.

'Valentine's Day is typically English,' I said hastily.

14

'We prefer to express our deepest emotions incognito. We're happy to say we're in love, but we don't like the risks involved.'

'We?' said Kristina, giving her enquiry a teasing inflection. 'Aren't you talking about yourself, Julian?'

She had been quiet since coming in to the house, fussing over the children and letting Raymond patter on, but now, perhaps under the influence of the champagne, she was beginning to relax. The directness of her remark was arresting, and my awkwardness returned. I found myself blushing.

'What's Ray been telling you about me?'

My brother was buried in the newspaper, chuckling over the sentimentalities. 'What's that?'

Kristina ignored him and smiled at me. 'I think you have had many valentines, Julian.'

I shook my head. 'My Valentine Days are over.'

She laughed. 'Who knows?'

'Listen to this,' said Raymond. ' "Darling PC. I adore your network. Let me access your software. Hard disk." Some frustrated boss wanting to roger his secretary, I suppose.'

'Please don't forget, darling,' said Kristina, 'about the intimacy you and I once upon a time have had in the office.'

There was a silence. Then Kristina gave a little laugh, as if she was enjoying the discomfort she was causing.

I watched my ebullient brother put the paper aside, quite crushed. In the past, Raymond had boasted to me of his winning ways with women, and I had imagined a mixture of comic gallantry, fellow-travelling libertinism, and old-fashioned sex appeal, but here suddenly he seemed unmanned. I, who knew so little of this relation-

15

ship, was fascinated to see Kristina's hold over him. I have a lawyer's interest in marriage, and my curiosity was aroused.

To smooth a difficult moment, I made conversation about the trivial nature of the British press. As if I had switched on a current, my brother's instinctive radicalism returned and he began to denounce the broadsheets of capitalism. Kristina's reaction said that she had heard this a hundred times before.

We finished lunch and then, light-headed with the wine, I said it was about time we set off for Jericho Lodge before darkness fell.

They piled into the van and I went with them, sandwiched between my brother and his wife.

The mist had cleared and the village was a tourist postcard in the pale sun. I pointed out the landmarks – the low, drab school, the flinty parish church, the corner shop, the newsagent, Mrs Williams' shoebox post office, the museum and the Tudor beams of The Royal Oak. Further on, we passed the gates of the Grange, the discreetly wooded mansion that has belonged to the Platts for the last four hundred years. I made a witty aside about bourgeois reactionary elements oppressing the rural proletariat, but Raymond was not paying attention. He was pointing out the sights of the country to Olga and Sasha, speaking German with an indifference to accent that even I could detect.

'This is not like Karl Marx Allee,' said Kristina.

I had never visited my brother's tiny East Berlin apartment, but I had a mental picture of a high-rise building inhabited by people in drab grey suits, worker ants in the workers' state.

'It will be good for the nippers to grow up in the country,' said Raymond.

16

Olga – blonde like her mother – with two front teeth missing, said something I could not understand.

Raymond translated. 'They want a dog,' he said.

'I want to have a dog also,' said Kristina. 'When I was a little girl I had a – how do you say? – a dackel called Anka.'

'We have a kennels,' I said. 'The owner's a friend of mine. I'm sure we can get you a puppy.'

'You do!' She turned and spoke to the children in German with a happy, sentimental expression I came to recognise as typical whenever animals were mentioned.

We reached the house. There were dark cypresses lining the short drive. I was reminded of the approach to an Italian cemetery. I had already resolved not to elaborate on the circumstances of the old lady's death. There was time enough for Raymond to catch up with village gossip.

The children shrieked with excitement as the van bumped over the potholes in the driveway. A black cat slipped across our path like a shadow. Kristina crossed herself.

'Lucky,' said Raymond, slapping the wheel.

'I thought communists had no time for superstition.'

'This communist does,' he replied. 'What is there to believe in any more?'

He switched off the engine and we climbed out. Raymond and Kristina stood and looked about them, arm in arm, an odd couple. The children were already racing across the lawn towards the shrubbery, a dark cluster of rhododendrons, exploring. In the porch, the rusty horse-shoe over the front door was tilted sideways, but I made no comment. I handed Raymond the key.

'When exactly did the old lady die?' he asked, as he turned the lock.

'Ages ago. Over a year.' I heard Kristina calling to the children behind us. 'It's been empty ever since.' I put my hand on his sleeve. 'I'm sure you'll like it, Raymond,' I said, looking at Kristina again. 'You'll make it your own in no time.'

'It will be nice to go upstairs at the end of the day,' he said, pushing the door open.

I had arranged for contract cleaners to give the place a good scrub. The air was heavy with disinfectant, and the silence was deathly. We walked from room to room with echoing feet. Spring light fell in bars across the floor. I wondered how my brother felt, but he was speaking to Kristina in German and I was lost. I walked ahead, slightly put out.

As we went up the panelled oak staircase to the bedrooms he caught up with me. 'Sorry, old boy.' He was out of breath. 'We were just saying what a good job you had done.' He took my arm, jerking his head in Kristina's direction. 'What do you think?'

'She's quite something,' I said.

'She's changed my life,' he said. 'I'm not exaggerating.'

'I can imagine it,' I said.

'Sometimes I can't believe my own luck.'

In the chilly master-bedroom, the view from the window was, I have to admit, a rival to my own cottage vista. A picture of the south of England on a spring afternoon. A view unchanged for centuries. A satisfying display of pastoral stability. A scene that, as light and seasons changed, would bring to mind Turner or Samuel Palmer.

'I like this.'

Kristina was standing between me and my brother, looking out, and the scent of her body was in the air.

'It's called the Garden of England,' I said.

'It looks to me,' said Raymond, 'as though the jolly old garden of England has become a bit of a concrete jungle these days.'

'You can still get away,' I replied, 'if you know where to go.'

'I think you like to get away,' said Kristina, stepping out into the corridor.

Downstairs again, Raymond shook me warmly by the hand. 'Thank you, frater,' he said, dropping into prep school slang. 'I think we're going to be very happy here.'

Outside, from the garden, there was a commotion. The children came running in. Olga's cheeks were rosy-red with the cold. Sasha was crying. My first thought was that they had been fighting.

Kristina caught them in her arms, soothing and motherly. 'Kleine Maus, na komm kleine Maus . . .'

I watched her instinctive tenderness and her absorption in their needs. Her hair was falling across her face and I experienced a sudden and disturbing thrust of desire.

My brother was explaining that the children had found a dead animal in the garden. We went outside to investigate. In the middle of the lawn were the putrefying remains of a rabbit. Raymond made a joke about funeral rites. We found a rusty spade by the side of the house and Raymond lifted the maggoty remains into the bushes.

'Nature red in tooth and claw,' he said. 'It will be good for die Kleinen to see what country life is really like.' He shovelled some earth with quick, decisive movements and then straightened up, flushed from the effort. 'No future for me in the old family business now,

I fear.' He was breathing hard. 'Tell me, is there much shooting done round here?'

'Pheasant and duck,' I replied. 'And clay pigeons and rabbits of course.'

'I remember Father used to shoot,' he said.

'I still have his gun.'

'Use it much?'

'Never.' I smiled. 'You know me, Ray, not really a man of violence.'

[3]

I could not, at first, put it into words, but I soon came to recognise that my brother's return had upset a routine, a habit of living. In the old days I could control my schedule, my comings and goings. Now I was no longer in charge. The telephone had always rung at odd times, the harbinger of another violent or unexplained death, but its summonses were like the occasional comma in a stream-of-consciousness novel. Suddenly the pages of my life were scattered with question marks. Did I want to join a family picnic? Would I play French cricket on the green? Could I recommend a good dentist? What should Raymond do about his life insurance policy?

I would hear the parp-parp of his car horn, look out of my window and see my brother's amiable, squashed face coming down the path towards me, another burning question on his lips. He carried his old briefcase like a dog with a bone. I have rarely known anyone so determined to make friends and find acceptance, and these enquiries became the rickety bridge of re-acquaintance between us. In the maze of contemporary English custom I was his trusted guide. I was happy to acquiesce. Hardly a day passed without my stopping at The Lodge to see how he and Kristina were getting on.

I was intrigued by their relationship, and she could see that. I found myself growing bolder in her presence, speaking of things I had rarely spoken of before. When I questioned Kristina about her first meetings with my brother and heard her frank, amusing replies I was quite charmed, as I suppose she intended.

'I was younger then, and I was impressed. Raymond seemed so eloquent and he always made me laugh,' she said, one day. 'He is not like you. He likes an audience. He must always perform. Yes, I was delighted by his humour and by . . .' she hesitated, 'by his absurdity.'

'But not any more?' I heard my rash enquiry with dismay and begged her to forgive me. 'That's my job,' I said. 'I ask too many questions.'

'I understand,' she said. 'You are looking for veri-fication.'

My liking for my brother's wife was unsettling but not so surprising. We were, I discovered, rather closer in age, less than ten years apart. I was taken by her sympathy and her wisdom. I liked her merry laugh, and the flirtatious way she tipped her head when she spoke, and the sound of her accent when she used words such as 'verification' and 'absurdity'. Her confidence and ease were infectious. I found myself opening up to her, against my nature, just as I could feel myself becoming friends with my brother. It was hard, in those bright spring days, to keep my feelings in hibernation.

I was not alone. Everyone in the village wanted to gossip about Kristina. I was like a public benefactor. People I barely knew would compliment me on my brother and his wife as though I was personally respon-sible. There were so many delightful mysteries to explore.

Where was she from? Was it true that her father had been a Red Army general? The enigma that seemed to lurk behind those heavy Slavic eyes was dramatised by Kristina's sense of herself. 'I am special,' she would say with that Mona Lisa smile, but she was not entirely joking. Neither she nor Raymond had any money to speak of, but she was always immaculately turned out and contrived to seem exotic in our narrow, red-brick High Street. When she was growing up, she had learnt to improvise. She could design her own clothes and knew how to combine what she had made with a simple elegance that was all her own. I am, no doubt, an unreliable witness, but in those early days she seemed to have both grace and style.

This was in attractive but perplexing contrast to her shambolic husband. There were unanswered questions buzzing around him, too. Was Raymond still a communist? Had he ever worked for the government? Was he, or had he ever been – as some people were suggesting – a spy? Usually, I assumed an ignorance that was perfectly genuine. There was so much that was still hidden from me. I see now that my reticence or my discretion, call it what you will, only served to stir the rumours.

I don't want to give the wrong impression. At this stage, no one felt any hostility towards Raymond. He was, in a way I never anticipated, the prodigal son. His capitulation to the forces of patriotism, Mammon and nostalgia reinforced my neighbours' unshakable British sense of superiority, and allayed their fears about a Europe ruled by the deutschmark. 'Raymond Rowley-Whyte says that the new Germany's not all it's cracked up to be,' they would report in a tone of anxious self-congratulation. They would never say this in my hearing, but I think they found my brother refreshingly open.

22

Perhaps because I know the hidden shames of the neighbourhood, their attitude towards me has always been reserved, an expression of respect. I am Death's secretary and they keep their distance, until circumstances force them within my sphere of influence.

Raymond and Kristina were inundated with invitations – to bring-and-buy sales, sherry parties, and garden club meetings. That light but steely filament of social obligation closed round them like a snare. Soon they were worrying about how they should respond. Raymond told me this as we sat in The Royal Oak enjoying a pint together one evening.

'Why not have a house-warming party?' I suggested. The locals were longing to have a good snoop round old Miss Nicholson's house. I saw Raymond worrying about the expense. 'I'll go halves with you.'

I suspected he was hoping for such an offer. He seemed relieved. 'You're a good sport, Julian.'

I took out my pocket diary. Perhaps because we were both in a convivial mood, we settled on 1 April, All Fool's Day. This, as it happened, was also Easter Monday, a national holiday, and an excellent choice. By then, as my brother observed, his goods and chattels would have arrived from Germany. As we left the pub, united in the fraternity of two pints and the satisfaction of well-laid plans, Raymond suddenly took me by the arm. 'I'm enjoying this,' he said. 'It's fun.'

'No regrets?'

He stood still. A cuckoo sounded in the tree close by. 'Frankly, it's a tremendous relief to be home.'

Months later, he reminded me of this moment – the quiet of evening, the bird, and the smell of the earth in spring – and remarked that, for him, this had been a turning point.

As the day of the party approached, The Lodge began to take on the appearance of a family home. A Mr Mover van brought several crates of books and assorted possessions from Berlin. After the men had gone, my brother stood in the front room and observed that a life of travel and ideology amounted to a pile of shabby paperbacks. Kristina dismissed his melancholy. She had inherited several sticks of furniture, pieces of quality, from her mother. These would soon add up to an air of homeliness and comfort. She seemed determined to make the best of their new circumstances. I pitched in, reminding Raymond that there was also his share of our parents' effects.

I was particularly conscious of the grandfather clock. This tall black sentinel had once stood in the hallway of our house in Tunbridge Wells, marking the hours with a musical chime. Over the years, its mechanism had become clogged with dust and its music had failed. Mother had wanted the clock to go to Raymond, but when I opened her will and discovered her wishes he was in Germany, and I did not imagine he would want me to ship it out to his tiny apartment. So I had kept it, wrapped in sacking, in the garage. I decided I would take it over one evening, as a surprise. When I showed him the clock case, lying in the back of my estate car, he laughed. 'For a moment, I thought you were showing me my coffin.' He ran his fingers over the dark wood. 'I remember this so well. When I was a boy I was terrified by this clock.'

'Mother wanted you to have it.'

'Did she now?' When he tried to lift the case the wires and weights jangled discordantly. 'It needs a complete overhaul.' He chuckled. 'Like me. We can ask those sale room wallahs what they advise.'

We had arranged to spend the next afternoon at a country auction. As we scrutinised the items for sale – tables, odd chairs, mirrors, leaking sofas, Turkish carpets, knick-knacks – I discovered that Kristina had quite an eye for antiques. I watched her playing with a Regency fan, fluttering to herself in front of a mirror.

'The perfect courtesan,' I joked.

She turned away sharply. She had not seen me watching her. 'Do you have any idea what a chauvinist you are?' There was a flame of anger in her cheeks. She threw the fan down and walked away.

I felt ashamed, dismayed at my lapse in behaviour. I stood alone, pretending to study an old map of Barbados. I wanted to acknowledge that I had run ahead too far. She was, after all, my brother's wife. When I caught up with her a few moments later, I made my apology with sincerity.

Now it was her turn to seem awkward. 'You must forgive me,' she said. 'It was not right of me to fly off the handlebar.'

I corrected her, with a smile. We rejoined Raymond and had fun, all three of us, bidding for candlesticks and table lamps.

By chance, it was at this time that I experienced a welcome and unexpected distraction. I came home one evening to find a message on my answering machine from Susan Crowe, an old girlfriend. Susan worked in the catalogue department of the British Library. She was a fellow graduate from Oxford who, like so many of our generation, had put their professional lives first. Lonely and vulnerable, worrying about her chances of having children, she was facing up to the approach of middle age with difficulty.

When I returned her call, I found her distraught. The

current boyfriend, a rugby-playing city slicker some years younger than she, had taken up with a woman his own age, behind her back. Susan, suspicious, had confronted him and thrown him out. Now she was feeling bruised and miserable and wanted someone to confide in. I was pleased she'd called. Our relationship had ended some years ago. We had lived together briefly and there was a time when I might have married her and raised a family. As it was, we had drifted apart, too alike to feel passion, too familiar with each other's faults to get along on a day-to-day basis. We had kept in touch, as old friends, and now she wanted 'a shoulder to cry on', she said. 'We all need someone we can lean on,' I replied, and was satisfied to hear a faint giggle at the end of the line.

I invited Susan down to dinner. On the appointed day, I left the office early with some excuse about visiting the morgue, and hurried to meet the train. I saw her first, wan and smudgy-eyed, her dark hair pulled back in a schoolgirl ponytail, carrying a neat little bag, like an evacuee from the city. Sometimes when, unobserved, we see our friends as strangers might see them we can feel the onrush of time, and sense our own mortality too. When she caught sight of me she brightened and almost ran and then I took her in my arms and kissed her. A casual watcher might have assumed we were lovers.

It was a pleasant March evening, warm enough for a stroll through the Lanes. We window-shopped arm in arm, furnishing houses we would never live in, while Susan complained about her work at the Library, moving slowly, as we reconnected, towards the recent dramas of her private life. I have, in my time, walked these back-ways with a number of women in this way, but just then I had no entanglements, despite the efforts of various Mansfield couples to fix me up with a suitable partner.

I had booked an early table at a famous seafood restaurant and by the time we had settled down for an evening of oysters and Chablis she had found her natural animation. I am quite well known in this establishment, and the waiters fussed over us as if we were courting. We talked on, oblivious to the other diners, and at about ten o'clock I made a reference to the last train, knowing, I suppose, that she would choose to stay the night.

We had not made love together in years, but we returned to each other's bodies with satisfaction. When she loosened her hair and relaxed Susan was still the cheerful young woman of my thirties, even the irrepressible girl of my history lectures. There was an affection between us that was real and deep, and our sexual life had meaning, even then, after all the interruptions. It was nice to fall asleep, slightly drunk, to the rhythm of her breathing.

The next day was Saturday. We had a late breakfast and then, because I was anxious to avoid my brother, we went for a long walk on the Downs. The wind seemed to blow our conversation hither and yon. I told Susan about Raymond and his family, and Susan's unerring instinct did not fail her. She asked about Kristina. I said I did not know what to make of her, but I spoke for longer than I had intended. After I had finished she was quiet for a while and then she said lightly that I was a silly boy who lost his heart too easily. She patted me as an older sister might have done.

'You'll get over it.'

'But there's nothing to get over.'

'No, of course not.'

'I've disappointed you.'

She shook her head. 'I know you too well.'

I stopped and put my arms around her. 'Friends?'

'Of course we're friends.' She sighed. 'That's the trouble.'

'If you stay tonight,' I said, chancily, 'you could meet her tomorrow. They're supposed to be coming over for Sunday lunch.'

'Are you looking for a romantic cover story?' She smiled. 'Or do you want me to fix the lamb for you?'

'I want to know if you think I'm crazy.'

'I don't need to meet this woman to tell you that.' She laughed. 'You've always wanted what you can't have.'

After the walk, we had a lazy day together. Susan played my CDs and read the newspapers. I dug the garden. The earth was alive with growth and every stem and branch was sticky with the newness of spring. Later, I persuaded Susan to improvise some dinner. I am an indifferent cook, and rely on take-away meals and pre-cooked food. It was good to watch her in the kitchen, while we chatted and drank wine together. To my relief, there was no intrusion from Raymond, and no telephone call from the emergency services. We went to bed early. When we made love this time, I regret to say I imagined it was Kristina whose body I was possessing.

[4]

When I was a boy, Sundays were dead days, and in my adult life I have kept up the routine of childhood, the reverie of solitude. I speak to no one. I listen to Wagner or Bach. I read the newspapers and my current book, a biography or a history. I potter and footle. I snooze. The only interruptions are from the police, calling to report a body discovered by ramblers. Occasionally, if I have been disturbed in this way, I will attend Evensong, join in

'Abide With Me', and shake hands with Francis Find-later, our parish priest. 'Suicide, murder, or natural causes?' he will ask, knowing my habits. I see riding-boots under his cassock. I will smile, and refer to his sermon with approval. It's a game we play. I am known for my discretion. Having Susan to stay was another variation in my schedule, but there was something about my brother's return that gave me the taste for it. I could feel my life changing, and it was an enjoyable sensation.

I woke early that Sunday and was sitting downstairs with an early morning cup of tea, lost in a reverie, when I heard Susan moving about in my bedroom. I reflected how different two people can be. Kristina's movements, as I had observed them, were swift and noiseless, and yet her presence was somehow always with you. When she spoke, it was as though every word had been chosen with care. Susan, in contrast, sorted the words after she'd spoken, revising her thoughts impromptu and discarding scraps of sentences on the wing.

Susan has an open and a vigorous disposition, and I have always been attracted to her for her energy and frankness. She is one of those people who can be unnervingly direct about herself and the people she meets. When we were together, there were times when she'd look in the mirror and announce that she felt as ugly as a dog. She has a way of asking straight questions and getting answers, and she will not flinch from risking offence. It's a kind of honesty that does not come naturally to me. I am inclined to conceal my thoughts. She speaks hers.

Raymond and the family arrived shortly after midday. Outside, in the village, neighbours were exercising their dogs, strolling to the pub, and playing football on the green. My brother was his gallant, breezy self. Kristina was in jeans, a plain white cotton shirt, and a sky-blue velvet jacket she had made herself. Olga and Sasha were in Sunday best, polished up like china dolls for this outing.

I had warned Raymond about Susan and had tried without much success to explain that she was just an old friend. 'Nothing serious,' I'd said, appealing to him as a man-of-the-world. 'That's not like you,' he'd replied. 'You're a serious fellow.' I'd laughed him off with a lightness I did not feel. Now I was wondering how Kristina would respond to the evidence of a woman in my life.

I introduced Susan. The children, who had become quite used to me, were shy in the presence of a stranger. Speaking slowly, I whispered to Olga that I had hidden 'surprises' in the garden. She was still having difficulty with the language. She said something to her brother in German and they ran off to explore. Raymond and Susan were shaking hands. I saw the cavalier look in his eye. Kristina was holding a bunch of daffodils. 'A nice little gift,' she said. She handed me the flowers, but she was looking at Susan. 'I have dreamed of this garden.' She smiled at both of us. 'It's what England is known for, gardens.'

Raymond nodded with encouragement, as if she was his pupil. 'The perfect climate,' he said.

I escorted everyone into the front room. The Sunday papers were scattered across the floor. 'Moderate, temperate, with no extremes.'

'And perfectly bloody,' said Susan, lighting a cigarette with a laugh.

'One of the reasons I left,' said Raymond. I noticed then, as I had noticed before, how he liked to introduce his life story into the conversation.

'What brought you home?'

'As I told Julian,' he replied, accepting a glass of champagne with a nod, 'I wanted to end my days here. Sometimes I feel a bit like an old elephant.'

Susan looked him in the eye. I recognised the gleam of candour. 'How old are you exactly?'

Suddenly, Raymond was almost sheepish. 'Nearly sixty.'

'Is this early retirement, or a search for roots?'

He looked at his wife with embarrassment. 'Let's say it was time I came home to Blighty.'

Kristina said something in German I could not understand, as she arranged the daffodils on a side table.

'I fear my three score years and ten are almost up,' murmured Raymond.

'Sixty is nothing these days,' Susan replied. 'People are starting whole new careers at sixty. What's that phrase? The silver generation. You've time to re-invent yourself.'

I saw that Raymond, who generally liked to be the centre of attention, was uneasy with this discussion of his mortality. I raised my glass to distract the conversation and we toasted each other. Then Olga ran in to show her mother what she had found in the garden, a stick of Brighton Rock I'd bought during my stroll with Susan. Sasha followed her, stumbling to keep up. Raymond, in better humour, began to sing, 'Oh I do like to be beside the seaside.'

I suggested we sit down to lunch and they crowded into my low-ceilinged dining-room. I was glad that all the adults seemed to be getting on well. I carved the lamb, serving the children first, as Kristina had instructed. She had warned me they would fidget, and fiddle with their food, and ask to leave. Susan pressed on, as I expected, with more questions. I concentrated on my duties as host. I could ask everyone for their verdicts later. Raymond was describing how he had met Kristina.

'She was my student. We met in my seminar on the history of the British Isles.'

Kristina made a face. 'You might say we were brought together by your kings and queens. That's rather funny, isn't it?'

'The reactionary enemies of the working class,' Raymond chipped in.

Susan laughed appreciatively. 'Are you still a member of the Communist Party?'

'That,' I said, looking up from my carving, 'is what everyone in the village is dying to know.' I saw the anxiety in Kristina's eyes. 'Don't forget that in Mansfield a communist is that slightly scary animal, a revolutionary.'

Raymond began to hum 'The Red Flag', then stopped. 'Do I look like a revolutionary?' he said, accepting a full plate of lamb. 'If I am a communist,' he went on, 'I'm a communist who wants to become that infinitely more dangerous beast, an English country gentleman.'

I exchanged a glance with Susan. We had already discussed Raymond's weakness for the good life.

Susan looked at him quizzically. 'Dangerous?'

'Listen,' said Raymond, happy to have an audience. 'I shall be mixing with men who have in their lifetime seen off both Nazi Germany and the Soviet Union. If I'm going to live in the country I shall follow country ways. I am too old to hunt and horses have never been my friends, but when the season is on I shall take my rod and line and pursue the elusive trout in the streams of Wessex. In the winter I shall take down my gun and blaze away at pheasant and rabbits with the best of them. Julian is going to give me Father's old Purdey. Where is it, brother? Gathering dust in the attic, I expect. Go on. Let's give the ladies a thrill.'

I had only just begun to eat but was intrigued to see the direction of my brother's thoughts. So I put down my knife and fork and hurried upstairs. After Father died, I had wrapped the gun in an old towel and hidden it in my wardrobe. Occasionally, in the way I had been taught, I would take it to pieces and carefully oil the parts, an oddly satisfying duty. Now I laid aside the wrapping and picked it up, feeling the weight and the menace. The gun had seen good service and its stock was scarred with use, but the barrel was smooth and cold. As I held it in my hand I could hear my brother's laughter downstairs and I could see him in the butts, banging away at snipe and woodcock with some ruddy-faced squires. There was, of course, no ammunition. I had never fired it, even into the air. When I took the gun downstairs the room fell silent. Raymond took it eagerly in his hands, turning it over for inspection. He raised it to his shoulder, squinting to take aim. Susan flinched but I saw that Kristina was unmoved.

'It's not loaded,' I said.

'I shall get some ammunition tomorrow,' said Raymond. 'I'm going to have fun with this.'

Kristina broke in seriously. 'What sort of fun are you talking about, darling?'

Raymond ignored her coolness. He was showing off to Susan. 'The feathered population of Mansfield had better look to their flak jackets. I shall become the Deadeye Dick of the neighbourhood.'

Kristina was looking strangely at the gun. She got up and said something in German I could not understand

and walked out into the garden. We watched her retreating figure in puzzlement. My brother laid the gun on the table with a forced laugh.

'What was she saying?'

Raymond started, as if from a reverie. 'Eh? What's that? Oh, some old Prussian proverb. She's worried that Olga and Sasha will catch their deaths out there.' He stood up. I noticed, once again, how easily his wife could deflate his ebullience. 'I'll go and see if they're okay.' He patted the gun. 'Kristina's right, of course. I'll have to keep this well away from the children.' He went out into the sunshine and I was left alone at the table with Susan. I had hardly touched my food.

'Well?' I said.

'She certainly has your brother where she wants him.'

'How does she strike you?'

'You tell me,' she replied. 'What do you see in her?'

'She's very . . .' I hesitated, unfamiliar with the words I wanted. 'Don't you think she's beautiful?'

'It's not what I think that matters.'

In the past, such vibrations in the conversation had a habit of becoming full-scale eruptions, but I was determined to remain unprovoked. 'It's not a fantasy, if that's what you mean,' I said. 'I suppose I like the way her mind works. I find her mysterious. I like the fact that she likes me.'

'That's obvious.'

'I'm sorry,' I said, and saw the needle quivering on the dial. 'You did ask.'

She looked hard at me. 'Let's leave Kristina out of it – frankly, that's your business – but I'd say your brother has a problem.'

'What do you mean?'

'He was lying to you.'

34

'Lying?'

'That was never some old Prussian proverb. That was a simple threat.'

'What sort of threat?'

She came over and sat in Kristina's empty seat. She took my hand. 'She said, my dear Julian, "I don't want that gun in my house" – my house, see – "and you move it from here at your own risk." And she meant what she said.'

'Raymond has always had a weakness for women who boss him around,' I said, with a lightness I did not feel.

'What about you?' Susan smiled. 'What are your weaknesses these days?'

'I don't need to tell you,' I replied, flirtatious again.

'Watch out, Julian,' said Susan, kissing me on the lips. 'You're not like your brother, and you don't want to be.'

[5]

Spring arrived in stops and starts. The countryside danced in the March sunshine and then a frozen sky held the land in suspended animation. There were storms at sea and a sycamore fell across the road outside my house. At times it seemed as if winter would never end. I recorded several verdicts of suicide.

I was a little gloomy on my own account. The optimism I'd experienced from my family's arrival in the village was fading. I had pretended that I could take a simple, almost brotherly pleasure in Kristina's company. Susan, plain-speaking as always, had put me straight. She had spoken, quite coolly, of my fascination for Kristina and had reminded me of the potential for jealousy in my dealings with Raymond. I had persuaded myself that her advice was uncomplicated by any residual feelings of her own.

I also had to contend with my own observation of life in Jericho Lodge. Whenever Raymond and Kristina spoke German in my presence there was what Mother used to call 'an atmosphere'. Even simple matters seemed to require negotiation. The acquisition of Jack, an undisciplined mongrel puppy, was the upshot of many hours' discussion, like the signing of an arms treaty.

The village saw none of this. As a keeper of secrets, I had to admire the way that Raymond and Kristina presented themselves in public. My brother, especially, was eager to play his part on the provincial stage, and threw himself into his new life with enthusiasm. His appetite for applause was not diminished by his advancing years, while his dismay at the changes that, as he saw it, had disfigured his native land only sharpened his appreciation of village traditions.

I knew the significance of this. For most of his adult life, Raymond's meal ticket had been the Communist International. In various guises – journalist, translator, lecturer, Party activist – the service of Marxism-Leninism had carried him all over the world, from Mao's China to Allende's Chile. He had visited Moscow and Havana as a privileged guest. His affiliations had given him a place in the sun, a way of life, and a source of pride. He had even written a concise history of the British Isles for his fellow comrades and been praised for it. But his now-discredited version of events was not the version shared by his new neighbours in the village, and I was intrigued to see what would happen at the house-warming party.

The party dominated everything. Among my neighbours, an invitation was a highly-prized trophy. Anyone who was anyone was going to be at Jericho Lodge that

36

Easter Monday. Some who, like the Pooles and the O'Malleys, did not at first receive one of Kristina's hand-painted cards did not scruple to make their disappointment known to me, the natural go-between. Others, like Mr Dacosta, simply buttonholed my brother in the village shop. News travels quickly in Mansfield. Soon there was talk of Kristina's traditional German cooking, of Raymond's purchases of wine, vodka and party balloons in Brighton, and some inevitable speculation about the cost.

A few days before the party I was sitting at home working quietly on my papers when there was a knock on the window. It was Raymond, with Jack, the new puppy, who bounced up and down, barking, at his side. I got to my feet. Some fresh air and a walk would clear my head. We set out purposefully. The long winter sleep was ending and now, as the first primroses appeared, the hedgerows were bursting with springtime. The lion of March was still roaring, but the sky was clear, a cold cyclorama of blue. We had just put the clocks forward and the evenings were getting lighter at last, like a headache that is slowly lifting.

'It must have been a shock,' I said, 'coming home.'

'You don't know me very well, Julian,' he replied. 'I'm a survivor. When I joined the Communist Party I was a middle-class refusenik. I adapted. My marriage failed, I got stuck in a rut, and I lost heart. I adapted. I emigrated to East Germany. I claimed it was for ideological reasons but the truth is that I was on the run. That's me, Mr Adaptable.'

'I remember that Father always used to say that one should manoeuvre oneself into the position of critic at the first opportunity.'

'You seem to have done that quite successfully,' he

observed with a smile. 'I'm not one of nature's pioneers. I was not born for the frontier, though I seem to have found myself in one or two rather exposed situations, as much by accident as by design. I'm a coward who has taught himself to be courageous.'

A pigeon whirred up out of the bushes, and the puppy barked with excitement. Raymond told me that, when the pheasant season started, he was hoping to join a local shoot. I did not mention Kristina's prohibition, and assumed he had negotiated a compromise. We returned from our walk in good humour, but with many things unspoken. I walked him to the turn in the woods that led back, via the bridleway, to Jericho Lodge and took my leave. I refused his invitation to drinks with an excuse about pressure of work, a rather unconvincing pretext.

The truth was that I did not wish to expose myself to Kristina's comments about Susan. Whenever I dropped by, Kristina would make teasing references to my 'girl-friend' and 'that charming woman'. To my annoyance, Raymond even went so far as to refer, in his jocular way, to my 'future ex-wife to be'. I told them both, with some vehemence, that our relationship had ended years ago. Kristina was not to be deterred. She wanted to know how I could sleep with someone I did not love. Eventually I found myself forced into a laborious joke.

'I'm afraid I long ago decided that I could not have a relationship with a woman that involved love.'

Kristina did not hear my irony. 'How can you say that?'

I became serious. 'Perhaps I don't trust myself any more.'

Afterwards, I revolved the conversation in my head and was unsettled. I saw that I wanted to provoke her and to show her that I was unattached. I determined to

38

avoid further discussions of that sort, especially in my fragile mood of uncertainty.

I took refuge in my professional duties, as I had done so often before. Each morning I pulled on my suit, knotted my sombre tie, and drove to the office like an automaton to administer the flow of provincial litigation – boundary disputes, breaches of the peace, and a multitude of minor legal wrangles. Once or twice a week, I conducted inquests at the coroner's court. A procession of the bereaved passed before me. Widows, mothers, step-fathers, foster parents, civil servants, shopkeepers, nurses, taxi drivers: it is my privilege to see the chaos of everyday life. Pain and misery is so often mixed with small, unheralded acts of dignity and heroism. I found myself expressing my feelings for Kristina through my comments from the bench. The court officer noticed a new solicitude in my observations and made a joke about tea and sympathy. I would study the bleached Polaroid photographs of violent death – car crashes, suicides, boating accidents – look down into the well of the court, and try to offer words of comfort to the solemn and frightened faces before me. This was a bizarre time, full of pent-up frustration. I see now that it was the prelude to a year of many bizarre moments, a year that would send me backwards and forwards and inside out.

The Easter holiday was approaching. Raymond, a belligerent atheist, made slighting references to 'Holy Joes' and 'bells and smells'. One evening, during one of these tirades, Kristina asked me if I would accompany her on Easter Day to the Roman Catholic church in Brighton. In one of our conversations about her childhood in East Germany, she had explained that the Catholic Church had been a refuge for opponents of the regime. Going to church was a way of expressing dissent.

39

She had divided her loyalties, embracing the faith but still working for the state.

I saw that it troubled Raymond to have excluded himself from his wife's presence before the Almighty, and I accepted with a certain guilty opportunism. It gave me secret satisfaction to take his place, and when the day came, I found something unaccountably reassuring about stepping into the candle-bright, incense-heavy atmosphere of the church. The children were excited. I had given Olga a doll as an Easter present, and little Sasha had a teddy bear.

'What's his name?' asked Olga, speaking with a slightly American accent.

I mimed a conversation with the bear. Kristina watched, laughing. 'He says his name is Bruno.' It was all I could manage on the spur of the moment. 'He is very fierce, but he'll be friendly if you and Sasha treat him well.'

We shuffled inside as a family with a great crowd of worshippers, making our way to the heart of the nave and finding a place with a good view of the high altar. A triumphant procession passed down the aisle while the choir sang the Gloria and then an old priest in gold vestments announced 'Christ is Risen.' I was bursting with joy at being so close to Kristina and part of her life, and at being away from my brother's watchful eye. I responded to the prayers and lifted my voice in thanks.

Afterwards, we came out into rainy spring sunshine with the faithful and made our way down the steps with the children holding our hands and making Bruno take the steps too. We sent Olga running on ahead to find my car.

'My mother's family was Catholic,' said Kristina. 'They came to Dresden from Poland, and when I was growing up I always identified with their suffering. I dreamed of baptism into a Church that understood pain and knew about forgiveness.'

'Do you go to confession?'

'I should.' She smiled. 'What about you?'

'I hear confessions in court every week. Who can confess the confessor?'

She gave me an odd look. 'Do you know who I would most like to put in your court?'

I shook my head. I wondered what she was getting at.

'Guess.'

'Honecker? Stalin? Hitler?'

She was shaking her head, looking at me with a fierceness that made me pause. 'Raymond.'

She continued to walk towards the car, but I did not keep step. I stood and watched her at a distance, puzzling over the many things about Raymond and Kristina that I still didn't understand.

[6]

I caught Raymond with an April Fool. On the morning of the party, I arranged for my neighbour, Joe Vaughan, the sports editor of our local paper, to telephone my brother and, in a suitably official but rustic accent, to enquire if he had a permit to give a party at Jericho Lodge. The local constabulary were concerned about the build-up of traffic in the vicinity, and besides it was a statutory requirement with rental property that social gatherings of more than twenty persons etc., etc. He should present himself at the police station, bringing his passport, his driver's licence and fifteen pounds. 'Just a formality, sir,' said Joe, winking at me. We hurried down to the police station. Shortly afterwards, my brother arrived, looking harassed. 'Very good, Julian,' he said. 'I didn't know you had it in you.'

I promised to make amends by helping out with the guests. When I came into the house at noon, I found Raymond adjusting a psychedelic party tie in the mirror. His hair was slicked down, not wild as usual, his face was shining, and I could detect the hint of alcohol on his breath. He was in high spirits. In answer to my question, he explained that Kristina would be down shortly. Taking my arm in the most familial of gestures, he gave me a tour of the arrangements.

I was impressed. He and Kristina had made a tremendous effort. The house was decorated with a profusion of spring flowers: daffodils, primroses in baskets, sprigs of pussy-willow, and displays of ivy and evergreens. There was a hand-painted banner, 'Welcome to Jericho Lodge', over the door, and on a long table in the dining-room, laid out like a medieval banquet, there were piles of cold meat, various salads, a salmon, and some strange-looking dishes I assumed to be German. Another table had serried glasses and a large white jug with a festive cocktail, my brother's concoction.

We had just completed our inspection and I was reassuring my brother on the magnificence of the display, when the guests began to arrive. In most instances I knew them better than Raymond did and I found myself acting as unofficial master of ceremonies. There were few absentees from the roll-call of village society. Lady Platt, Mrs Boyle, Colonel Matthews and Dr Stephenson were among the first to arrive. Everyone was curious to see inside old Miss Nicholson's house.

The party was going with a swing when Raymond turned to me. 'Have you seen Kristina?' I looked around and shook my head. 'I say, frater,' he was speaking confidentially, 'would you pop upstairs, tell her that most of the guests have arrived, and suggest in the nicest possible way that she gets herself down here PDQ.'

I hurried up to the master-bedroom. The door was ajar. I knocked. There was no answer. I knocked again. This time a very small, faint voice invited me to come in. I entered slowly. Kristina had her back to me but she greeted me by name, a sad murmur. She was sitting on the bed, half-dressed in jeans and a bra, staring at herself in the mirror. Her silky hair fell over her face and her high cheekbones were blazing with despair. I was shocked and embarrassed to find her this way. Awkwardly, I apologised for my intrusion and explained that I had been sent. She did not reply. I was about to back out, unnerved by this display of indifference, when she patted the bed beside her. 'Please. Don't go. I can't stand it.'

So I came and sat next to her, another irrevocable but undeniably pleasant step in our strange relationship. We had never been alone in such a condition of intimacy before, and the knowledge that half the village was below, oblivious, gave me an odd thrill. I remember noticing a tiny birthmark on her shoulder. Kristina was quite unselfconscious about her *déshabillé*. We did not touch, of course, but I could feel the warmth of her body. I said I wanted to understand why, on today of all days, she was upset.

After a long silence in which I could hear the party hubbub downstairs she pushed the hair out of her face. 'I can't explain.'

I was frustrated that she would not tell me. Privately, I believed that she could explain if she wanted to.

'You have to come downstairs,' I said. 'You have to.' I told her how hard Raymond was working. He was

43

waiting for her. There were people who wanted to meet her. After all the build-up, she could not disappoint them. I spoke like an advocate, arguing my brother's case. 'It's much better to get it over with in one fell swoop,' I said encouragingly.

'One fell swoop? I don't understand.'

'It's a phrase, an expression.'

She smiled. 'It sounds funny to me.' She repeated it again, 'One fell swoop,' and stood up, pulling herself together. She paced in front of me, barefoot and half-dressed, choosing her clothes from the wardrobe. She was thin and beautiful. Her breasts were small and rested lightly in her bra. Her skin was the colour of watery silk. I watched her disappear into the bathroom. Kristina was a swift, almost professional, dresser. She returned in a matter of moments, elegant and yet not too formal, in a little black dress. I stood there, leaning against the window, while she sat in front of the mirror and began to dab at her face with make-up, like an actress preparing for a first night.

Just at that moment I wanted so badly to know what she was thinking. Was this casual intimacy a kind of flirtation, or was she so beaten down by her predicament that she did not care how she seemed? When I caught her eye in the mirror, she became suddenly self-conscious and for a moment I was encouraged to see that she was capable of a certain shyness in my presence.

'You've been crying,' I said.

'It's silly, isn't it?' She began to apply mascara. 'My heart goes up and down like a bouncing ball. One minute happy, one minute sad.'

I wanted to say that I understood her state of mind. The reckless half of me wanted to lure her into an admission of mutual attraction, but the sober half of me

44

feared the risk. Besides, I was still wrestling with my conscience and was almost too paralysed to utter anything sensible. Finally I said, 'I think you have a lot on your mind.'

She ignored my invitation to speak of herself. 'Is Susan with you?'

I was disappointed. 'No,' I said. 'You don't understand about Susan,' I replied, watching her put on her earrings.

She laughed. 'I think even you don't understand about Susan.'

She turned round, tossed her head and hurried to the top of the staircase. I followed at a distance and heard the momentary hush in the hall as she appeared before them, the Snow Queen from the Steppes. 'Darling—' Raymond's delighted and relieved exclamation was drowned in the noise of greetings. I stood out of sight and I heard Raymond almost shouting. 'You must come into the dining-room, darling. There are so many people who want to meet you, so many new friends . . .'

When, finally, I made my way down into the crowd, unnoticed, I was glad on my brother's behalf, to see that the turnout was almost complete. There were the Rogers and the Cottons, the Willetts and the Evans, an habitual clique. Over by the bay window, the Reverend Findlater was holding forth to Barbara, from the pub, about the prospects for the Flat. Nearby, but scarcely on speaking terms, was the librarian Michael Watkins, our self-appointed local historian and resident snob. Standing by the fireplace, was the village shopkeeper, Leslie, and his sister, Shirley, brash and assertive, pricing up the room with a practised eye. Next to them, leaning on a stick, was Mrs Simpson, the headmistress of the local primary school, a quiet disciplinarian who was none the less fond of a pre-prandial sherry. She was chatting to Dr Stephenson and his wife, Alice.

Outside in the garden, children were playing in the long grass, fighting and racing up and down. There was to be a fancy dress competition in aid of Oxfam in the village hall later that afternoon and some of the children were dressed up as Napoleon, Bo-Peep, Nelson, the Merrie Monarch, and various characters from Beatrix Potter. This event had been organised by James Curran, our popular scoutmaster. He was in drag himself, crammed into an Ugly Sister costume he had worn on several occasions over the years. Curran could always be relied upon to entertain the village, and no one ever publicly questioned his proclivities. I have always held that we are a private race who cherish eccentricity and love to gossip. But put the members of an English village in an unfamiliar environment and they will indulge the baser aspects of curiosity. Many of the guests were snooping about as if this was a stately home recently bequeathed to the nation.

I did my best to act as interpreter and guide for my brother in this social labyrinth. There's hardly a family in the village that has not, at one time or another, come to me for advice or assistance. Their secrets are my secrets. Tax, property, marriage, divorce, inheritance and death: there was no story here whose plot was unknown to me. In my experience, it is the middle classes who are loudest in their protestations of innocence, and their social inferiors who prove the least guilty. High and low, they trust me because I am affable but self-contained, sympathetic yet discreet. I seem to offer no threat.

A number of guests had brought gifts – Irish teatowels, painted mugs, bottles of elderberry wine, chocolate cakes, tea caddies. Someone else had come with a

Union Jack, which seemed rather pointed. To one and all, Raymond was generous with his thanks. He confided, with amusement, that the vicar had given him a Gideon Bible. 'I'm probably beyond redemption now,' he murmured. I could see that he was pleased by the collective welcome and the offer of a place in our little society.

After about an hour, when the house was full and the guests had stopped arriving – some, indeed, were making preliminary gestures of departure – and the ground floor was crowded with people balancing plates and wine glasses, Raymond jumped on to a chair in his impetuous way, and banged his glass with a knife. A hush fell over the room.

'Ladies and gentlemen,' he began, 'or should I say, comrades.' There was an uneasy flutter of laughter. 'I shall not detain you long, but this auspicious occasion demands a few words of explanation and many more of thanks.'

'Bravo,' said a voice at the back.

'I remember, only a few months ago, sitting on the balcony of our little flat in East Berlin, as was, and saying to my dear wife, Kristina – where are you, darling? – yes, there you are – saying, "How nice it would be to be back home in England." And she said, "You are always dreaming." And I said, "Let's see about that" – and it was then that I wrote to my dear brother Julian – thank you, Julian – and thus it was that my dream began to come true . . .'

I wondered if he would stop there but quickly realised that years of speechifying at official gatherings had accustomed him to something more long-winded. He was, as it were, just clearing his throat. The familiar phrases were rolling out, but he was doing it well, and when he approached the end the party was with him, touched and grateful. 'I ask you all to raise your glasses to home, to the village, to Mansfield.'

'Mansfield,' echoed the guests.

There was a scattering of applause. He had spoken from the heart, with elegance and a certain style. I was, in some obscure way, proud of the ease with which he seemed to be slipping back into English life. I had always dreaded his disruptive potential and was relieved that he seemed disinclined to make the kind of trouble he had in the past. Kristina's reticence towards the village was another question altogether, and it was one that would preoccupy my thoughts in the weeks to come.

The party took up again. Many of the guests stayed in their groups, content after the initial handshake to stare at Raymond and Kristina as if they were stars from a TV soap opera. Often, the villagers directed their conversations about my brother to me, the unofficial interpreter. Mrs Boyle, the secretary of the Conservative Association, wanted to know if Raymond was 'still a commie'. I told her, politely, to ask him herself. She replied that she did not expect straight answers from Mephistopheles.

I worked my way across the room to where Raymond was standing. He had been cornered by Michael Watkins, who was offering Raymond a tour of the local historical sites, especially the field where the RAF had shot down a Messerschmitt during the Battle of Britain.

'Of course,' Watkins was saying, as I joined them, 'the bodies were removed for a military funeral, but you can still see the remains of the airframe. I had hoped to preserve it, but I could not raise the funds.'

'Perhaps it is better to forget these things,' said Raymond.

Watkins became very pompous. 'As an historian, Mr

48

Rowley-Whyte, you must know that people who forget the past are doomed to repeat it.'

'I say that people who have not learned to forgive are in danger of damaging the peace in the world.'

Watkins was upset. 'I say,' he said, flushing with indignation, 'whose side are you on, anyway?'

My brother was rather impressive. 'Our side lost,' he said quietly. 'Now I'm on no one's team. It's a peculiar but quite pleasant feeling.' He looked at Watkins with disdain. 'You don't know what I mean, do you? You couldn't. You're English. Excuse me.'

A momentary frisson of disharmony ran through the party like an angry dog. Conversations faltered. Heads turned. Minute social realignments were made. It was shortly after this that Watkins, who had fussily retreated, used a particular word in association with my brother, a word that had not, I think, been heard in Mansfield before.

[7]

The first time I heard Michael Watkins refer to 'the Stasi' I remember seeing the lilacs in my brother's garden out of the corner of my eye. As I listened to my neighbours discussing the New Germany, I noticed, not for the first time, how this subject will always provoke at least one Englishman to say, in a poor German accent, and apropos of nothing, 'Ve haf vays of making you talk.'

A vain, well-groomed, intrusive little man, Watkins had the bibliophile's love of order and method, and the assertiveness of the self-taught. There was nothing he liked better than to stroll, a tiny general, between the stacks, reviewing his troops, adjusting a spine here, a

49

jacket there, in an atmosphere of reverent hush. He would share his knowledge in a way that other men might show off a new car. Mr Watkins was pleased to inform us that this fateful term was an abbreviation of the German word 'Staatssicherheitsdienst', a literal translation of 'state security service'. Mr Watkins said that, according to his understanding, it was this 'Stasi' that was the source of Germany's troubles.

Many of us were quite ill-informed about the recent changes in German society, and the conversation soon turned to the likely fate of Mr Gorbachev, but I made up my mind to explore the matter further for myself at the first opportunity. Apart from my curiosity about the Stasi, I was still puzzling over Kristina's enigmatic remark about putting Raymond on trial.

When Raymond and I met in The Royal Oak to conduct a post-mortem on the party, I found myself asking questions with a blitheness that was, in retrospect, horrifyingly naive.

I knew at once that I had touched a raw nerve. Raymond took a handful of peanuts, tossing them into his mouth in a single, anxious gesture.

'People talk about the Stasi,' he said, 'but, take it from me, old boy, most of what you hear is exaggerated.' He smiled weakly. 'It was just a bureaucracy, a typically German bureaucracy.'

'How did it affect you?'

He repeated my question, staring into his ale. 'It's what people want to hear about, I suppose.' He looked round the pub, the atmosphere of warmth and relaxation. 'Everyone was affected, but I have nothing to regret,' he said. 'Nothing to be ashamed of.' The satisfaction he had taken in a successful social occasion was forgotten. 'Look, no one who has not lived in the GDR, as I have, can possibly understand the system.' I recognised the pain in his expression and saw that he suspected a deliberate provocation on my part.

'People like Michael Watkins are so provincial,' I said, with a belated access of tact.

'When I meet people like that I remember why I left,' he said. 'No,' he repeated. 'Je ne regrette rien.'

He seemed so defensive that I put the subject to one side for a moment. We sat in silence briefly, observing the other customers at the bar. One or two had been at the party and came over to offer thanks. I found myself, searching for a neutral topic of conversation, comparing English and continental drinking habits. I said I'd prefer to live in Italy, not France or Germany, and Raymond asked me how often I had been there. I described holidays in Tuscany, showing off local knowledge and a certain familiarity with Italian cuisine.

As we talked, I realised that there were years of my life and experience that meant nothing to him. He had dropped off the family map, only checking in, long-distance, at Christmas and birthdays, and sometimes not even then. He was like an explorer who had gone native, returning home to twenty years of unopened letters and disconnected relationships. I found that in his new, English guise, it was a pleasure to sit and talk to him. In retrospect I must say that he was, for all his faults, one of the sweetest and most natural men I have ever known.

There was though something about his vulnerability that made me cruel. After several minutes of chat, I returned to the question of Germany. I was curious to know why he had inflicted this experience on himself for twenty-five years. 'Surely,' I said, 'you didn't have to wait for early retirement to come home?'

He blinked like a fighter taking a punch. 'We are still

getting to know each other, Julian,' he replied. 'You are a pragmatist. I am an idealist. I dreamed of a better world. I even devoted myself to trying to change the world and in the end I found that it was I, not the world, that was being changed.' He picked up his drink. 'Changed for the worse, alas.'

'Come on,' I said. 'You've everything to look forward to.' I could not disguise the envy in my voice. 'You have a gorgeous wife. You have the pleasure of seeing your children grow up in a new society.' I got up and went to the bar and returned with two fresh pints.

He looked up, as if from deep thought. 'Gossip – that's the problem.' He began to whistle, a nervous tic I'd noticed before.

I was puzzled. 'What do you mean?'

'We'll always report on what the chaps next door are getting up to, won't we? I mean, it's in our natures.'

I was at a loss to follow his train of thought. It occurred to me that after the restrictions of his life in the GDR, he was having difficulty adjusting to our open society. They say that newly released prisoners take time to adapt to the multiple choices of democratic life. I tried to reassure him. He had nothing to fear from village tittle-tattle.

'You have nothing to hide,' I said.

'No,' he shook his head. 'That's right.'

'People will always talk,' I went on. 'It's mostly harmless. In a few more months you'll just be part of the landscape.'

'I hope so.' He sounded unconvinced. 'I hope so.' He had a tendency to repeat himself when he was anxious, and I saw that my enquiries had stirred up unhappy memories. 'Let me tell you another thing about the famous Stasi. They really were a bit of a standing joke to most people. Everyone knew they were watching.

Frankly, I'd have been disappointed if my phone hadn't been tapped. It's like going to the doctor's. They're privy to all your secrets, but they don't tell anyone, so what difference does it make?' He took a deep draught of beer. 'Most of it was just trivial gossip, anyway.'

'In this country,' I said, 'people gossip about sex. Who is doing what to whom. I think you're safely out of risk in that department.'

'Are you kidding?' He gave me a rueful look. 'I have a young wife. You've just told me yourself how attractive she is. In my position, you always imagine the worst.' He gave a self-deprecating laugh. 'Like some comic grey-beard from the Merry Wives.'

I heard myself saying with some vehemence that he was being silly. That was the word I used. Silly. Not ridiculous. Or paranoid. Silly. Now it was my turn to laugh. 'You make Mansfield sound like a village in Hell.' I looked him in the eye. 'You forget,' I said. 'I have lived here happily for years. Nothing ever happens here. It's as dull as ditchwater.'

'I expect you have enough drama in your own working life.' It was his turn to probe. 'Have you ever thought of writing a book about your work?'

'I've thought about it,' I replied, 'but I've been too lazy to do much. I've kept diaries. I write case-notes. A long time ago I tried my hand at fiction, but the problem was confidentiality. And time. What about you?' I was eager to move the subject forward. 'You have all this leisure. Wouldn't it be a good idea to have a project to focus on?'

'The party executive wants me to revise my history of England,' he said, 'but it all seems rather irrelevant. If anyone talks about Marx now, it's Groucho not Karl.' He smiled. 'I thought I'd make a start by collecting my articles and pamphlets. Until we left the apartment in Berlin, I didn't realise how much I'd written over the years.'

'Good idea.'

We stared reflectively into our pints. The hubbub of the bar did not intrude.

'By the way, I'd like to visit Father and Mother's grave again. Would you come with me?'

'I'd be delighted. Anytime. At your leisure. You know how I love old graveyards.'

'The truth is, Julian, I'm not in a hurry to take on more work. I should like to enjoy my family. I'd like to be useful in the community, grow vegetable marrows, and watch cricket on the green.' He looked at me with candour. 'It's nice to be an ordinary person again.'

I was surprised. 'Were you not – if you'll pardon the expression – an ordinary person in Berlin?'

He shook his head. 'If you were English or foreign, you were always slightly different, however long you lived there. My students were always asking why I had come.' He looked at me, and I saw his confidence returning. 'They were like you, Julian, they could not understand what I was doing.'

'Why not?'

'I had certain privileges, you see. I could cross the border into the West whenever I chose. I could buy things, little luxuries like cheese and coffee. And I could read things that were forbidden.' He looked away. 'So people always treated you – ' he searched for the word, ' – with envy.' He sighed. 'I was never able to shake that off. I was always a marked man.'

[8]

In the argument between my head and my heart I told myself that I felt sorry for Kristina. Mine were the attentions of sympathy, not love. The flowers and fruit that I laid on her kitchen table were symbols of neighbourliness, not the shy gifts of a suitor. That was my contention, and my fantasy. I see now that my passion for her was like water dammed up by familial constraint. Once a breach was made, the surrounding countryside would be devastated, with all of us clinging to the wreckage. For the moment, however, I believed I was just responding to her circumstances, an attractive German woman coming to terms with life in a foreign country.

When my brother had been an expatriate in Berlin, Kristina had enjoyed all the advantages of language and citizenship. She could meet a man or a woman in the street, hold a conversation in a threadbare Konsum, exchange words with a dog-lover in the Volkspark, and have a reasonable chance of identifying something of their past and status, and of being known in return, the unconscious transaction that occurs between speakers of a shared language.

Now she was the outsider. Her social radar was no longer receiving signals. Raymond had persuaded her that the children should be brought up in the country, and she had acquiesced. When I pressed her, she confided that she thought it would be an interesting adventure. She had always been curious about England. Whatever the true value of this statement, there was no denying the price she had paid. In Mansfield she was cut off from the pleasures of the metropolis, the galleries and concert halls that would have stimulated her imagination. She loved her children, and fussed over their needs, but she was also trapped by the domesticity, the world of painted faces, gingerbread men, and bed-wetting. She wanted to find work that would get her out of the house. In Berlin, she had worked as an interpreter and translator, but her secretarial English was not yet good enough for her to work at temping as a typist. I offered to give her instruction in legal and business English, and it was through these lessons together that the first cracks began to appear in the dam.

Now Jericho Lodge was open to the world, buzzing with air and light and activity. The garden was full of noises – grass-cutting, hammering and birdsong. An empty corner of the village was alive again and when I found I could not avoid the place I attempted, through grammar and syntax, to establish a mode of normality to my dealings with my brother's wife, however hard that might be. I would sit beside her in the evenings, and take her through the week's exercises. We would laugh together over the absurdities of the English language.

'I am your Pygmalion,' I said, as we sat one evening with her books scattered across the kitchen table, 'and you are my Galatea.'

She was puzzled. 'Excuse me?'

'My Fair Lady.'

She smiled. She understood.

Raymond came in, catching the end of the conversation. I was embarrassed. He began to sing, 'I'm getting married in the morning,' in a Stanley Holloway voice. He had a good baritone and knew the words by heart. He went out, still singing. I looked at Kristina. 'The rain in Spain stays mainly in the plain.'

She laughed. 'He loves those songs. He saw that show when he was still a young man.'

'Before he left.'

She nodded. She pushed her books aside. 'I was five years old when Raymond came to Berlin.'

'And I was fourteen.'

It was then, and on subsequent evenings, that she began to tell me about herself. We had the language books open before us, but we made few references to the subjunctive or the past participle. If Raymond came in, she would break off and refer with studied amusement to an oddity of phrasing.

I learned that she had grown up in Dresden. Her mother, Anna-Maria, was of Polish origin, but had been raised a German.

'My grandparents left Poland after they were married.'

'Did you know them?'

'They died in the war.'

There was something about the way she said this that discouraged further enquiry. In a moment, she took up her story again. Her father, Reinhardt Oswald, was an academic, a professor of classics. He had been conscripted by the Nazis and captured by the Russians just before the fall of Berlin. He had suffered terribly in Siberia as a prisoner-of-war and had not been released until 1952.

I was surprised at this.

Kristina shook her head. 'Many thousand Germans did not return, if they were lucky, until the Fifties.' She sighed. 'That is how it was then.'

Oswald was a member of the SPD, and he had met Kristina's mother soon after his release from captivity. They had married within a year, and Kristina, their only child, had been born just after the Hungarian uprising.

'I had a good childhood,' she said, 'but it was so short.'

Her father had never recovered from his imprisonment and had died when she was still a little girl. Her mother, whose middle-class background had handicapped her academic prospects in the university world, had managed to get a teacher's job in Dresden.

'My mother worked so hard for me,' she said. 'I was everything to her.'

Then tragedy struck again. Her mother was found to have breast cancer and Kristina's adolescence had been dominated by her illness. She had died when Kristina was nineteen.

'After that,' she told me, 'I had my daring time.'

'What sort of daring?'

'My government work.'

She had always been anxious to escape the provincialism of the society, and had trained in languages. Now, without a family, her work became her life. Translation and interpreting offered opportunities to work with foreigners, and sure enough the authorities were only too pleased to have a beautiful young German woman escorting visiting dignitaries around the city, inspecting showcase factories and institutions, and providing a commentary on the heroic successes of the GDR. The job had been well paid and responsible, and soon she was transferred to East Berlin, a significant promotion.

'Then I had freedom,' she said. 'I could do what I liked.'

'Did you?'

She gave me her enigmatic smile. 'I have always done what I liked.'

Throughout these years, she had remained committed

to her Church. 'God was my little private protest.' The more she worked for the state, the more she longed to escape her duties. 'I hated what I was doing,' she said, 'and then I came to hate myself. That was when I decided to go to university.'

'And so you met my brother.'

'I think I was always looking for a father,' she said. When she was introduced to Raymond, he was an impressive, much-travelled, even romantic figure, and she had fallen for him. 'East Berlin was so boring,' she said, 'and so provincial. Foreigners always seemed appealing.' I was interested to discover what other relationships had preceded Raymond, but she did not volunteer the information, and I was reluctant to ask. Kristina liked to ration what she told me, session by session.

Once, early on, when we were alone, she said, 'It is odd to see you and Raymond here together.'

'I think we are very different.'

'He says you were not friends.'

'He was a stranger. I did not know him.'

'Oh,' she said, with a distant look in her eyes, 'no one really knows him. Perhaps he does not even know himself.'

On another occasion she said, 'He asked me to marry him a week after we first met.' She laughed. 'I refused.'

'Why did you change your mind?'

'He persuaded me,' she said. 'Perhaps in my unconscious I wanted to come to England. You cannot understand how bad it was to live in East Berlin.'

I was intrigued. 'Did he always plan to come home?'

'How do you say? In his secret heart, he always did,' she replied. 'He is a patriot.' She smiled. 'But I am not.'

'What are you?'

'According to your police authorities, I am an alien,' she said. 'So here I am,' she concluded.

'A long journey.' There was something incomplete about her narrative, but I could not put my finger on it. 'And already so many adventures.'

'Too many,' she said with feeling. She sighed. 'Yet, do you know Julian, sometimes I feel as though I have only just started.'

I always liked it when she used my name. Our routine was well established now. I would ask questions, and she would talk about her early life. In return, she would quiz me about my own career.

At first, I had answered stiffly and with caution, but, like a convalescent with a physiotherapist, I was learning to take risks and to express myself in new ways. There was optimism and energy in the air, and though I had not used such words to anyone, even Susan, I felt myself to be falling in love. It was so hard for me to utter this word, even to myself. The experience was both new and forbidden. What did this love feel like? My descriptive powers, such as they were, came from the lexicon of the law. I lacked the words to put my fascination with my brother's wife into an acceptable vocabulary. Instead, I continued to hover indecisively near the subject, unwilling or unable to do anything myself, hoping against hope that Kristina would take charge for both of us. What I did not realise at the time, and only now understand, is that those who are passive in love will always suffer for it.

[9]

One morning Kristina rang to say that Raymond was unwell. 'He has a pain,' she said.

'What sort of pain?'

'He says he has a pain in his chest. I think it is no matter. He is always complaining.'

I knew that Raymond was something of a hypochondriac, and sure enough his mysterious attack faded as suddenly as it had occurred. 'I'll have a check-up with the quack, just in case,' he said, when he rang to announce his recovery.

'Nothing like a check-up,' I said.

'If you don't mind, old boy, I'll park the wife with you while they do the tests. She has a bit of a thing about the medical profession.'

I happily went along with his plan. Raymond, who liked to make a fuss about his health, turned a routine matter into quite an occasion, as if determined to be the centre of attention. Kristina would leave the children with a neighbour, and then drop him at the doctor's. In deference to her distaste for hospitals, she would come to my office and kill time reading magazines. I did not resist Raymond's scheduling, but made a contribution of my own. I would show Kristina some of the sights of Brighton and we could all meet up on the pier at five o'clock. We could have ice-cream and visit the fortune-teller. Raymond agreed. 'Let's make a day of it,' he said. Inside, I was singing. I would be alone with Kristina.

When the day came I slipped out of my office at the appointed hour to find Kristina waiting for me in reception. She was, in my eyes, more beautiful than ever. Her hair was loose and sensual, not braided as usual, and her face was smiling, not remote and inward, as it could be. She was dressed for an outing, and I was only sorry that our promenade could not be a head-turning stroll through Knightsbridge or down the rue de Rivoli.

'How is he?'

'He will be better once he has spoken to the doctor,' said Kristina, dismissively. 'That is always his way.'

We set off on our walk, like truants, in high spirits. The road sloped down to the esplanade. Our feet rang on the pavement. The afternoon was still, the sea like glass. Sounds carried, the cries of children and the shriek of seagulls. We watched a boy in a canoe paddling up and down, dipping his oar into the water, silver on the blade. On an impulse we descended to the shore, dropping out of sight below the promenade. Our feet sank into the beach and Kristina took her shoes off. We played ducks and drakes. We did not speak much. I think I was happy to experience the joy of companionship. The little waves beat feebly on the shore. The calmness was deceptive. This was a killing sea. I had seen bodies pulled up on these stones. Yet today there was no hint of the dark forces that could be unleashed here. Behind us, in the lee of the seafront, local traders were painting and decorating, preparing deck-chairs for the summer crowds. Like a Regency tart, the old resort was getting ready for another hectic season. At length, slightly out of breath from our exertions on the shore, we climbed up to the pier and, avoiding the photographer with the Polaroid and the monkey, crossed over to the boardwalk.

When I was a boy, my parents had occasionally brought me here, a solitary child with strange fantasies in his head. We would drive down from Tunbridge

Wells, visit the aquarium, marvel at the octopus and the seahorse, and worry about the likelihood of rain. Father would pursue antique-shop bargains in The Lanes, and Mother would gaze wistfully at fashions she could not afford. We would have a pub lunch and Father would complain about the cost of living. Later, I would be given a pound or two to spend on the amusement arcades. Looking back, I realise they didn't know what to do with me, just as I had almost nothing to say to them. I associated the pier with escape, loneliness and impoverishment. I remember watching a family of children chasing each other in a riotous game of tag. They wore cowboy hats and Red Indian feathers, waved toy guns and swords, and were lost in their game. I felt envious of their carefree fraternity. That was a long time ago. Now I was walking with Kristina and I had lost my voice, I did not know where to start. I was tongue-tied, as I had often been with my parents.

When we stepped on to the boardwalk, I experienced that old sense of departing the world of responsibility. Here, we were on the margin. The town was behind us. We were over the sea, oily and menacing through the cracks below. We had escaped. Almost at once, as if this was expected of people on the run, Kristina took my hand, quite gently.

'Don't have anxiety,' she said.

I smiled. 'I'm okay. Are you?'

I could feel the tension and so could she. We were entering a danger zone.

'It's nice,' she murmured with reassurance.

'I'm sorry,' I said. 'I'm not used to this sort of thing.' Then I said nothing, feeling only the warmth of her fingers. Whenever I recall that moment I remember the happiness and often there are tears in my eyes. I could not think what to say or do, but I knew something was happening. Inside, there was singing and laughter, and my heart was carousing. All my defences were down. With a single gesture, Kristina had reached out and made contact. I had written long, intimate letters to her in my head, proposing such moments of escapism, but I had never sent them. Now that I was with her and could say anything I wanted, all I could think of was the impossibility of what we had just begun. I had been waiting and waiting, but now I was fulfilling my desires, I was lost. I remember shaking my head in silent dismay.

She seemed to know my thoughts. 'Nothing is impossible,' she said fiercely. I felt her grip tighten. 'You are such a lonely person, Julian.'

'Do you understand that?' I wanted to throw my arms around her and embrace her, there and then.

'I understand.' She sighed. 'In Germany we call it Einsamkeit. When you are alone you are cold. It is warmer with another person.' She squeezed my hand in hers. 'I am going to make you warm again.'

We stood by the balustrade and followed the gulls bobbing on the water. A male was chasing two females, an apparently random movement that developed meaning as we watched. We laughed and pointed and said little. The watery sun was strengthening and burning hotter on our faces.

After some minutes, we continued our stroll up the pier, still holding hands. I found I was glancing over my shoulder, conscious that we might bump into one of my clients or someone from Mansfield. Kristina noticed my anxiety and slipped her hand out of mine. I took her arm, moving from suitor to brother-in-law. We did not need to hurry down this road. Time was on our side. Vaguely, at the back of my mind, was the fear that

Raymond would find out. I could hardly explain or justify this behaviour to myself let alone my brother.

We reached the end of the pier. A colony of fishermen trailed lines into the sea. A few silver fish lay on sheets of newspaper. When I saw plastic picnic boxes filled with worms, my mind jumped to mortuaries and graves. A young man with a mop and pail was pasting up advertisements for the summer season. I bought us each a toffee apple at a stall. A procession of tankers inched across the horizon in misty silhouette.

Kristina looked out at the Channel. 'I have always loved the sea,' she said. 'When I was growing up, it was a place of longing. In the summertime, my mother would take me to this island on the Baltic, Hiddensee. It's very beautiful there, you know.'

'I should like to see it.'

'The Baltic Sea is very calm,' she said. 'But in those days it was forbidden, of course. I would look at the horizon with despair, knowing I could not get out. Your sea is different. When I look at these waves and when I see the ships out there I think of freedom.'

'We have the sea in our veins.'

She laughed. 'I thought it was ice that was in your veins.'

'I have been afraid.'

She squeezed my hand again. 'Don't be afraid.'

We turned away and walked into the amusement arcade. At first we watched boys in leather jackets take on the forces of the universe with nonchalant co-ordination. Then Kristina took the wheel of a Formula One racing car and began to negotiate the computerised, Virtual Reality of the course, laughing at her collisions. When the game was over and the car had stopped I saw a new light of enjoyment in her eyes.

We were still there, rolling coins down a chute, when I saw Raymond hurrying towards us. He seemed relaxed and cheerful. I knew that in his self-confident mood he would detect nothing. Kristina kissed him on the cheek, a married, affectionate kiss. I was relieved to return to our easygoing threesome.

'The quack says I have the cardiovascular system of a fifty-year-old. The heart of an ox.' He clapped his hands together. 'Good news, eh?'

'What a relief,' I said.

'I feel ten years younger already,' he went on. 'Now, what about this fortune-teller?'

I smiled. 'There's also a young woman offering to decode the secrets of your signature.'

'Come on, Julian, I think it's high time we all had a really reliable guide to the future.'

[10]

About a week after our visit to Brighton, my brother and I took advantage of the May Day Bank Holiday, a cold Monday, to visit our parents' grave together. We had stood there once before in discord and hostility and I wanted – perhaps we both wanted – to make peace with the past.

Raymond was a lovable character, but rather more of a shambles than I had bargained for. When he boasted about his doctor's admiration for his cardiovascular system, I sensed he was troubled by something in his mind, a fear or a worry that he could not mitigate or console. This interested me. My forensic mind was still weighing up what Kristina had said, and I was also considering the various tell-tale remarks my brother had

66

made to me in unguarded moments. I have to admit that there was nothing I wanted so much as to have him, in a manner of speaking, answering my questions under oath.

It was a cold morning, but bright, with fluffy white clouds and a strong, invigorating wind which ruffled the countryside with shivers of movement. As we left the village, a troop of Morris dancers was forming up outside The Royal Oak, but I did not pause. I like to do what I've set out to do. I took a picturesque route, away from the main roads, down tree-shaded lanes reminiscent of Arthur Rackham illustrations.

The church was in a secluded hollow and its graveyard rose up the slope behind, vanishing into a line of trees; beech, hazel and fir. We stepped through the lych-gate and the familiar, almost soothing, chill of the cemetery crept over me like the hush of nightfall. A woman with a bunch of wilted flowers was pushing a pram. Rooks were cawing high in the beech trees. Otherwise we were alone. This was my territory. I led the way.

The plot was easy to find. A simple grey headstone. Two modest parallel impressions in the ground. My parents' names and dates. R.I.P. The salt of the earth, now side by side. Adversity overcome. Long, full, reasonably happy lives. 'In death they were not divided'. The phrase popped into my head from nowhere but I did not utter it. We laid some flowers on the turf. Mother's funeral now seemed a world away. Raymond stood there, lost in thought. I observed a sympathetic silence. Then we walked slowly down to the foot of the rise and sat on a sunny bench out of the wind.

'When my time comes,' said Raymond, 'I'd like to be buried here.' He looked away, up into the trees, as if his spirit was soaring there.

'A place like this,' I said, 'brings you face to face with yourself.'

I knew he was watching me carefully. 'What has Kristina been telling you?'

'Hardly anything,' I said, with some truthfulness. 'For some reason, she seems reluctant to talk about you.'

In another context that might have been a cruel thing to say, but my brother seemed relieved by my words. 'That's good,' he said. 'I'd rather you heard things from the horse's mouth.'

'I'm happy to hear your side of the story, so to speak,' I said, as brightly as I could.

I have often observed from the Bench the compulsive need we have for sharing secrets. People blurt out the truth as though they cannot live with their lies. Man is, I believe, a moral animal. That's one conviction I share with the communists. Despite all the progress we have made, we still believe in punishment and retribution. I have often seen witnesses admit things they simply cannot keep down. But if I had hoped to find in Raymond a spirit of remorse, I was mistaken.

'There is no story, Julian. There's my life, of course, but as I've told you already I have no regrets.' He scowled in the direction of our parents' grave. 'I'm sorry to disappoint you.'

I fumbled in my coat. 'I was reading Conrad the other night. I came upon this passage. I wrote it down.' I pulled out my wallet and found the scrap of paper. '"A transgression,"' I read, '"a crime, entering a man's existence, eats it up like a malignant growth, consumes it like a fever."' I looked at him very hard. 'I hate to say this, Raymond, but I think you are like that man,' I said.

My brother looked grim. 'You'll have to explain yourself, Julian. I don't know how often I have to repeat this. I have nothing to hide.'

In my courtroom manner, sympathetic yet firm, I said I thought it was he who had the explaining to do. 'Everyone knows you were part of a totalitarian regime. I simply can't accept that you have nothing to answer for.'

Raymond nodded, as if he was making up his mind to co-operate. 'Let me tell you my story,' he said, 'and let me admit where I feel a sense of failure. And then tell me if you think I have anything to be ashamed about.'

'You must understand,' I said, 'that I am only asking the questions that someone in my position would ask. It's really just a professional habit.'

'I understand.' I watched him compose his thoughts. 'When I first went to Berlin as a young communist,' he began, 'I thought I was making a stand for the working class. I believed I was joining the movement for world revolution in our time. I thought I was John Reed in Leningrad. What I didn't see, because I didn't want to see it, was the need the authorities had for western defectors. No wonder they fixed us up with jobs and cars and nice flats to live in. We were like gold.'

'I remember a letter you wrote to Mother,' I said. He looked at me with interest. 'You described yourself as a showcase communist fleeing from the corrupt capitalist West.'

'Did I now?' He laughed. 'I certainly thought I was mixing with the people of Berlin on equal terms. I quickly discovered how wrong I was. As I've told you, I could always use my passport to cross over to the western sector. I was aware of a resentment on the part of ordinary East German citizens who did not have these advantages, but I didn't make the connection.'

'What connection?'

'With the methods of the regime. In those days I wouldn't admit the evidence of my own eyes. If you had asked me about it then, I would have said it was the price the working class had to pay to achieve a classless nirvana.' He was shuffling the gravel with his feet. 'There were so many inconsistencies in those days, I didn't pay much attention . . .'

I tried to picture him in his proletarian cloth cap and his grey trousers, a mini-Brecht figure with a bundle of theories and a big heart shrivelling at the sight of this regimentation and control. He was, as I have observed before, a most unlikely communist.

He was turning over the past in his mind. 'As a foreigner, of course, I was both a prize exhibit and at the same time incredibly vulnerable. I could be expelled at any time. I was always open to blackmail. Plus, I had made an emotional investment in the place. As you know, having divorced Maureen in England, I quickly married Eva, from the ministry. I later discovered that she had been planted on me. So even that part of my life was not my own. We like to believe in free will and end up coming to terms with an oddly deterministic universe, don't we?'

I wondered what exactly he was getting at, but I sensed it was better to say nothing. He had his point of view and it was right to let him explain it at leisure.

'You are looking at a man who has lost his faith. My working life was centred on the communist ideal. Now what have I got? A pewter bust of Lenin, three volumes of "Kapital", and a map of the world that's as useful as the Ptolemaic projection.'

'You have Mother's legacy, I suppose.'

'For an ex-communist, a modest inheritance is something of an embarrassment.' He gave a bitter laugh. 'It's all a bit of a joke.'

'History is full of jokes.'

'You talk about History, Julian, as if it was a mathematical abstraction. Look at me. I am History. I feel my life is wasted.'

'You should draw a line in the sand,' I said, encouragingly. 'Put your demons behind you. You're not too old to enjoy the future.'

He considered me coolly. 'You don't give up, do you? If I wasn't married to her, I'd imagine that Kristina had put you up to this.'

'Put me up to what?'

He sighed. 'There is one thing I feel awkward about, just one thing. If I tell you about it now, will you let the subject drop?'

'Of course,' I said, feeling a sense of triumph. 'What is it?'

He collected his thoughts. 'To cut a long story short, I was a university teacher with colleagues from all ages and backgrounds. I had the charge of hundreds, no, thousands, of students. We all had to do it.'

'Had to do what?'

His expression registered a moment of disquiet. I saw that the words were not coming so easily. 'File reports and fill in stupid forms. It was only routine information.'

'Routine information?'

'About the students.' He was anticipating my questions now. 'I had no choice. I was bound to give it to them. No one will ever understand the extent to which we were all spying on each other.' He shook his head at the recollection. 'Yes, I became an informer for the Stasi soon after I arrived in Berlin.' He glared at me. 'Satisfied?'

'The state police,' I murmured. 'Staatssicherheits-dienst.' I admit that it gave me a certain perverse thrill to see the look of pain in his eyes as I rolled the fateful syllables on my tongue. There was nothing in our new-found friendship that would ever stop me asserting control over his future.

'You have to understand the strange position I was in.' His nervous smile was like a wound. 'I was a cog in a machine. I was part of the system, as we all were.'

We had disputed this many years ago. He had argued that every society has its secret side, its unaccountable agencies. I was half expecting a justification of that sort, but he took the conversation in another direction.

'I learnt that if you do something for the system, then the system will do something for you.'

'What else did you do for the system?'

'I used to go to the libraries in West Berlin, the American library, the British Council library, and the university library. I would read the English and American press, and make reports.' He smiled blandly. 'It was hardly a hanging offence, Julian.'

I did not reassure him. I found his lack of remorse annoying me. 'What sort of reports?'

He screwed up his broken face as if I was ripping off a bandage. 'One of the ironies of spying on the West is that almost all the information you need is printed in the newspapers, or published in official documents. It was just a question of ploughing through newsprint looking for occasional nuggets. I had access, so it was easy for me. It was low-level stuff, of no real importance.'

'Did they pay you for what you did?'

'Oh yes, they paid me.' I heard the anger and frus-tration in his voice. 'If you want to satisfy yourself that I was suffering for this, I can confirm that my life was not a happy one. After Eva, there was a succession of women, but I didn't trust any of them. That was why Kristina was so special.'

'She was different?'

'Yes, she was different.' I was glad to see that he did not smile, as I had feared. He seemed troubled still. 'Now you can see why I was so anxious to leave.'

It was as though he had jumped several steps in a complicated argument. 'I don't understand.'

'I had to get her away from there. I had to make a clean break.'

I could see that he was upset, but I knew that this was the moment to explore the matter. Sometimes I think I see the world like a film director, and with a calculated detachment. At such moments, I want those who are in my movie to obey my every whim.

'I'm glad you did,' I said, inviting further explanation.

He was rubbing his face awkwardly with his hand, and now he stood up, as if wanting to leave the scene of his embarrassment. I followed him, listening attentively.

'So you see, yes, I do have some minor demons, and yes, I did want to escape a little – no harm in that – but not in the way you think. I have no regrets. Reading English newspapers in West Berlin is not such a crime,' he said. 'The information I passed was dull stuff. You shouldn't torture me about it.' He bent down to pick a flower for his buttonhole. 'It's easy to be judge and jury after the event.'

We were standing on hallowed ground, at the entrance to the sanctuary. The medieval door creaked in the wind. I was silent. He claimed to have no remorse, and no regrets, and yet he was deeply worried. There were implications to what he had said that I did not understand. I would have to discuss these with Kristina, at the right moment.

'Thank you, Ray,' I said. 'I appreciate hearing your story. You were part of a system that failed.'

'It is hard to put it right out of my mind. I'm doing what I can to keep busy here.'

A bird flew out of the porch. Raymond started, and then laughed at himself. 'Jumpy,' he said, almost apologising.

'If you believed in this', I said, pushing open the church door, 'you could see a priest and get it all off your chest.' We went inside, greeted by the musty smell of pews and ecclesiastical hangings.

'What has the Church done? It's a cruel state, perpetuating centuries of hate, discord and superstition.'

I smiled. 'I see you are still anti-clerical.'

'I should like nothing better than to find a meaning in things.'

'Perhaps you should write it all down.'

Now it was his turn to smile. 'The True Confessions of a Reluctant Informer.'

I was serious. I could see a plan. 'You could write it down and then, if you wanted, you could place it with me. I would only open it and read it after – after your death.'

He seemed cheerful at last.

'My memoirs. Posthumous fame. Don't forget, young Julian, that I'm going to be around for some years yet. The doctor told me so.'

SUMMER

[1]

That was the summer I discovered the meaning of family. I became expert in the noises children make and learnt to distinguish between a grizzle, a whine, a howl and a sob. I found that silence is not always golden but can suggest mischief, the prelude to juvenile chaos. I grew wily in the ways of childish manipulation. I was, I told my brother, like a remote, self-satisfied tribe whose treasured, secluded ways are upset by the invasion of a demanding intruder. I had to adapt or become extinct. I liked to say, indulgently, that it was good for me.

At first I was awkward, not myself. Then, as Olga and Sasha and in due course their friends from the local school became bolder, I acknowledged the surprising pleasure of playing games and practising card tricks. I found I was good at making up stories and, when I enhanced these with details from my work with the dead, could induce a satisfying *frisson* of fear in my listeners. There was nothing that these kids did not relish. They would terrify themselves with macabre tales of decapitation and disembowelment and then beg me to play hide-and-seek, or kick a ball around my garden. I came to look forward to these interruptions. My brother referred to his children as 'the Visigoths'. From time to time, he would murmur, 'I hope the Visigoths aren't bothering you, Julian.' I would smile and say, quite truthfully, that a change was as good as a rest.

My brother was keen for his family to grow up bi-lingual and when he saw me teaching his wife, he pressed me to help with the children, too. At school they would learn English. At home, he and Kristina used German.

My task was to balance the domestic ticket. I worried that this would confuse them. Raymond replied that German was essential for the Europe of the future, and if his children had divided loyalties then that was their inheritance. Why should they not have the best of both worlds? I was not so sure. I feared they would be bullied. 'Don't you realise,' I said, 'how much some of us still hate the Germans?'

We had crossed swords over such matters in the past. Raymond always wanted to believe in the brotherhood of man. I, the cynical young capitalist, had sneered at this. You could not extinguish nationalism, I had argued. The Wall had come down, and I could rightly claim to have won the case. My brother was the loser, but he refused to concede. The old arrogance was still there. He resisted my questions about the past and claimed it was the future that mattered. In those early days, it seemed that his mood of optimism might survive unchallenged.

Outside, the May air was full of rain and sun. The crab-apple and garden lilac, the cow-parsley and the new leaf of beech and willow, and the great candelabras of horse chestnut in the lane all unfurled together in an explosion of growth. The land around grew fat and green. Everywhere there was sappy new life, impressionist colour and light. From nowhere, it seemed, trees and bushes would sprout long, trailing stems, and patches of bare earth would become choked with couch grass, bindweed and ground elder. Beyond my spiky privet hedge the daffodils bowed their heads and died, and were replaced by poppies and rambling roses. When I walked in the woods under the canopy of young beech, with the sunlight filtering through the leaves, and the bluebells rippling underfoot, I felt as if I was underwater, drowned in creation. The days lengthened and the spell of summer took hold of our imaginations.

I am a keen gardener. At this time of the year, I like to come home from a day lost in labyrinths of litigation or struggling over the causes of death, and unwind in the shade of my medlar tree. I'll pour myself a glass of chilled white wine, sit in my deck-chair and survey the scene at sunset. The sights and sounds of the country will accompany my reflections. Above the pasture at the end of my land, swallows and house-martins will be hawking for insects. Bugs and slugs move in the dampness at my feet and the undergrowth stirs and rustles with hidden movement. Perhaps I'll read the *Evening Argus*. Eventually I'll take up secateurs or hand-fork and start to prune or weed. For the first time in years, I found I was growing seeds in the greenhouse.

The seeds were Kristina's gift. When she and the children came over, I was often gardening and Olga and Sasha would question me about what I was doing. One day, Kristina handed me some seed packets. 'Here you are, Mr Green Fingers,' she said, patting me on the head as I knelt on the ground and prepared the potting compost in a tray.

I showed Olga how to space the marigold and nasturtium seeds. Kristina watched, humming a song, 'Geh aus mein Herz und suche Freud . . .', words I came to know by heart.

We covered the seeds with earth and marked the tray with the packet, and I explained that it would be a week or so before the seeds sprouted. Olga wanted to know why. 'Nature is slow,' I said. 'You have to be patient.' I looked up at Kristina. 'Good things take time.' I expected her to speak, but she remained silent. After the episode on the pier our relationship had changed in subtle, almost invisible, ways and I liked to think that the quiet pleasure we both took in doing ordinary things together was part of a deeper understanding. I was still persuading myself that I could handle the situation with discretion, like a case.

I was relieved to see that within little more than a week there were tiny green shoots breaking the surface. The children came almost every day to monitor the progress of the plants. We placed them in two separate trays, labelled 'Olga' and 'Sasha', and it amused me to see the rivalry that developed over how fast the plants were growing.

When I teased my brother with observations about the competitive nature of humanity, he would simply laugh. 'I shall teach them that all the seeds were planted equally and deserve an equal chance,' he said.

'And I shall teach them that there are good gardens and bad gardens,' I replied. It was, as I say, all very good-humoured.

Some days later, when it was time to transfer the seedlings from the safety of the greenhouse to the flower-bed, Olga and Sasha came to help. As I was burying the little roots in the earth, Kristina, who was watching, remarked in that strangely hypnotic accent of hers, 'The more you bury things, the more they come to the surface.'

'If they have life,' I said. I dug in the dirt with my fingers, plunging deep into the cool ground to turn the soil over. 'The dead do not trouble us.' One by one, I took the seedlings out of their tray. Olga and Sasha had lost interest in the planting and were running across the grass. We were alone.

'They take after their father,' she said.

'I think they take after you.'

She picked up a stone, and then tossed it away. Her wrists were so slender, and I admired the deftness of her hands.

'Would you like to be married?'

When I looked at her, returning her glance, she turned her eyes away. 'To the right woman,' I said.

'To Susan?'

I shook my head, quite instinctively. 'Not to Susan.'

'I think you are afraid of women,' she said.

'Unlike my brother.'

We both laughed. Every time we shared a joke I felt myself inching closer to that point of no return. What we were contemplating was taboo, and we both knew it.

Then, quite suddenly, as I smoothed the earth into place, I cut my hand on a piece of broken glass. I felt a stab of pain. There was blood dropping on to the ground and running down my wrist.

'I've cut my hand,' I said stupidly. I stood up and hurried back towards the house. Behind me, I could hear Kristina calling to the children in German.

I was in the bathroom, holding my hand under the cold tap to cleanse the wound when I felt a touch on my shoulder. 'Let me help you,' she said. Then she took my hand, put her lips to the wound, and sucked the blood into her mouth.

I felt her tongue, her teeth, her lips. Involuntarily, I closed my eyes, as if I had to make this into a dream. To believe or not to believe. I looked down at the nape of her neck and the tiny blonde hairs. It was all I could do to stop myself caressing her with my free hand.

The moment passed. She straightened up, looked me full in the face with excitement and then pushed my hand back under the water.

81

'There's a medicine box in the cupboard.' I watched her cross the room. I was aroused, embarrassed, unsure. I have led a sheltered, rather dull life. These were new experiences.

Kristina reached up and, following my instructions, lifted a biscuit tin off the shelf. Mother had given me a tin of cheese biscuits when I'd first moved here. It was a house-warming present which summed up our relationship completely.

Kristina took my hand and dried it with a towel. I obeyed her like a small boy. The blood was stopping and the wound was clean. She squeezed some salve on to the tip of her finger and began to work it into the cut.

'It's quite deep,' she said.

I felt the ointment bite. I said nothing.

Then she took a pair of nail scissors and cut a strip of lint, dressed the wound and bandaged my hand. The bandage was clean and warm. I felt whole again and reassured.

I hardly knew what I was doing, but then, with my free hand, I pulled her towards me and kissed her on the lips. There was no blood to taste, but she tasted wonderful anyway.

We were still kissing when Olga and Sasha came upstairs, looking for their mother.

I have never felt so exhilarated in my life.

[2]

My hand healed. I cannot speak so confidently about my heart. The green days of May became the short nights of June. In the fine weather we enjoyed that year I would sit out in my deck-chair, looking towards the Downs, letting the swish-swish of the sprinkler lull my thoughts while I battled with my conscience. I would sit there, alone, often with a bottle of malt whisky to hand, sometimes until eleven or twelve. When I heard the chimes at midnight from the parish church across the valley, I would rise, lock up, and turn in, hoping that my night would not be disturbed. Sleep did not come easily in those weeks. I was going round and round in my head, a rat on a wheel. There was no one, literally no one, I felt I could turn to. Once, I drove to Brighton and loitered by the Roman Catholic church we had attended at Eastertime. The old priest appeared eventually, moving watchfully, like a tortoise. Our eyes met. I almost stopped him, but something held me back.

The truth is that there was part of me that was relishing this secret. I was coming alive. I had made my declaration at last and I believed it had been answered. I thought I had found something and had been found in return. Whenever I told myself that it was a forbidden love, I found myself revelling in the discovery, not recoiling from it, as I should have done.

In my confusion, I telephoned Susan and invited her down for the week-end. I wanted to see what had happened to my emotions. Her visit was a disaster. She knew within minutes of her arrival that something was different. When she asked about Kristina, I replied that she and Raymond were settling in nicely.

'Are you still in love?'

'Oh, absolutely.'

We chatted about nothing, strolled in the garden, and admired the Judas tree she'd given me some years before. At her insistence, we went for a walk through the village. I dreaded that we might meet Raymond or Kristina, and steered her, on the pretext of a new exhibit, into our little museum, three poky rooms in the mock-Tudor craft centre behind the hairdresser. Old Mrs Lane, the curator, welcomed us with the greedy eyes of an inveterate gossip.

As we came back to my house, Susan put her arms around me. 'Let's go upstairs.' She could feel my hesitation. 'Are you seeing someone?' I brushed her question aside with a sarcastic comment about the women of Mansfield. When I kissed her I realised how preoccupied with Kristina my heart had become, but I pretended that nothing had changed. After we'd made love Susan began to cry. I was humiliating her. It was obvious my mind was elsewhere. I protested again, blaming my work, and somehow we managed to make up.

The evening drew on, and to keep the pretence of the week-end alive I took her to an expensive restaurant in the Weald. The conversation meandered, faltered and then died. We drove home in silence. In the morning we read the newspapers like an old married couple, hardly speaking. Susan left after lunch with an excuse about meeting a friend from America but we both knew that whatever there had been between us was finally over. After she had gone, I found myself wishing I had spoken out, but somehow the reality was harder to address than the fantasy version I'd enjoyed dallying with before.

I was shy of my feelings, inhibited by anxiety and shame. From almost every point of view, I was in the wrong. There was something so terrible about my emotions that, even when I was alone with Kristina, I found myself avoiding the obvious discussion. This was an inhibition she seemed to share and, in my innocence, I imagined that her reticence was to do with me.

About two weeks later, when my wound had contracted to a purple scar, Kristina said simply, 'I'm glad your hand is better.'

84

I smiled, and shared a nervous look with her. 'I was afraid it might become infected,' I said. 'But it seems to have been okay.'

Raymond, who was with us at the time, said blandly, 'That was a nasty cut. I'm only just realising that the countryside is just as dangerous as the city.'

So, once more, we pretended that nothing had really happened between us, even though I, at least, had my dreams and many waking moments full of her presence.

The children were also in my thoughts. They were a constant reminder of that outrageous kiss. They knew that something strange and important had taken place. They did not say anything, but they knew, and their knowledge frightened me. Whenever they came round to my house I detected a nervousness towards me. They no longer quite trusted the easy terms of our relationship.

It was with these anxieties in mind that I arranged to go on a residential course one week-end in late June. From time to time, the Coroners' Society organises these sessions for its members in some provincial conference centre. We will assemble to brush up on the latest aspects of the law and hear lectures on subjects such as 'Deaths in Police Custody and Prisons'. We are a scattered tribe, working alone, and it is pleasant to meet up and talk shop, so to speak.

On this occasion we were to foregather on the campus of Exeter University. It was a relief to shut up the house, throw a suitcase into the back of the car and take the motorway to the west. Mansfield had become rather claustrophobic and as I approached the broad sweep of Salisbury Plain my heart began to lift.

The real interest of these occasions lay in the extra-curricular activities – the drinks in the bar, the walks round the cathedral precincts, and the gossip in the deserted common rooms. Our society was, essentially, an all-male affair, and we had the clubbable air of a part-time regiment. It was an unwritten rule that one did not bring wives or partners, and I believe those few women coroners who did attend felt somewhat excluded from the jollification. When they were not flirting with the more attractive members of our group, they tended to sit together, no doubt passing adverse comment on the rest of us.

As far as the formal part of the week-end went, there was an enjoyable session entitled 'Sexual Asphyxiations' with slides, and then a panel discussion on 'Conflicts of Interest' which provoked a lively debate about where, in certain extreme circumstances, a coroner's loyalties might lie. I did not, I regret to say, admit to my questionable verdict on old Miss Nicholson, but others described how at times they felt obliged to interpret Jervis, the coroner's bible, with a certain elasticity. At these gatherings I am known for my conservatism, my adherence to the rule book. Indeed, it was my reputation for reliability that resulted in my being elected, to my surprise, to the council of our society.

On the final evening there was a dinner, an informal affair with jocular toasts and speeches, concluding by way of entertainment with a police video of the Lockerbie disaster. Afterwards, a number of us sat up in the college bar and reminisced about the bizarre experiences of our peculiar trade. More than once, one or other of our number would shake his head and observe, to general approval, 'Well, it only goes to show that fact is stranger than fiction.'

Inwardly, I was hoping that when I returned to Mansfield something – I did not know exactly what – would have changed. I am inclined to adopt a *laissez-faire* approach to things, and in my various emotional entanglements over the years I have tended to let matters take their course. I believe in Fate. Perhaps, during my absence, something had occurred that would break the impasse. As it turned out, there was a development, but it was not one that improved the situation to any degree. On the contrary, it only made matters worse.

When I returned home I found, among the bills and circulars on the mat, a note sealed in a plain white envelope.

'I must see you. Kristina.'

No date, just the urgency of that imperative. I was staring at it, stupid and indecisive, and was about to make an exploratory telephone call, when I heard a dog barking, followed by footsteps coming down the path. Without turning, I knew it was Raymond. He was sweating from his walk, and his manner was less spirited than usual, even a trifle forced. Jack, the puppy, was jumping disobediently at his side.

'Hello there, bwana. How was the busman's holiday?'

I guessed that he had been watching out for my return. His appearance was too pat. Behind the mask of jollity, I sensed there was something on his mind.

I put Kristina's note into my jacket pocket. 'It was nice to get away,' I replied.

'Pack up your troubles in your old kit bag, what?' He tied the dog to the gate. Once inside, he dropped into the armchair by the fireplace with a sigh.

'Troubles?'

'Just a manner of speaking.'

'Cup of tea?'

'Spot on, old boy.'

As I waited for the kettle to boil I took Kristina's note from my pocket and shredded it into the bin. I was certain that Raymond had not seen the handwriting on the envelope. I reflected that it was a good thing he did not have a key to the house. When I carried the tea things into the sitting-room, Raymond was sprawled back in the chair, hands folded across his chest, twiddling his thumbs.

'Something on your mind, Raymond?'

He looked at me strangely. 'Kristina.'

I passed him a cup of tea, affecting detachment. 'So what's up?'

I looked at him more closely. He seemed indefinably older, and shrunken into his clothes. Without his customary bonhomie he seemed weaker and more vulnerable. When he spoke, it was almost to himself, as if he was unfamiliar with admissions of weakness.

'If I anticipated difficulties about coming home, they were of the Rip van Winkle variety – comic misunderstandings and inevitable readjustments. I know this sounds corny but I thought that I could live in the present and look forward to the future. And I thought Kristina could be part of this.' He paused to take his tea. 'It seems that I was wrong.' He directed a searching look towards me. 'How well do you think you know Kristina?'

I know my laugh was nervous. Was he playing with me? 'Well, so-so. I mean – how long have you been back? Four months? I like her immensely, of course, but—'

He put his tea cup down with a clatter. 'Can you imagine how I would feel if I thought my wife was involved with another man?'

I was strangely calm. 'I imagine you'd be – pretty upset.'

'Upset?' There was rare anger in Raymond's answer. 'I'd be devastated.'

88

I considered the situation judiciously. 'Do you have any reason to suspect that she's seeing someone?'

He stood up. 'That's a hard question to ask of any man in my position.' He began to pace up and down. 'I have a suspicion, that's all. Who knows? I may be getting things out of proportion again.'

As in a cross-examination, I saw my opportunity. 'Again?'

'I love her, Julian. I – I have kept her at some cost, you see. There have been times . . .' He dismissed the thought with his hand. 'That's not important now. I love her, and yet . . .'

I was interested. 'How can you be so sure?'

He shook his head. 'Her thoughts – her emotions – are somewhere else. I've seen it before. I mean, she has lost all interest in me.' A look of regret passed across his face. 'We sleep apart.'

I felt he was studying me like a card-player with a tricky hand, but I am professionally expert at giving nothing away. 'I'm sorry,' I said, and then I heard myself asking how long this had been going on.

'Hard to say. It's on and off. Her mood varies.' He shrugged. 'Months, probably.'

A question always offers a good disguise. 'You mean since you arrived in England?'

'I suppose so.' He seemed doubtful.

Now I was cruel. 'How was your sex life . . . before?'

'Before what?'

For a moment I wondered if he was trying to trap me, but I dismissed the notion. 'Before you left Germany.'

He smiled with embarrassment. 'I'd say normal.'

I could not resist the temptation. 'What's normal, would you say?'

'Oh, come on, Julian, don't be ridiculous. You know what I mean.'

I apologised, blaming the habits of work. I tried to make amends. 'Is there anything I can do to help?'

He looked at me with gratitude. 'Would you talk to her on my behalf?'

Perhaps, in retrospect, that was the moment I should have made some kind of admission and said, I am the other man. As it happened, of course, I said nothing of the sort. I simply shook my head in a simulacrum of sadness and murmured, indistinctly, that of course I would speak to Kristina if he thought this would help.

His relief was painful to witness. 'I know she thinks the world of you, Julian.'

'She's my sister-in-law, Raymond, that's all.' The evasion – I will not call it a lie – came out easily enough. 'I'm touched that you'd want to confide in me. I know how difficult that is for you.'

'Please.'

He was imploring me and it appalled me to see how good I felt about it. He was in my control, and it gave me a surreptitious thrill to see how reduced he had become.

I feigned anxiety. 'What should I say? I'm not very good at this sort of thing.' I made a little joke. 'I'm used to dealing with the dead.'

He did not smile. 'Get her on her own. Tell her about my fears.'

'What exactly are they?' I could not help myself. 'Is it someone in the village?'

'Good Lord no.' He seemed to find my suggestion almost comical.

Now I was suspicious, and I had with difficulty to suppress my anxiety. 'I'm not sure what you're getting at, Ray. It's not as though she's had much opportunity to meet someone new.'

'Why should it be someone new?' he replied. 'There's always the past.'

I realised with surprise, and some relief, that we were speaking at cross-purposes. Presumably he was referring to the years before they'd met. This did not seem to offer much of a threat to either of us. 'That's a big subject,' I said. 'I wouldn't know where to start.'

'Find out what she's up to. Say – say that she has reasons – I concede that – but say that we have so much to offer each other. Say—' He was waving his arms, becoming his animated self, and as he recovered his spirits I felt my pity for him fade. 'I don't know, Julian. You'll have to play it by ear.'

I nodded, happy at the influence I had been given over his life. 'I'll have to choose my moment.'

'Of course, of course.' His submissiveness was pathetic. I could torture him for as long as I wanted. I could do nothing for a week, ten days even, and he would have to suffer patiently. 'Take all the time you want,' he said. 'We don't want to blow it.'

I noticed his attempt to turn this into a shared project and again I turned the screw. 'I don't have much experience in this line. Have you any tips?' I was curious to discover how he, the ladies' man, would respond.

'Talk to her about me. Ask her what you like. Don't mind my feelings. If there is another chap, the chances are he's German.'

'Someone you know?'

'Maybe.' He seemed uneasy at the idea.

'You're sure it's from the past?'

'Who else could it be? She hardly knows anyone here – apart from you.'

I did not want to encourage this line of enquiry. 'It's pointless to speculate, Ray,' I said, 'you're only causing yourself pain. I'll do my best. Just leave it to me.'

As I watched him lumber towards the door it occurred to me that, when the moment came, it would be safest to report that Kristina was 'seeing' no one, and that his suspicions were misplaced.

He lifted the latch on the front door and turned. 'I really appreciate this, Julian.'

'No problem, bro.'

I put out my hand and he shook it, like a businessman sealing a contract.

'I knew I could rely on you,' he said.

As he walked up the garden path to collect the dog, he was actually whistling, as if his mind had already been set at rest.

After Raymond had gone, I telephoned Kristina and announced my return. I asked how she was and accepted her reassurances. She apologised for the letter. Raymond had been annoying her, she said. She was better now. She was okay. She sounded slightly out of breath and anxious, as if afraid of being overheard. I explained I had a few things to sort out, and would come over in a day or two. Again, I asked if she was all right, and she said she was. I said I had some new ideas about the kind of work she might do in the neighbourhood. Finally, I rang off. Raymond would be home soon.

I sat for a while, alone with my thoughts. Eventually I left the house and went for a walk. I found myself heading towards the cemetery, but this time I did not linger among the headstones, but made my way into the gloomy interior of the church. The nave was deserted. I sat in front of the east window, watching the summer light go down behind the cross. I felt drained of energy, and yet at the same time curiously elated. I felt a kind of mischief creeping over me that was new and not unpleasing. I felt as though I was passing out of the familiar world of order and responsibility, into a *terra incognita* in which I could invent the rules. It was as if I was becoming one of those characters who came before me in court, and the idea that I should become my own case study was strangely appealing. Intellectually, I had always maintained that life was only of value when we risked it. In practice I had strenuously avoided such a gamble, but now I was beginning to entertain the idea of a mild flirtation with a certain provincial badness.

[3]

I made my visit. I went to my brother's house one afternoon when, by special arrangement, he was out shopping. I came as an envoy, but the message I carried was full of double meanings and hidden clauses. In my heart I was full of doubt and excitement.

It was a fine summer's day. I parked my car out of sight in the driveway, like a stranger or a travelling salesman. I had decided in advance to approach the house across the lawn, checking the out-buildings *en route*, in case Raymond had decided to stay and witness my mission. The Sussex countryside was languorous in the heat and nothing stirred. As I reached the back door, I felt a surge of adrenaline.

Inside it was cool. Kristina was in the kitchen, making bread. She had flour on her nose, but she was wearing make-up and underneath her apron she was dressed as if for a dinner date. I was glad to see that I was more than half expected. When I went up and kissed her, she turned her face to avoid my lips. I put my arms around her and hugged her. She was nervous, perhaps because she knew we were alone.

'Raymond is out shopping,' she said, taking off her apron and twirling round, like a model, suddenly girlish. 'Do you like it?'

'It's beautiful.' In my eagerness to find compliments I became absurd. 'To me you are always beautiful, so beautiful.'

'Julian.' She was laughing.

I was smiling too. 'I can't help myself,' I said, pressing my face into her hair. 'I'm falling in love with you.'

She pulled away from me, and went back to rolling out the dough on the kitchen table. She was muttering to herself in German, a mannerism of anxiety with her. 'Tell me. You have come for a reason. What's the matter?'

'I came here because I was sent.'

'What do you mean?' she challenged. Her cheeks were shiny with exertion and her eyes bright with annoyance. 'Didn't you want to come?'

'I always want to see you.' I was dismayed at our misunderstanding. 'What I mean is that Raymond asked me to see you.'

'Why?'

'When I returned from the conference last week he came to see me. He told me he suspects that you are, as he puts it, seeing someone else.'

'He always suspects that. He is the most jealous man in the world.'

I wondered about the dark forest of animosity I might have stumbled into. 'That's why he sent me. To find out.'

'No—' Kristina began to laugh again, covering her face with her hands.

'It does have its funny side.'

She came up and put her arms around me. 'This is like the Boulevard-Theater.' She was still laughing. I saw she was on the edge of mild hysteria. 'I can't imagine – I mean, it's like a dream – or a nightmare.'

We began to kiss. I pulled her towards me and this time she did not hold back. 'My love, my love . . .' This was a moment I had dreamed about. 'Darling . . .' I held her and for a moment I said nothing.

She kissed me. 'Geliebter, Liebster . . .'

I lost myself in her taste, her smell. This was my dream come true, and I surrendered myself as if for the first time. I wanted only newness and renewal. 'We must tell him,' I said. 'The longer we're silent, the worse it will be.'

'What can you say?'

'I can tell him the truth.'

'The truth?' Her laughter returned, and she was mocking me. 'Does anyone know what is the truth?' When she saw my seriousness she grew quiet. 'With feelings, it is so difficult.'

'Don't you trust yourself?'

'I need time,' she said with a sigh. 'My heart needs time.'

'So when he asks about you,' I said, 'I'll just say that we talked.' I had rehearsed these lines many times. 'I'll say that the subject of your marriage came up and you assured me that you loved him. You told me that there is no one else. As we say in English, I shall put his mind at rest.'

'You will deceive him.'

'I have already deceived him.' I saw Raymond's squashy, trusting face and his breezy openness and I felt ashamed.

There was a silence in the kitchen. Kristina fiddled with a scrap of dough. 'Perhaps I am a very bad person. Perhaps . . .' The rest of the sentence was lost in her reticence.

I took her hand. I felt the flour on her fingers. 'No,' I shook my head. 'You are not at all a bad person. Anyway, nothing has really happened.'

She lifted the tray and carried the bread to the oven. 'Do you want something to happen?' A wave of heat filled the room. I thought, We could go upstairs now and make love and he would never know. Kristina closed the oven door with a clunk and turned to face me, flushed with her cooking, the question still unanswered between us.

'I'm afraid,' I said, and I heard my words echoing in my mind.

'You are right to have fear,' she replied. 'You are seducing your brother's wife. That is a sin.'

There was something provocative in the way she used this word that gave me a moment of uneasiness. It was as though she was making a deliberate appeal to my worst nature. I dismissed the thought. I was in love. Such false notes simply did not register.

She came to me and kissed me again.

'What do you feel?' I asked. 'Deep down.'

'I feel – I feel that for many reasons I cannot stop myself, Julian.'

I felt she had rarely spoken my name so intimately and I was stirred to hear it. 'I know,' I said.

'I feel – I don't know exactly what I feel. Perhaps I could explain it in German, but in English . . .'

'Tell me in German.'

'You would not understand.'

'I could use a dictionary.'

'You see—' She was almost triumphant. 'We hardly know each other. You will find . . .'

'What will I find?'

She looked away. 'I'm not what you think . . . Or what you hope for.'

I laughed. 'People always say that.' I kissed her again. 'However bad I find you to be, I'll still love you.' As I said this the thought came to me that perhaps I loved her because she offered the prospect of transgressions.

'Careful, careful.' She moved away from me. 'You don't know what you are saying. "Love" is a big word.'

'It's a word I can handle.'

'You are a good man and you have a good place here. You should watch out.'

'We are a secret. I'm very good at secrets.'

'That is good.' She seemed relieved. 'I don't want anyone to know about this.'

'Especially Raymond.' I drove an imaginary golf ball down a mossy fairway. 'He would be destroyed if he found out.'

'He must not find out,' she said fiercely. 'Never.'

'Raymond says you don't sleep together. Is that true?'

She looked down. 'Yes, it's true.'

I think she understood what I wanted to ask. 'I don't love him any more,' she said, after a moment. 'I did love him once, but now . . . now I cannot.'

The anger in her voice surprised me. It was as though she had a reason, even a grievance to sustain this. 'You have his children,' I said.

She gave me a hard stare. 'They are from another

time. I thought – I thought I did love him then.' She was speaking with the greatest difficulty. 'I was wrong.'

For a moment I did not reply. The finality in her voice discouraged further questions and there was something in her tone that made me fearful, though I could not exactly say why.

'Tell me about Berlin,' I said. 'It's the part of your life that's still a mystery to me.'

'How English you are,' she said, not smiling. 'I am not in your court now, you know.'

'I'm sorry. I can't help it.'

Kristina began to clear the table, clattering the baking things into the sink. I sensed our time was drawing to a close. 'You English are all the same.' She seemed to know what I was thinking. 'When it comes to matters of the heart you don't know how to be serious. Once upon a time I thought that was the smart way, now I'm not so sure.' She squirted detergent into the water and began to wash up. 'What can I tell you about Berlin?' she said, as if humouring me with politeness. 'It was my home, and it was where I became a woman.' She looked up from her work with a strangely intent expression. 'I can tell you that I miss it every day of my life.'

I imagined that she missed her friends and her mother tongue. 'If I learn German perhaps you can teach me about my emotions.'

'There's only one way to learn a language,' she said.

This sounded like an invitation. I put my arms around her as she stood at the sink, and kissed her on the back of the neck.

She broke away. 'He will be back soon,' she said. 'He never stays out long.' She pulled out the plug and began to dry her hands. 'Sometimes I wish he would never come back. Is that terrible?'

'It's understandable.'

'He loves it so much here. It makes me a little crazy sometimes. He loves the house. He loves the village. He loves the countryside. It's hard for me. I'm foreign. I am not part of this.'

I wanted to ask her more, but I was thinking of Raymond and his imminent return. 'In his letter he told me that he'd come home to die.'

'He says that all the time. He thinks it's amusing.' A vehement look came into her face. 'It's not amusing to me.'

I began to compose my thoughts. Raymond would expect an answer. I would have to construct a plausible account of my conversation with Kristina. I did not see how I could do this with much credibility if Kristina did not love him. I wondered grimly if I was being set up to confront my brother not with some imagined infidelity but rather with the end of his marriage.

I said goodbye. I kissed her again.

'What will you say?' she asked.

'I will give him the reassurances he wants me to give him.'

I was conscious of being poised to make another small but significant move and, like a chess player, I was calculating the range of possible responses. Part of me was saying, Stop now before it is too late. But then I told myself that I had said this too often before. I should take the plunge into an adventure, and experience the thrill of freedom.

I hurried away through the garden, climbed into the car and accelerated out of the village, hoping not to pass Raymond on the way. I wanted to arrange my thoughts in private, alone. I parked in a lay-by high on the Downs, overlooking the village, and watched the summer gliders hovering in the thermals. I reviewed my feelings for Kristina, and my obligations to my brother. I began to form a plan that would enable me to keep my options open. Then I came back to Mansfield by the circuitous back route.

As I passed The Royal Oak I saw that the annual Midsummer Fair had arrived. The fairground people were setting up hoopla, coconut shies, helter-skelter and electronic games in the field behind the church. This was one of the high points of the year. I decided I would take Olga and Sasha there on Saturday.

[4]

The telephone was ringing as I reached home. Raymond was eager to know what had happened. I asked if he was alone in the house, sure in the knowledge that he would not be. I said I'd prefer to discuss such a delicate matter face to face, and then, because I could sense his anxiety, I added, 'You have nothing to worry about.' I was rather pleased with this formula: it was at least half true. Raymond said he would come over at once. I argued that this would look contrived. He began to worry that Kristina suspected something and I said he should relax. I suggested we discuss the whole business on Saturday when, I proposed, I would take the children to the fair. He could deliver them to my house, or collect them afterwards, and we could have a few minutes alone. It would seem more natural, I said. I wanted time to get my story straight.

A few minutes later I was in the kitchen preparing a simple evening meal of pasta, salad and cheese, when Kristina rang to say that she, too, wanted to go to the fair. I wondered what had happened in the interval. She sounded tense and I reacted badly to her agitation. I explained that Raymond and I had spoken, though of course she knew that.

'I told him not to worry,' I said.

'Is that what you feel?'

'What else could I say?'

There was a click on the line, probably a harmless electronic blip. I experienced a moment of panic. Was Raymond listening on the extension? I began to chatter about the fair. Kristina's anxiety turned to irritation.

'I don't understand what you're talking about.'

I said, lying, that I had to go out on a job and would call back later. As it happened, I did not telephone until the next day, speaking from my office between appointments. Raymond answered the phone. I suggested that we all go to the fair.

'We'll have some moments alone together. We can make an arrangement then,' I said. 'Don't worry.'

Although I like to prepare for every eventuality, each occasion has its own, unexpected logic. The visit to the Midsummer Fair was no exception. In anticipation, I was afraid that Raymond would broach the subject of our conversation right there in Kristina's presence, leaving neither of us anywhere to hide from our embarrassment. He was certainly capable, if the past was any guide, of such behaviour. In the event, we were caught up in the excitement and there was no opportunity. We, the Whyte family, found ourselves on show and we had to play our part in the village pageant as a happy family enjoying an afternoon out.

I was grateful for the carnival mood for I was in a state of high anxiety. Perhaps we all were. Raymond and Kristina threw themselves into the event with enthusiasm.

My brother, the jocular atheist, accepted an invitation from Reverend Findlater to guess the weight of the pig and then, with exaggerated shouts, tried to put the tail on the donkey. Together, he and I shied at coconuts and missed. Kristina bought raffle tickets in aid of Ethiopia. The children went screeching down the helter-skelter. I proved to be a crack shot with an air rifle and won a goldfish which I gave to the kids. Then I bought them candyfloss and gallantly held our trophies while Raymond and Kristina took them on the dodgems. I was an avuncular figure from a story book to the curious eyes of the village. Mr Curran, accompanying a party of boy scouts, even made a jocular reference of this sort. I was conscious only of the dangerous and discordant ideas in my head.

When they returned, Kristina decided that enough was enough. She was concerned that the children should not become over-excited. As we walked back through the village to my house for tea, Olga, whose English was improving rapidly, turned to me and said, 'Julian? Do you love me?'

I had been expecting trouble ever since Olga and her brother had discovered me with Kristina. We had explained the moment away by saying that Uncle Julian had hurt his hand and Mummy was kissing him better, but I was under no illusion that we had heard the last of it. I had feared what the children might say to their father in the privacy of Jericho Lodge.

'Of course I love you,' I said.

'Do you love Mummy?'

There was a silence, and I had an unnerving moment of panic. I knew that both Raymond and Kristina were watching me. Then I said, with an almost indecent glibness, 'No one loves Mummy as much as Daddy does.' I gave a light laugh, hoping to signal a change of subject. I hoped that my performance was both natural and yet not self-consciously so, smooth but not too easy, in a word, credible.

But Olga had not finished and there was little I could say to stop her. 'Julian?'

'Yes.'

'When Mummy was crying this morning Daddy said she didn't love us any more.'

Kristina took her daughter by the arm. 'Olga!'

I looked at Raymond. He was at a loss. He seemed broken and miserable. The secrets of the family were spilling into the open. There were undercurrents here that I still did not understand. I realised that I had to take charge. I said, 'Look, Kristina. I think you should take the children home. I'll go for a walk with Ray.'

I almost pushed her away. Olga and Sasha were too startled by the sudden flurry of adult activity to react. Olga could be in no doubt that she had done something wrong, and that in speaking her thoughts she had broken some grown-up rule.

Raymond and I began to stride purposefully down the road in silence. After some minutes Raymond, who was puffing along next to me, said 'Thank you Julian.'

I did not reply. Now, finally, I would have to come up with a story that he would accept. I knew, as I had always known, that I could not pretend that there was nothing wrong between them. I had said, 'Don't worry,' but that was an interim measure. I had to convey that there was cause for concern while also suggesting that all was not lost. I wondered what Kristina had been crying about.

I pointed ahead. There was a five-bar gate, and beyond that the Roman Road, a roller-coaster of white chalk. I indicated that we should leave the highway before opening up the conversation. There, we paused for breath. We were both out of shape. Around us were hop gardens and oast houses and cornfields, the green and gold of Kent. The sun was still high in the sky. This was the England the Normans had invaded, the England to which Raymond had so much wanted to return.

After some moments of silent contemplation, we began to walk again and as we found our pace I started to speak, letting my sentences punctuate the rhythm of my stride. 'You must know,' I said, 'that Kristina wasn't necessarily honest with me. Although we spoke at length, I had this sense that there were things she didn't say, things she might have been holding back.'

'You know what women can be like,' he said. 'Kristina is no exception.'

I waited for him to go on, but he was not forthcoming. 'To me,' I went on, 'she seems like a woman with something on her mind. I have seen that often enough in court. The sentence that remains unfinished and the shrug that avoids the question.'

'I've told you before that life in Germany had its own special complications.'

'Is she running away from something? Is that what Olga was talking about? You know, Raymond, I can't help you if you won't be frank with me.'

He took out his handkerchief and mopped his forehead. He was flushed with exertion and also with my directness. He did not quite know how to respond, though he knew it was wrong to be angry.

'Coming to England was her idea, too,' he said defensively.

'The problem is that things have not turned out as she hoped. She finds she doesn't understand the people. They don't understand her. Some of them, men like

Watkins, can seem quite hostile. She probably blames you for this.' I felt my imagination take wing. 'I think she wishes she was somewhere else and she sees you as an obstacle to that.' I delivered the *coup de grâce*. 'There's no doubt that, for the moment at least, she's fallen out of love with you.'

'Probably for quite understandable reasons,' he said.

I was encouraged to have his agreement, and did not probe more deeply, as I should have done. I accepted, at face value, the idea that this was a relationship going through a bad patch. I felt the confidence of a lecturer demonstrating a complicated theorem to a class. We walked in silence for a few paces and then I continued. 'You know this can happen in any marriage. Kristina has had a lot to adjust to. I've tried to help—'

'You've been wonderful,' he interrupted.

I waved his compliment away. 'All I've tried to do is to make her see that you are desperate for her love.' Now I was reaching the difficult part of the equation. 'That's what Olga meant just now. To Kristina, I am an alternative. She knows no one else. If there is another man in her life of course it's me.' I was pleased with the elegance of my wording. I had told him, but in such a way as to deceive him. I wondered how long this formula would hold. 'Yes,' I continued, 'Kristina has invested me with a significance I can do nothing about. Inevitably that reflects badly on you. It's something we both have to live through.' I had another inspiration, my QED. 'It is no doubt the fate of brothers in this situation, different as we are. Think of all the sisters who have fallen in love with the same man.'

Raymond was taking all this in, treading heavily across the chalk. 'She did not mention anyone else?'

'Should she?'

He shook his head. He seemed pleased. There was a new optimism in his demeanour. 'Is there anything I should do?'

I watched the wind furrowing the crops in the field, and was touched for a moment by the mystery of nature, the mystery of existence. The natural world seemed effortless in a way that we, with our consciousness, can never match.

'Have confidence,' I said. 'Don't worry so much about her.' I could hardly credit what I was saying. How quickly he had passed into my power. 'Kristina is busy building her nest here, seeing the family is settled. Leave her alone, but don't ignore her. She will come back. She is your wife. You have your children. I am here to help you. All is not lost.'

I trotted out these words of advice to my brother as I had so often trotted them out to the hopeless and the bereaved in my court. A sentiment is a great balm, especially if it is delivered with feeling. It is amazing how frightened people can be soothed if you look at them calmly and keep talking.

When I go back over these events I know I sound treacherous, manipulative, even cruel. Yet, at that precise moment, part of me sincerely wanted to help Raymond sort out his life. I even thought I believed that there did not necessarily have to be a catastrophe between him and Kristina. I've always held that life is renewable and that our tenure in this world is not beyond redemption. The irony, as I saw later, was that it was I who was getting things wrong, as much as Raymond.

I have to say, in my own defence, that my brother seemed reassured by my words. The extraordinary feeling of power that I had over him was like a rush of blood to the head. Suddenly, he was old, vulnerable and dependent. When I had been growing up the conversation at home had always seemed to swing back to Raymond. I can still hear Mother saying 'Raymond tells me . . .' or 'Your brother thinks . . .' or 'Raymond's going to . . .' as though what I said or thought or did was of no interest. He was a rebel, a source of worry, and finally a great disappointment, but he was her firstborn and special in a way I could never be. Sometimes it seemed as though no one else was allowed to have deeds or opinions. How I resented it, and how I raged inside. Of course, I'd concealed that, as I'd concealed everything else. My whole life was a great act of concealment, and all the time I was waiting to get even, waiting for my moment. Here, at last, my time had come, and this great balloon of egotism and vanity and conceit and self-importance had been deflated and brought down. I sensed I could dispose of my brother in any way I chose, and yet at the same time I felt pity for him, and a strong desire to help.

If I analyse it carefully, I find I have to admit that I had my own interests in mind as much as Raymond's. I wanted, to use an expression that always made Kristina smile, to have my cake and eat it. I wanted my relationship with Kristina to remain undiscovered, free from scrutiny. I wanted to explore this forbidden territory I'd stumbled into, living my life as I'd always lived it, enjoying my position in society. Also, I wanted to control things, to pull the strings, as I controlled things in my work.

I see now that this idea of playing God with my brother's destiny was an illusion. I was not in control at all. I was simply wrong. I thought I was deceiving Raymond but in fact I was deceiving myself and when I finally recognised the true nature of the situation I found

I had gone too far down my chosen path to be able to turn back. Only then did I realise that it was I who was out of control.

We walked on through the hot afternoon. As Raymond's agitation subsided, his pace slowed. The chalk was dry and brittle underfoot and unyielding. 'Imagine having to work this land,' he said at one point. 'Imagine having to dig it day after day.'

'Imagine being a grave-digger,' I replied.

'Grandfather used to talk about digging graves,' said Raymond.

'I never knew him,' I said.

During one particularly strenuous climb we paused to catch our breath. The trees below were massed in regiments of green. Rooks were cawing monotonously in beech trees at the foot of the escarpment. Far, far overhead, an aeroplane was tracing vapour across the sky, like the scratch of diamond on glass.

'You're a good fellow,' said my brother after a while. 'I can see why everyone admires you.'

'What do you mean?' I was embarrassed. 'Don't be silly.'

'No – you have been honest with me. You have admitted that Kristina has some kind of crush on you. That was brave.' He raised his hand to stop me. 'Don't be alarmed. This is between us. It will go no further. You can rely on that. It makes perfect sense. I am not concerned. It is, in an odd way, only what I deserve. Your words make me want to treat her better. I have not always done that. I must learn to be sympathetic. I have been accustomed to ruling the roost and getting my own way, especially with women. I must recognise that in my retirement I have to share. Thank you, brother.'

Then he put his arms around me and kissed me.

[5]

In the course of my duties as coroner I am often the trusted recipient of secrets. I had always treated these confidences quite straightforwardly and with a certain detachment. It so happened that as my own life began to deviate from its harmless provincial routine, I found myself doing something quite uncharacteristic. I held an inquest at which, for the first time in my professional career, I compromised the trust invested in me.

One evening a few days before Sasha's sixth birthday, the telephone interrupted my seclusion, as it often does. The air was heavy and the sky dark with an approaching thunderstorm. I was reading the newspaper and listening to Beethoven's Fifth. I can often intuitively guess when such phone calls will be the harbinger of bad news, and this time was no exception. I sensed tragedy, and I was right.

A young man, an airman at the local base, had been found dead in his quarters. Foul play was not suspected. He appeared to have taken an overdose of sleeping pills and, in accordance with the regulations, the commanding officer was ringing to notify the death. I gave my usual response – routine instructions to call the doctor, the police and the undertaker – and thought no more about it until the court papers arrived on my desk a few days later. Sad though it is, young people commit suicide quite often, and I am no longer surprised by it.

The case, when it came before me, turned out to be peculiarly painful. Three young Royal Air Force fliers had shared living quarters in a rented cottage just off the base. They were all in their early twenties. When the two survivors stood before me in the witness stand they seemed impossibly young. I was reminded of wartime photographs of pilots waiting to scramble against the Luftwaffe in the Battle of Britain. These boys had done everything together, flown, trained, studied, holidayed, and partied. Naturally enough, in the way of things, two of the boys had found girlfriends and the third, who had not, had been left behind. His companions had become involved with their girls and there was no longer any place for him in their lives. Apparently, he'd had little success with girlfriends himself. As a single man, it was awkward for him to accompany his friends on their outings. He was the gooseberry. It was said that he'd drifted into a lonely, introspective and finally self-destructive mood. In despair, it was thought, he had ended his life. Needless to say, his two friends were devastated.

The truth, as I uncovered it, was far more complex and tragic. The young suicide was revealed to have been a homosexual who had only recently acknowledged his sexuality. His upbringing had been sheltered. He had never known what it was to be with other men and he'd only recognised he was gay after he had joined the RAF. There, he had fallen in love with the more dashing of his two house mates, a tall, blond games player of stereotypically limited sensibility. He had feared to confess his love. Homosexuality is still illegal in the armed forces, but his own inhibitions were enough to prevent him from making a clean breast of it. While the three fliers had gone about together in a gang he had been able to cope with his secret. Once his companions had found women – who were also in court on the day of the inquest, and both quite attractive – he had slowly gone to pieces. *In extremis*, he had killed himself.

I, alone, was privy to this catalogue of despair because, before he died, the young man had written a letter and sealed it in an envelope marked 'For the coroner', a not unusual practice among suicides. I believe that words addressed to an anonymous authority can sometimes temper the awful solitude of death.

My office always treats such documents with discretion. Envelopes and packets are left for my eyes only. When I scanned these pages it was as though their author was speaking to me in the confessional. I found his frank admissions of secret sexual desires strangely compelling. We had a bond, he and I.

In his letter, the boy begged me to protect his parents, conceal the truth, and return a verdict of 'suicide while the balance of the mind was disturbed'. If that had been all I had to cope with I should have had few problems. But that was not all. Inside the first envelope was a second letter, also sealed. Once the inquest was over, he wanted me to pass this to his house mate, the object of his desires.

I knew, without even opening it, that this would be a love-letter from beyond the grave, the declaration he had been unable to make in his lifetime. I was well aware how devastating such a revelation would be to his friend. As I have often observed, a coroner's responsibilities lie as much with the living as with the dead. Decency and honour mean nothing to the deceased. It's the living who care, not the dead. There was, in such circumstances, a strong argument for destroying the letter, unopened, unread.

The case came before me one afternoon, in the usual way. The courtroom was exceptionally full. There was much local interest and the newspapers were there. The deceased had been part of a large, tight-knit RAF community. The young man's parents, bowed and silent; his two friends, in uniform; their girlfriends, tearful and sombre; various officers from the squadron: it was a sober turn-out.

When the tall young pilot who had found the body took the witness stand, he began to cry and then broke down completely. I remained calm but my secret fear was that he would blurt out something that revealed an understanding of the true nature of his friend's anguish. Speaking very quietly, I asked him to take his time and describe what he had found. I have discovered, over the years, that if you address a witness in soft, personal terms, even in moments of great distress, they will forget the intimidating circumstances of the court and talk as if you were alone. So I waited for a moment or two and then prompted him with the simplest of questions. Death is often uncomplicated, and this one had been no exception. The young airman told me how he had gone to his room one afternoon and found his friend dead in his bed. He confirmed that the lad had been depressed.

'Thank you,' I said. I looked him in the eye. This was the boy I was supposed to give the letter to. I watched him return to his seat, shaken and pale. I saw his girlfriend lean across and comfort him.

The rest of the inquest unfolded without incident. After various witnesses, including the base commander, had spoken, I made my summing up. I did not refer to the letter I had read, except in the most general terms. I expressed my condolences to the family of the deceased and recorded a verdict of suicide, blaming acute mental depression associated with the stresses of his chosen career and the aftermath of the Gulf War, a convenient alibi. As I spoke, I could see out of the corner of my eye the second letter lying on the desk in front of me, still unopened.

The bereaved filed out. In the car-park outside the court house I saw the two young men hugging each other in grief. They were, as I have said, absurdly young. There was something about their girlfriends, arm in arm, in tight black skirts and sheer black stockings, a certain heartless chic, that made me perverse.

I crossed over towards them. The young men saw me coming and composed themselves in the face of authority. In a few simple, dignified words, I explained that there was one duty I still had to perform on their friend's behalf. They nodded, serious-faced. I could see they had no idea what to expect, and their ignorance gave me a dark, illicit pleasure. I reached into my coat, took out the letter, and handed it to the tall young pilot. 'He asked me to give this to you,' I said. I saw the young man hesitate. 'What does it say?' he asked. 'I have no idea,' I replied. 'That is not my responsibility.' He took the envelope with thanks and put it into his tunic. I watched the group of young people move away to their cars, and I knew exactly what I had just done.

[6]

For some days after our walk along the Roman Road, I received no interruptions from the inhabitants of Jericho Lodge, though Kristina was never far from my thoughts. Then, perhaps a week later, my brother telephoned to say that two of his 'chums' from Berlin, now settled in England like himself, were, as he put it, 'popping over on the Sabbath for a spot of lunch'. Would I care to join them? I hesitated for a moment and then replied that of course I would be delighted. I was glad to hear no trace of tension in Raymond's voice. I was anxious to establish a level of normality in my dealings with my brother and, besides, it would be interesting to meet some of his former comrades-in-arms.

His two visitors were both ex-communists, but there the similarities ended. Eric Payne and John Moore could not have been more unalike. Payne was thin, precise and eager to please. He and Raymond had, for some years, taught at the same institution in Berlin. They had both written books. Raymond had published his history of England. Payne was the author of several 'tomes', as Raymond put it, about the role of the East German revolution in the transformation of post-war European society, jargon-laden works of propaganda printed on cheap grey paper. Payne's colleague, John Moore, was a large man, an industrial chemist, a Londoner, dark, heavy and rather melancholy, awkward in company and without much small-talk. Payne was happy to sparkle in his own neurotic, ingratiating way, but until the arguments started Moore could provide only a dull social glimmer.

After a few minutes of polite conversation in which the two visitors quizzed me about my brother, I realised with dismay that Kristina had not appeared and, making an excuse, I left the guests for a moment, and went to find Raymond. He was in the kitchen, wearing a ridiculous frilly apron. There was a tumbler of sherry on the side. He had obviously been drinking. As I came in, he was fiddling with a salad. The radio was burbling in the background.

'Where's Kristina?'

'Oh.' He was strangely off-hand. 'I suggested she take the day off.'

'Raymond.' I was shocked. 'She's not your house-keeper.' I was about to say that if this was the way he treated his wife it was hardly surprising their marriage was in trouble, but something restrained me. 'What did she have to say about it?'

'She was delighted,' said Raymond. 'She finds Eric and John a bit of a handful.'

'They seem perfectly okay to me.'

'They remind her of things she prefers to forget.'

'What sort of things?'

Raymond was slicing a cucumber with concentration. He did not look at me. 'I say, old boy, lay off the interrogation today, will you?' There was no mistaking the warning in his voice. 'Go and top up the guests, there's a good chap. Lunch will be ready any minute.'

I did not press further, but went back into the living-room. Raymond always has a chess set drawn up, ready for battle, on the table in the window, and during my absence the two visitors had begun to play. I stood and watched as they moved the pieces rapidly into the middle of the board, attacking and parrying along familiar lines.

'We used to play almost every night in Berlin,' Eric explained. 'John usually wins, don't you, John?'

Moore frowned and moved a knight forward. 'I'm not in a winning mood today,' he said in his strong South London accent.

Raymond came in, whistling cheerfully. He glanced at the board. 'Queen's gambit declined,' he said. 'Ah, the old ways are the best ways.' He flourished the oven-cloth. 'Luncheon is served, comrades.'

We followed my brother into the dining-room, now

furnished in a simple farmhouse style. The meal was heavy and Germanic, with roast meat and overcooked vegetables. The only concession to the summer was the watery bowl of salad. The three older men around me ate their food like school dinner. The wine, a lively Bordeaux, was a supermarket bargain, one of my brother's interests, and Raymond, ever the good host, kept our glasses full.

My chief memory of this occasion is the vehemence of the conversation. Even when comparatively small matters were under discussion there was a degree of personal commitment to positions taken and opinions expressed that could only have come from a lifetime of ideological debate. The arguments raged on all afternoon, regardless of social niceties. I was glad we were alone. Eric and John lacked the usual bourgeois graces, and indeed seemed to be openly contemptuous of them. Yet at the same time they were obsessed with rightness. Everything had to be correct. Justified. Doctrinally pure. These men were zealots, and now that they were back in the West, they were zealots without a cause. I began to sympathise with Kristina.

We discussed everything under the sun, or so it seemed. The conversation ranged from American imperialism in Panama and Nicaragua, to the crisis of capitalism, the repression in China, and the ecological disasters in South America. Occasionally, we went back in time and hashed over the Vietnam War, or the Cuban intervention in Angola. For each of these topics there was, I discovered, a party line, an interpretation that fitted Marxist-Leninist theory, even if they could not quite agree on the fine definition of that theory. That, so to speak, was the fun of it: there was endless room for dispute.

If there was one subject that really got them going it was the failure of Communism, the collapse of their church. This was a source of pain and puzzlement to which they returned again and again, an aching wound they could never soothe. In Eric's words, they had shaken hands with the *Zeitgeist* and found themselves dragged down to Hell. Round and round they went, sifting through the events of the last decade for clues to the sudden disintegration of the Soviet edifice. As the afternoon stretched out, Payne revealed himself to be a Stalinist of the old school. For him, the present troubles had to be traced back to the Twentieth Party Congress. Khrushchev's speech was when the rot set in. Moore, naturally, disagreed. Reform had been essential. Mistakes had to be admitted. Openness and re-construction, *glasnost* and *perestroika*, had been vital. My brother blew hot and cold as the argument flowed backwards and forwards. I might as well have not been there.

'We have to admit,' said Raymond, 'that no one liquidated as many communists as the communists.'

'Call it by its real name,' said Moore. 'Call it murder.'

'There is a price to idealism,' said Payne. 'We were trying to change the world. We were young and we had ideals. We wanted to build up something new. We felt we were making a new society, and we were, you know, we were. Our sails were filled with the wind of Utopia.'

'We were flying,' observed my brother wistfully.

'Oh, don't get me wrong,' said Moore. 'I'm still a Marxist, very much so. Marx said that capitalism was going to dig its own grave, and believe me, it is, isn't it?'

Occasionally, I made a pertinent observation of my own, but they hardly seemed to notice. By mid-afternoon we had finished three bottles of wine and the table was spread with the remains of the fruit and cheese. My brother offered port and brandy. I went into the kitchen and made another pot of coffee. When I returned, the conversation had moved on.

'She's quite at home here now,' Raymond was saying. 'She's taken to English life like a duck to water. Wouldn't you agree, frater?'

'She seems to be making friends in the neighbourhood,' I said evenly.

My brother glanced at me with gratitude. 'I'm glad to be home. The kids love it here. The wife's happy. What more can I say?'

'You've done well,' said Moore, directing his attention towards my brother. 'Don't I remember Kristina saying she would never leave Berlin?'

I looked across at Raymond. He could not dissemble in front of his old comrades as he had with me.

'Perhaps you do,' he replied. 'Things change.'

'Ah, the beautiful Kristina,' said Payne mournfully. 'La belle dame sans merci.'

I was interested in this comment. 'Did you know Kristina before she married Raymond?' I directed my question at Payne, but it was Moore who answered.

'Oh yes,' he said. 'We all knew Kristina.'

My brother interrupted. 'If you worked for the government as she did, you were bound to know all the expats.'

'But you were the lucky one,' said Payne, brightly. 'You succeeded where others had failed.'

Moore shook his head and I wondered if he had been a disappointed suitor. 'I take my hat off to you, comrade. None of us thought you would keep her.'

Raymond was playing uneasily with his orange. 'The sedge is withered from the lake, and no birds sing.' He might have been speaking to himself. He looked up at his two former colleagues. 'Yes,' he said. 'I have kept her.'

'Cheer up,' said Payne, winking at me across the table. 'It may never happen.'

'At the end of the day,' said Moore, 'everything has its price.'

'Kristina always seemed like an expensive woman,' said Payne, 'but I imagine she is worth every penny.'

'A remarkable woman,' said Moore lugubriously.

My brother brightened at the compliment. 'Nice of you to say so, John.'

In the silence that fell over the room I found myself wondering what these peculiar visitors could tell me about Kristina's past, but I could see that Raymond would not thank me for prolonging this particular conversation.

'How are your other wives?' asked Payne, matily.

'Both flourishing,' said Raymond. 'Both flourishing at my expense, God rot 'em.'

'La belle dame sans merci,' said Payne absently. 'You have heard about our little conference, I expect?'

'Naturally.'

My brother seemed on surer ground, and entered into the discussion with animation. Payne and Moore were organising a kind of 'Whither Socialism' affair in July. I noted as they discussed the programme and the speakers how they seemed to be painfully recreating the world they had left. Faced with a new world of choice, freedom and opportunity, they preferred the limitations of the past.

'How would you like to chair one of the sessions?' said Moore.

'Sure,' said Raymond. 'I'd be absolutely delighted.' He seemed eager to participate. 'Anything I can do to help.'

'You don't mind appearing in public on a platform?'

Raymond looked embarrassed and began to bluster. 'Why on earth should I?'

'Oh,' said Payne vaguely. 'I just thought – I mean you get all sorts of questions. People say such wild things nowadays.'

There was a pause. I watched Raymond consider the point. His pride was battling with his anxiety, and I guessed his pride would win. 'No problem,' he said. 'I really have nothing to be ashamed of.' He smiled at me weakly, 'I'm no stranger to controversy.'

Moore and Payne looked at each other. 'Well, that's settled then. We'll look forward—'

Moore stopped. He had heard – indeed, we had all heard – a car pulling up outside on the gravel. Raymond glanced out of the window on to the driveway. 'That'll be Kristina,' he said. 'Heigh ho.'

An extraordinary transformation came over the lunch table. An air of alarm, almost of panic, set in. The three older men behaved as if surprised in the middle of something disreputable. The two visitors rose to their feet with excuses. Raymond looked at his watch, made an exclamation, and began to clear the dishes into the kitchen.

'We'll stay and wash up,' said Payne.

'Not to worry,' said my brother. 'I can cope.'

'Well, perhaps we should be on our way,' said Moore. 'Good to miss the worst of the traffic.'

Kristina came in, with the children running before her. They stopped when they saw the room full of men and went quiet. Kristina directed a cold, polite smile at the visitors and began to speak German in what I took to be a greeting. Moore and Payne spoke back, awkwardly. Their unease was only too evident. Within a matter of minutes they were gone. Silence descended and once again Kristina and I were alone.

'An interesting lunch,' I said, as we cleared away.

'How were the fellow travellers?' asked Kristina.

'They argued about everything.'

She made a face. 'They always argue. They talk about principles, but they have no morals.'

'Oh,' I said. 'They seemed to like you.'

She stopped by the table. 'What did they say about me?'

'They were very complimentary,' I said. 'I think they were both rather keen on you.'

She turned away towards the kitchen. 'That is an impertinence.'

'I don't understand.'

'They are typical English hypocrites. In Berlin, they always made jokes about me marrying Raymond.'

'Then perhaps you were wise to stay away.'

'I am sure of it.' Raymond came in, and she changed the subject. 'We had such a nice time. I took the children to the bird sanctuary.'

'She loves birds,' said my brother, as though his wife was still absent.

Kristina looked at Raymond. 'What did Payne mean by "See you in London?"'

'They asked me to a conference,' said Raymond, with the defiance of a man who has been drinking all afternoon. 'I said Yes.'

'But—' There was anger on her face. 'You said you would never do that again. People will ask questions. You know how I hate that.'

'Well, you won't be there, will you?' He was leaning on the table. 'I can handle it,' he said. 'Can't I, Julian?'

'I don't think I should get involved in this,' I said.

'You damn well get involved in everything else. What's the matter with you today?'

'When is it?' asked Kristina.

He named the date, a forthcoming week-end at the beginning of July. I tried to intervene, as a peacemaker, but Kristina cut me short.

'How can you forget Sasha's birthday?' she said accusingly.

'I'm sorry,' said Raymond. 'It slipped my mind.'

I saw his pleasure in the afternoon with his friends evaporate in a sentence. 'I'll tell you what,' I said. 'Raymond can go to London and I'll take you and the kids on a surprise outing, a mystery tour.'

Kristina was recovering her temper. 'Thank you, Julian,' she said, with a pointed look at her husband. 'That would be lovely.'

'Great idea,' said Raymond. 'We'll have a special birthday celebration when I get back in the evening.'

'Perhaps,' said Kristina. 'You have no need to hurry home if you are enjoying yourself.' She went into the sitting-room.

Raymond shrugged, 'Sometimes,' he murmured, as we cleared up together, 'sometimes I think I can do nothing right.'

[7]

I settled on Box Hill for the outing with Kristina and the children. I would enjoy expounding on the literary associations of the place, and from a recreational point of view we would have an agreeable drive there. If the weather was favourable the children could play in the open spaces while Kristina and I prepared Sasha's birthday picnic. This well-known beauty spot also appealed to my darker side. I know that many a body, violently dead, has been discovered in the picturesque undergrowth.

As luck would have it, the day was fine. We dropped Raymond and his briefcase at the railway station and set off, just after nine o'clock, across country. The children, confined to the back of the car with the dog, were in an excitable mood. Sasha had been up for hours, pestering his parents for presents. I was excited too. I'd put a bottle of champagne on ice in the cooler, a surprise for Kristina. There was quite a party atmosphere as we accelerated away from the station yard.

'One is one and all alone and ever more shall be so,' I hummed. I could see Raymond in the rear-view mirror, still waving. I regret to say that his departure lightened all our spirits.

Kristina looked at me. 'You are happy.'

'So are you.'

We smiled at each other without restraint. I was light-headed at the prospect of having Kristina to myself for the day. Raymond was not expected back until nightfall.

It is less than an hour's drive from Brighton to Box Hill, and we made the journey in good style, singing songs and playing I-Spy. In my presence, the children spoke to their mother in English and I noticed that they were using the language with new confidence. If you had seen us, bowling along, you might have supposed that I and my attractive wife were taking our two young children for a day in the country. We looked like a happy family, and in a way we were. Not for the first time since

Kristina and her children had come into my life I found myself regretting that I had no family of my own.

It was one of those lazy July days when time seems to stand still. The heat swirled on the road and the oncoming cars shimmered with a metallic reflection of the glare. When we reached Box Hill I parked in the shade, in front of a fine view. Sasha and Olga jumped out and began to explore. Jack followed, barking with excitement. Kristina called after them, but I reassured her. 'There's plenty of other families,' I said. 'They're safe enough.'

We were not alone on the hillside, but we managed to find a secluded patch out of the sun. Kristina laid a tartan rug on the grass. I put down the cooler and took out the champagne with a flourish. 'Here's a little surprise.'

I was delighted to observe that she was blushing. 'You are very good to me, Julian.'

I had planned this moment. 'I love you,' I said, handing her a glass. I had been apprehensive in anticipation, but it did not seem difficult to speak like this out of doors.

'You should not say such things,' she said.

'Do you love me?' I was becoming reckless. 'You must tell me.'

'Of course I love you, Julian, but not in the way you mean.'

Now that we were alone, I hoped she might be less provisional, but there was something, it seemed, she could not ignore. I thought I detected a look of despair and excitement in her eyes.

We touched glasses and I began to question her about her feelings. Alone in the countryside with this beautiful woman, and the champagne nipping in my throat, I found myself saying, 'I want to make love to you, Kristina.'

'Here?' She laughed in mock alarm. 'Julian!'

'No.' I had the seriousness of the ardent suitor. 'I want to sleep with you. I want to wake in your arms.'

'You are all the same,' she interrupted. 'All you are thinking about is your dick.'

'That's not a word we use in polite society,' I said, with a smile.

'I'm sorry.' She lowered her eyes. 'I pick up my language from my children. They bring it home from school and I do not know how to correct them.'

'Anyway,' I said, dragging the conversation back, 'how can you say that? I love you for yourself.'

She was quiet then. 'But it's impossible. You know that. Have you forgotten? I am married to your brother.'

I had not forgotten. I had turned the problem over in my mind a thousand times. 'Could you imagine getting a divorce?'

Now I had shocked her. She looked away. She sighed. 'You really want me, don't you?'

The champagne buzzed in my head. I leaned across the rug and kissed her. This time she did not hold back, but opened her mouth to mine. We were still kissing when the dog bounded up on to the rug and we heard the children racing through the bushes with shouts of 'Jack! Jack!'

Kristina and I drew apart quickly. I was anxious about what Olga might report to her father.

I watched them approaching across the grass. 'Hi, kids,' I said. 'Time for lunch.'

'Please can I have my present now?' said Sasha.

'Of course you can, it's your birthday.' I rummaged

for my gift, and watched him unwrap it. I had chosen a child's cassette recorder, something he had asked for. The little boy was struck dumb with pleasure and amazement. It occurred to me, as Kristina prompted his shy Thank You, that it would be good to have the children on our side.

We settled down for lunch, a fine display of sausage, fruit and cheese. 'A proper German picnic,' said Kristina. I confess I could not wait for it to be over, for the plates to be cleared away, the scraps thrown to Jack, and for the children to be off again in the bushes. I wanted to lie on the rug with Kristina, alone and undisturbed.

The children refused to comply. They sat and played on the rug. Sasha, who was delighted to play with his new tape recorder, making up voices and fiddling with the rewind button, was keeping an eye on his mother, and so, I sensed, was Olga. Occasionally, they would speak to her in German and she would reply, but rather offhand. I hoped that she, too, wanted to be alone with me. But the kids would not go.

After a while I went over and threw the champagne bottle into the overflowing municipal dustbin. Superstitiously, I put the cork with its torn gold foil into my pocket as a souvenir. Then, like a bored paterfamilias, I read the Saturday newspapers, half listening to Kristina's voice. From time to time she'd encourage the children to go off and 'explore', but they resolutely preferred to stay, and if I was them I would have done the same. In my impatience, I made a mistake. I took out a five-pound note and suggested to Olga that she take her brother to buy an ice-cream.

'I don't want an ice-cream,' said Olga. 'I want to go home.'

Sasha joined in. 'It's my birthday. Why can't we go home now?'

'It's too soon,' I said. 'We've only just arrived.'

'We've been here for ages. It's a horrid place,' said Olga. 'Why can't we go home?'

Olga started to cry, and then Sasha joined in, and they both ran to their mother. Kristina comforted them in German. I stood up. 'Let's go for a walk,' I said. 'Then we can go home.'

The children's mood passed, but all hope of solitude and privacy had gone from the day. We folded up the rug and set off through the bushes and along the slope. There were other families having picnics on the grass, observing the summer rituals. Olga ran ahead, her blonde hair flying. Sasha took Kristina's hand and then mine and we began to swing him, higher and higher. He became very excited. 'Again.'

Kristina shook her head. 'That's enough for one day.'

Sasha began pleading, but Kristina was firm. The little boy slipped loose and ran after his sister. I took Kristina's hand in mine. I found it warm and secure and trusting.

'You have nice hands,' she said, turning my fingers over.

'You have nice everything.'

She made a face. 'You have no idea.' A look of pain came into her eyes. 'I think I am not a nice person.'

'I prefer an honest person.'

'Don't talk about honesty,' she replied. 'Honesty is the word we use to hurt our loved ones.'

When I looked into her eyes for an explanation, she shook her head. 'Not now.' She pulled me towards her. 'I don't want to spoil our day out.'

127

We stood still and kissed. I remember there was children's laughter in the distance, but we were not disturbed. I could feel her body close and warm and urgent against mine. I wanted to believe that our lives were being twisted together into that rope of intimacy that makes a relationship, but secretly I suppose I knew that I was being tugged into something that was far beyond my experience.

The afternoon wore on. We walked, rested, played hide-and-seek, bought ice-cream, strolled on some more, and dawdled in the shade. When the shadows began to stretch out across the dry grass it was time to go home. We made our way back to the car with burning faces. The upholstery was hot to touch and the steering-wheel was a ring of scorching Bakelite. Sasha began to cry again. We laid out towels and rugs and coaxed the children, like nervous animals, into the back seat. Once we began to roll downhill from the car-park the evening air cooled the interior and filled our heads with lightness and longing.

For a while we drove without speaking. The cars on the other side of the road flashed by, punctuating the silence. At last, Kristina said, 'I wonder if Raymond is having a good time.'

'I'm sure he is,' I replied. 'He'll be in his element, arguing with the comrades.'

When we reached Mansfield I drove Kristina and the children straight to The Lodge and unloaded the picnic things into the hall. I hesitated by the driver's door. Kristina, on the way to the house, turned. 'Don't go just yet. Come in and help me.'

The house was cool and still. The Mr Mover boxes were still in the kitchen, as though Kristina and Raymond were not fully settled.

'When do you think Ray will be back?' I asked.

'Later.' She gave an indifferent shrug. 'He'll ring before he catches the train. I'll go and collect him, or he can take a taxi.'

She went up to bath the children and get them ready for bed. I sat downstairs in the sitting-room and watched cricket on television. This room was furnished in a heavy, Germanic style that was not to my taste. I found myself wondering how I might decorate it differently.

After a few minutes, Sasha appeared in a dressing-gown, with his hair combed down. He was ready for bed. He was carrying *The Tale of Samuel Whiskers*.

'Will you read to me?'

I patted the seat next to me, turned off the television and began to read. In due course, Olga and Kristina joined us and sat on the sofa as I read on. Sasha curled up against me and fell asleep. Kristina picked him up and tiptoed out, carrying him to bed. I finished the story.

'I liked that,' said Olga. 'It was very frightening.'

Kristina returned, and told Olga to go to bed. I sat on, staring into the evening light. Eventually, Kristina slipped back into the room like a shadow. She sat down and kissed me. I put my arms around her. I could feel myself losing control and all the more so, knowing we would not be disturbed. Suddenly she pulled away.

'Shall I make you some supper?'

I did not know what to say. Everything seemed suspended. 'I'll have a drink,' I said.

We stood up awkwardly and went into the kitchen. I opened the fridge and poured us both a drink while I watched her prepare a meal. 'This is good,' I said. 'I'm getting to feel quite at home here.'

I could hardly breathe. We were standing on the edge. Then the telephone rang.

Kristina hurried to answer. I heard her speak in German and knew at once that it was Raymond. I wondered, with a sinking heart, what arrangements she was making to meet him. When she came back into the room there was a strange look on her face.

'Raymond says he is staying up in London tonight. The conference finishes tomorrow but he wants to stay for the morning session.'

'Is he having a good time?'

'He sounded drunk.'

'Those comrades,' I said.

Kristina put her arms out towards me. 'Come,' she said.

[8]

Raymond made only the most perfunctory enquiries about our day on Box Hill. He had returned on the train next day, picking up where he had left off, as though nothing had happened. Kristina was not surprised at his reticence. 'He talks of honesty,' she said, 'but all he knows is lies.'

Everyday life went on, but there was nothing mundane about my experience of it. My prayers had been answered. I had discovered the meaning of risk. I was a player in the kind of domestic drama I might have read about in the newspaper. I was surprised to discover how ordinary the extraordinary can seem.

I arranged for Kristina to hire a nanny. Jane Parry was a pleasant, round-faced local girl who looked after the children in the daytime, and went back to attend to her elderly mother after six. I had successfully defended Jane's late father in a motoring dispute, and I knew his daughter would be reliable. I reinforced my role in these new domestic arrangements by purchasing a car-phone, an executive toy that Reverend Findlater, for one, openly coveted.

Kristina was now free to visit my house alone. Occasionally, in the lunch-hour I would drive home from the office that summer, a twenty-minute journey if I was speeding, and I would find her laying food on the table, or opening a bottle of chilled white wine from my cellar. I would bring her flowers, clothes, perfume. Sometimes – quite often, in fact – we never touched the food. Kristina was a woman of great sexual appetite, a lover of refined sensuality whose physical presence became my obsession.

I was fearful that our adulterous meetings at my house would excite comment and arranged, whenever possible, to meet Kristina on neutral ground and even at Jericho Lodge. I have to say that Kristina showed all the determination of a woman who generally got what she wanted. She was adept at encouraging Raymond to conduct his researches in London. In this way we were able, from time to time, to spend the night together. For a few hours I could persuade myself that somehow we would find a way of sharing a life, even if it meant banishing Raymond from the scene. Alone in the house Kristina became relaxed, almost serene. In retrospect, I think it was during these evenings that she was most herself with me.

'See,' she said, one evening when Raymond was away and the children had gone to bed. 'This is where he sleeps now.'

She pushed open the door into the spare bedroom. It was cold and empty. There was a narrow bed with an eiderdown, a centenary poster of Lenin in a wooden frame, and a small bedside lamp. The walls were white and bare. There were no books.

'Spartan,' I said.

'He prefers it like this.'

I embraced her. 'That wouldn't suit you at all.'

I had come to the house and found her watching television while she browsed through the tempting, brightly-coloured pages of a mail-order catalogue. When I questioned her, she replied that she'd like to go to America.

'Raymond says you want to go back to Germany.'

A disdainful, almost haughty, look came into her eyes. 'You can't trust Raymond.' She pulled me urgently towards her. 'You must take things from my lips.'

We kissed. I held her, but she was not with me as she had been before, and I was disappointed.

'Would you really go to America?' I said. 'You have only just moved to England.'

'There is no work for me here. In America I could support myself.'

'What would you do?'

'I would interpret and translate.' A look of pride came into her eyes. 'I know how to survive.'

If Raymond was to be believed, she knew only too well how to survive. I could imagine Kristina shopping in chic boutiques and lunching in fashionable restaurants. Our little interlude would be soon forgotten. I was dismayed by the thought. 'I've heard America is a terrible place.'

'That's just what Raymond says.' She laid the catalogues aside. 'You pretend to be so different, but to me you are so alike.' She stretched out her arms. 'Come with me to California,' she said, drawing me towards the bedroom.

And so 'California' became our code-word for intimacy. When we were in California we could escape the reality of the world we had created. It was, in truth, a place we aspired to but rarely visited. We would talk of 'California' with the longing of gold-rush prospectors who have heard stories of fabulous wealth, but in the day-to-day run of things, our wagon wheels were bogged down by the impassable Rockies.

I was utterly absorbed in our affair. I thought I was experiencing something I had never known before, an equality in love. When we were alone we were passionate and tender. When we were in company we were discreet but satisfied. We said we did not want to hurt anyone's feelings, but we were also anxious not to become the object of scandal in the village. There was always the fear that people would notice Kristina's comings and goings. My brother did not challenge me with the lies I had told him. He pottered about in an uncomplaining way, and spoke gloomily of his memoirs. Looking back, our behaviour was an outrageous affront to his good nature.

It was now mid-July, approaching August, high summer, that moment in the year when the days seem endless and time itself becalmed. Whenever we had the chance we would go off on our own for walks in the country. We would make love in fields under mackerel skies. Kristina seemed, in my eyes, to become more beautiful with each day. She began to behave more spontaneously. She laughed and took pleasure in things. There was still a part of her I could not reach, a shadowy, reserved part of her mind she would not share, but I was not concerned. I told myself that I would reach that part over time, and must be patient.

I must admit that in the distraction of my love for Kristina I treated my work with less and less attention.

Invariably now I found myself hurriedly scanning the relevant documents on my way to court, yawning on the Bench, and occasionally missing important steps in the legal argument. Only the sharpest visiting lawyer would have noticed that I was not on top form, but I was not happy with my performance. Throughout my career I had prided myself on my professionalism, fearing the charge of provincial incompetence, and now I was vulnerable. It was this disagreeable sensation that persuaded me to leave the world of the unsaid and put my desires for the future into words.

Kristina and I were lying in bed. We had just heard the clock on the mantelpiece chime two. In a few minutes I would have to put on my suit again and drive back to my office as if nothing had happened. I told her that I was fretting at the lack of honesty and uneasy about our clandestine ways. I said, speaking directly, that I wanted to live openly with her. My imagination ran on and I spoke more freely than I had ever done before. As far as I was concerned, even if we had to move elsewhere to avoid a scandal, it would be worthwhile. Raymond was getting in the way. His presence was oppressive and tedious. He himself was not content. Using words more appropriate for my office, I said that we had to confront the issue head-on.

Kristina was startled to find me in this mood. She said I was not myself. She said that men and women could become like animals when driven by sexual passion, and she seemed to speak from some kind of personal experience. I asked her what she was referring to, but she brushed the question aside. She began to caress me.

'You must calm yourself,' she murmured. 'At the moment, this is only an affair. In the future, who knows? You must be patient.'

I did not answer. Her words and her reasonable manner made me fearful. I drove back to my office in a cloud of anxiety.

Meanwhile, I had no idea what was going through my brother's mind. For one so ready to express an opinion on art, politics or religion, he had become curiously reticent about emotional matters, at least where they touched him. He could debate *perestroika* but he shied away from a confrontation about his wife's behaviour. I wondered why, when he had been so vociferous in the past, he was holding back now. He was like a dog that wants to bark but knows he will be punished if he does, and I puzzled in my mind over the reasons for his circumspection.

Then, one evening in early August, when the swifts were massing over the village, tracking insect swarms in the fading light, he appeared on my doorstep shortly after my return from the office. He was carrying Father's gun.

I was in the kitchen, clearing away the lunch that Kristina and I had not eaten. Her scent was still on my body. I did not expect him to notice that, or even her flowers in the vase on the table, but for a deranged, impossible moment I thought he had come to kill me.

'No luck?'

'No luck.' He laid the gun down by the door. 'I shall have to take lessons if I'm to bring anything home for the family pot.'

I offered him a drink. I was glad to have him alone, and on my home ground. We sat outside in deck-chairs with ice clinking in our glasses. The whirling swifts, like ash from a bonfire, were swooping and passing overhead with astonishing precision, screaming through the dusk in formation. We watched the strange black shadow

135

disappear across the trees and then scatter across the Downs.

'Weird,' said Raymond.

'An ancient compulsion,' I replied. 'You see it every year.'

He sequestered his thoughts for a moment, tilting his glass. 'How's tricks?'

'Busy.' I heard my own reticence and to make conversation began to describe the case of the homosexual airman. I knew he was fascinated by the stories I encountered in my work.

'People trust you, don't they?'

'A dog's obeyed in office.'

'No.' He shook his head. 'It's you they trust. They all tell me how reliable you are.'

I smiled nervously. I did not like the direction the conversation was taking. I sensed the threat in his voice. 'Are you suggesting that the village has been misled?'

He rattled his drink. 'I'm saying that the village loves to gossip. Jane's in the house all day. She's not blind, Julian.'

'Jane is a sensible girl,' I said. 'Everyone knows you have to be discreet with nannies.'

'And are you?'

'Discretion is my middle name.'

My reply seemed to galvanise him. 'You do understand,' he said, 'that I still love my wife.'

'I understand.'

'I believe in a certain loyalty to the institution of marriage.'

'So do I.' I offered him the bottle. 'As a matter of fact, much of my professional life is occupied by the institution of marriage.' I had been waiting for this opportunity. 'Tell me something, Raymond, what exactly were your friends talking about the other day?'

'What do you mean?'

'They seemed rather over-familiar towards Kristina.'

'That was just our circle. From the outside, it might seem a trifle louche, but I can assure you it was perfectly regular.' He studied his drink. 'I've told you before, life in Berlin had its compromises, but we survived.'

'On hypocrisy?' I said.

'Call it what you like,' said Raymond. 'I'd rather be in a house without a roof, and call it home, than live in the street.'

'This is not Germany,' I said. 'Perhaps Kristina sees things differently now.'

'Perhaps.' He seemed strangely confident, and seemed to dismiss my suggestion with ease. 'That fellow Watkins has been asking a lot of questions, you know.'

'Watkins is a professional nosey-parker. He's always been like that. People are curious here. They talk all the time.' I mentioned an unwanted teenage pregnancy that was causing some agitation in a certain well-to-do household. 'It doesn't add up to much in the end. So long as you don't upset the apple cart, they'll let you lead your life pretty much as you choose.' I refilled his glass. 'Nothing in your life, or mine, is in danger of doing that.'

'You're very confident about that, aren't you?'

I could see that my reasonableness was irritating him. I followed a lazy butterfly settling on the buddleia at the back of the house.

'You and I just happen to be rather good at secrecy, Raymond.' I watched the bubbles rising in my glass. 'It may not be the most attractive trait in the world, but it comes in handy in a place like Mansfield.'

137

[9]

I am accustomed, as a lawyer, to expressing dramatic events in a matter-of-fact way. I use language as a pathologist uses a scalpel, to probe and dissect. My words will be detached and impersonal. Here, in my own life, I have reached the point where it is hard to sustain such a neutrality. Briefly, it was in late summer that we – my brother, Kristina, and I – reached a crisis.

July moved into August, and imperceptibly the days began to shorten. It was the time of school holidays, half-empty offices and long week-ends. The leaves on the trees became dry and dusty. The fields were golden, like a loaf. Topaz dragonflies skimmed the village pond. The cycle of the land went on. Harvesting began. On the uplands, the farmers were already ploughing again, turning over the soil for the next crop.

At night I would lie alone in bed thinking about Kristina. Often the smell of her body was still on the sheets, and sometimes I would make a point of not bathing until morning to keep the memory of our love-making warm around me. I would put on music downstairs, turn up the volume and stare into the dark while the great singing chords of a Chopin nocturne filled my upstairs room like an anthem. Then I would feel tears pricking in my eyes with love and longing for Kristina, the joy and the pain she had brought into my life. I would lie there listening to the pedals mingling the sounds of the keyboard so that it was as if four hands not two were playing and I would wonder to myself: how will this end? Love, like death, would be bearable and easy if we could know the outcome, when and where we would die, how and when we would fall in, or out of, love.

As well as the intimacies of passion, Kristina was teaching me German words I wouldn't find in the dictionary. At first, I was slightly embarrassed by these terms, but I could see she was amused to utter profanities in the seclusion of the bedroom. It was between the sheets that I learnt the meaning of 'voegeln'. Sometimes, when I was not hurrying back to my office for an afternoon appointment, we would sit in the shade at the back of the house and entertain each other with coarse, impromptu limericks about young ladies from Geneva and Siberia. Kristina was demure and metropolitan on first meeting, but I discovered she had an earthy sense of humour.

And then one day there were no laughs. When I tried to soothe her, she rose from her chair and stalked away down the garden. After a few moments, wondering what it was that had upset her, I followed. Kristina heard my approach through the long grass at the bottom of the garden and half-turned. I saw she had been crying.

'I'm sorry,' she said. 'I'm not myself today. I don't feel well.'

I took her in my arms. 'It's that time of year. We have been so happy. Now there's only autumn to look forward to.'

'Last night I dreamed I was with my mother in Poland,' she said.

I was about to ask her what that meant, but she shook her head and turned away. I sensed that she was struggling to tell me something. I stepped aside and began pulling long tendrils of bindweed from the wild roses that blow along my fence. My fingers snagged on the briars and I remembered the fairytale story of the princess in the tower.

'Imagine a hundred years of thorns,' I said.

She did not reply at first. 'I think I may be pregnant,' she said. Then she began to cry.

I threw the weeds aside and put my arms around her. I did not speak but I pressed my hands, scratched and bleeding, against her body.

'Aren't you pleased?'

'I don't know what to do.'

'What do you mean?'

'Raymond will kill me.'

I shook my head. I knew the likely course of anger and its violent manifestations. Raymond would torture himself, no doubt, and then he would turn his anger towards me. He was an old-fashioned communist: it was his credo that the passions should be allowed free expression, unhindered by bourgeois convention. Kristina was not at risk. I kissed her. She was so dear and vulnerable to me. 'Let me tell him,' I said. 'There's time.'

'Time for what?'

'Time to find the words and the moment.'

'You don't understand. I do not want the child.' She broke away from my embrace. 'I will have to get rid of it.'

I was shocked at the urgency and directness with which she spoke. 'Don't you want—?'

'Please.' She stopped me with a look of pain. 'It is my decision.' She turned away. 'You cannot understand.'

There was no more to be said, and when we parted there were few words. I wanted to be alone with my thoughts. I felt like the witness to an accident, but the more I turned the matter over in my mind, I realised that I was the accident's victim. The prospect of a child made me understand more than ever how much I was in love with Kristina, and yet her response was anything but loving. I was in a turmoil, not knowing where I stood, or what to do. In the crisis in which I now found myself I wanted above everything to confront my brother with the news. It was not just that we had reached the limits of discretion. In an odd way, I thought that he might become my ally in my hopes of saving the child.

[10]

In the end I spoke to Raymond down by the seashore, beyond the reach of gossip and convention. Mechanical diggers, excavating the Channel Tunnel, growled through the mud and chalk behind us. The melancholy roar of the waves on the shingle was a sad accompaniment to what I had to say. Occasionally, to punctuate my recital, I would pick up a stone and watch it splash into the grey water. Sometimes, in the past, I had been here, or near here, in my official capacity, to watch another swollen, disfigured, waterlogged body pulled from the sea. I could not help wondering, as I spoke, if this would be my brother's choice.

His first response was resigned. 'I suppose it was inevitable,' he said, almost to himself. 'I should have expected it. After all, the physical part of our marriage ended long before the Wall came down.'

It was odd to hear him calibrate his life against the public events of his time, but it was perfectly in character. For Raymond and his colleagues, History was almost a member of the family. 'She wants an abortion,' I said. 'Is there anything we can do to stop her?'

'You know Kristina as well as I do,' he said. 'Once she has made up her mind . . .'

'I'd be happy for her to have the child,' I said. 'Of course I'd pay.'

'Of course you'd pay.' His laugh was bitter. I saw his anger coming towards me like a storm on the horizon. 'You lying, two-faced, deceitful, lousy bastard,' he said. 'How could you do this to me?'

'I'm sorry.'

'I'm sorry. Is that all you can say?'

'I don't know what else I can say,' I replied. 'It's not as though you didn't know.'

'I had my suspicions, of course, but I did not know.'

'You will always turn a blind eye,' I said. 'That's the way you are.'

'I pushed it to the back of my mind.' He threw a stone into the water. 'I told myself I would behave well, whatever that means. Give me credit for that, won't you?' He sighed. 'And then I gave up.'

He leant forward and buried his head in his hands.

I have said before that my parents considered the show of emotion to be a sign of weakness and I have always kept my feelings on a tight rein. Kristina had begun to break down that reserve and now here was my brother crying for the hurt I had done him. I was not shocked but I was touched. I put my arm around him as we sat there and let him weep. I might have done the same if he had been in my courtroom.

It was a cold summer's day. We did not speak. Holiday-makers, bundled up in anoraks, straggled past with crunching footsteps. I was conscious of their stares. Raymond and I never looked like brothers. I imagined their speculations about the two men miserably hugging each other on the shore.

After some while, Raymond composed himself, stood up, and went down in his shoes and socks to skim stones across the wavetops. I sat and watched. He was careless of the waves. The sea beat remorselessly on the shingle. I watched the ebb and flow begin, and cease, and then begin again. The stones skittered and jumped and sank. The tide is a great renewer, washing at the margin of human misery, and giving hope.

Then the sun burst from behind the clouds and the sea sparkled. It was suddenly hot. I took off my jacket. A seagull cried, and for a moment I was nine years old and Father in his khaki shorts was building a castle for the tide while Mother packed away the family picnic into a basket. I had been alone then, and I was alone now.

I wondered, in my detached way, what would happen next. He would turn and compose himself, but how? Once he had thought things through, how would he respond? Would he threaten? Would he talk of divorce? I rehearsed these scenarios in my head. I have seen many variants of these plots. The repertory of jealousy and revenge is oddly limited.

Eventually, he came and sat down next to me again. The hems of his trousers flapped in the wind. He began to unlace his sodden shoes and expose his white feet to the sun.

'At first I thought I would like to kill you,' he said, looking out to sea. 'But then I realised that even this cloud has a silver lining.'

I was pleased to see his rational side at work. 'You are being very nice about this,' I encouraged.

'In an odd way, I am reconciled. If I have to share my wife, I would rather share her within the family.' He looked at me with sudden candour. 'There was a time, once, in Germany, when I thought I had lost her for good.' He held up his hand. 'No, I don't want to talk about it now, but nothing you do can be as bad as that.'

As he spoke, something fell into place in my mind. 'When you wrote to me about coming home, you spoke of the urgency. That was why you wanted to come back, wasn't it?'

'That was part of it,' he admitted. 'My thoughts had been directed towards England for some time. That was a catalyst, I suppose.' He wiped an imaginary blackboard with his hand. 'Let's not go into that just now.'

'I understand,' I said.

'So here we are,' said Raymond, sadly. 'Where on earth do we go from here?'

'I don't want to cause trouble,' I said. 'Does that sound very strange?'

'Not really.' He seemed to be thinking aloud. 'I suppose there's no reason why things should not go on as before.'

'Would you like this to be kept a secret?'

He seemed relieved to hear the word. He was, at heart, afraid of scandal, and after a lifetime of adventure, anxious to avoid controversy in retirement. 'As a matter of fact, yes, I would. I hate the idea of village gossip.' He brightened. 'Perhaps we can all be one happy family.'

'I hope so,' I said.

There was a pause. He threw a stone and then another.

'You can sleep with Kristina,' he said, as though settling something in his mind. 'We shall remain married. We may not love each other, but at least we can stay together.'

In anticipation of our conversation I had resolved that I would suggest separation, even divorce. Now the moment had come I found I could not press him as I

144

had hoped. 'You have Olga and Sasha,' I said, comforting him in a way I had not intended. 'They love you.'

'They don't need me. You could look after them.' He rubbed his eyes with his hand, a painfully childish gesture. 'You could be their daddy.'

'I don't want to be their daddy.'

'You damn well pick and choose what you like, don't you?'

I saw the clouds of anger massing again, and adopted a more conciliatory tone. 'I agree that it would be nice if we could all be together.' I heard my forced laughter. 'In some parts of the world this arrangement would be quite natural.' I tried an appeal to his philandering nature. 'One is never too old to . . .'

When he looked into my face, I saw how tearful and weak he was. 'Are you suggesting that you pimp for me?' He shook his head in dismay. 'I thought you were Mr Safe, my steady-going, sensible kid brother. Now I realise you are just like everyone else.' He considered me with a certain curiosity. 'Did you set out to seduce her?'

'Of course not.'

'Please don't tell me you fell in love.'

'That's what it felt like.' I put my hand on his arm. 'I did not seduce Kristina. She came to me of her own accord. There was nothing I could do.'

'It takes two to tango, old boy.'

'Then you can say that she taught me how to dance.'

He looked at me oddly. 'She is certainly quite familiar with the dance.'

I voiced an enquiry I had been nurturing for some time. 'When it came to the dance floor, as it were, back in Berlin, am I right in thinking she was quite a professional?'

For a moment I was afraid he would evade the question as he had evaded other questions in the past, but then something of the gravity of the occasion, the roar of the sea, the grating of the waves on the shore, made him honest. 'Yes,' he said. 'When I first met her, she was doing quite a bit of dancing. Those government interpreters were all the same. Escorts. Is that the word?'

'Like Eva,' I said.

'But that's the point. She was not like Eva. She did not disguise what she was doing. She was quite up front. She was also looking for a way out of the world she had fallen into.'

'And you were her escape route.'

'In a manner of speaking. Olga and Sasha are mine by the way. Every marriage has its ups and downs. Heigh-ho.' He stood up. 'I fancy a turn along the beach.'

We trudged into the wind. On this part of the shore we were alone. A solitary wind-surfer was cutting through the choppy water in front of us like a champion.

'You have reached a dangerous age,' he said at last. 'You should know what it means to have children, but you're not the marrying type. This is a good solution.'

'I don't insist on your approval,' I said. 'I have no right to. But I appreciate your generosity.'

'Now, brother. No speeches.'

He quickened his stride and moved ahead. I did not hurry to keep up. I followed, turning over the conversation in my mind. After a few minutes, he stopped, and turned away from the wind. We began to retrace our steps. With the breeze on our backs it seemed calmer, almost warm. We crunched back to the car-park in silence. A Mr Whippy van was parked by the life-saving station. I bought two cornets. 'A nice day by the sea,' said the ice-cream man sarcastically.

146

'It could be worse,' I said.

'It could always be worse,' said the ice-cream man, handing me the change.

We sat on the wall and ate our cornets. As the afternoon drew on, families straggled off the beach to their cars. I was about to speak, to suggest some kind of formality to our arrangement, but something told me that this would be a mistake.

'Perhap . . .' I began, and stopped.

'Perhaps what?'

'Nothing,' I said.

'You know, Julian, you have been greatly improved by my wife's attentions.' He laughed freely for the first time that day. 'You have become almost human.'

For a moment I could not reply. He had shocked me with his words. In my position, I rarely hear the truth from those around me. 'Perhaps I've seen too much,' I said. 'It's not healthy living so close to death.'

He shook his head. 'For someone in your position, your life has been quite sheltered. In a situation like this you seem to understand so little.'

'Well, you don't tell me much,' I countered in a bantering spirit.

'There was a time when she wanted another child,' he said.

I was surprised. 'You would not let her?'

He hesitated. 'It did not seem appropriate.'

'Appropriate?'

I saw him hold back, and then think better of it. 'To be perfectly honest, sport, there was some question about who the father was.'

'I see.' In a way it was a relief to have my suspicions confirmed. 'I thought there might be something of this sort. Who was he?'

'I'm a bit surprised Kristina hasn't mentioned him to you.' Raymond finished the remains of his ice-cream cone with relish. 'His name,' he said, speaking like a prosecuting magistrate, 'is Walter Krokowski.'

AUTUMN

[1]

Autumn fell. Scarves of mist floated in the hollow of the Downs. When the sun was high people spoke of an Indian summer. At night it was often cold and damp. Local schoolchildren rambled the hedgerows for black-berries and when the frosts came there was talk of the Devil. At week-ends, bonfires seasoned the village air. I went to the garden-centre and bought spring bulbs, daffodils and crocuses, with a heavy heart. When I handed over my credit card at the cashpoint and glimpsed the scar on my hand, I experienced a terrible nostalgia for what had been. The harvest festival came and went. 'All is safely gathered in,' we sang. But nothing felt safe to me.

I kept what Raymond had told me to myself. I was not ready to confront Kristina with my knowledge of Walter Krokowski. In a perverse way, I wanted to pre-tend that nothing had changed. I was assisted in this delusion by Kristina herself. Not long after my seaside walk with Raymond, she calmly informed me that she was not pregnant, after all. It had been a 'Fehlalarm', she explained, a false alarm.

'I think you are sorry,' she said.

I did not know what to admit. 'Have you told Raymond?'

'He knows,' she replied enigmatically.

When I referred to the news, Raymond answered that whatever our differences we could agree that it solved a problem. He seemed almost to relish his role as the complaisant husband. 'Have you mentioned our German friend yet?' he asked, tormenting me with a knowing smile. I took refuge in evasion, and made excuses to myself that I did not, in my heart of hearts, believe.

Despite everything that had passed between us, Kristina and I were still hopelessly tangled up together, but when we tried to return to our old ways, we found we had lost the summer's freedom. Outside in the countryside, the fields were empty, the waves uninviting, and the hillsides ploughed up. We began to visit out-of-season hotels by the sea, inserting adulterous rendezvous into our daily routine. I bought Kristina a second-hand Mini from Kevin Carey, the owner of the Texaco garage. A buck-toothed operator with a squint, Carey was not slow to enquire about my need for additional transport. 'It's a gift,' I explained. 'My sister-in-law needs to get about the place when her husband's away on business.'

'She's a nippy one, your Mini,' said Carey, patting the bodywork. 'You can park her anywhere. The perfect car for your modern woman, Mr Whyte. Fast, light, and inexpensive.' He gave me a wink. 'You should tell that husband of hers to watch himself.'

When I reported this conversation to Kristina, she gave a bitter laugh. 'Why is it the woman who is always the fast one?' she said.

Kristina loved her little car. I would sit at the wheel of my Volvo in some deserted sidestreet and watch the snub-nose Mini squeeze into a nearby parking space. Kristina would get out, a marvel of elegance in those dismal purlieus. I'd join her with a guilty kiss, and we'd check in to some tatty one-star tourist hotel, registering under false names, paying in cash and trying not to worry about the cost. For the first time in years, I was overdrawn at the bank.

For a few weeks, before our strange relationship took its final turn, we became familiar with the sun-bleached backways of Brighton, Newhaven and Hove. Our rule was never to stay in the same place twice, and I would take unlikely detours to and from my office in search of some desolate new 'vacancy'. If a lunchtime rendezvous was impossible, we would meet after work, go to the room, undress in a hurry, and have sex between the grey, thin sheets. Sometimes I felt, like Oscar Wilde, that it was the wallpaper that was killing me. At other times, as I watched Kristina fastening her bra, or brushing her hair in a cheap plastic mirror, I would affect a spirit of gallows humour towards our situation. Then I would put on my suit once more and we would leave, pretending to go out for a meal. I suspect we fooled no one.

I had initiated these outings in a spirit of optimism, hoping against hope that a change of scene would renew our relationship. Soon, I discovered the price of the compromise I had made with my brother and came to regret the pact I had agreed to by the seashore. Secrecy gave me a transitory thrill, but it also defined the terms of our meetings. Neither of us was being honest. As the weeks passed, and my knowledge of Walter Krokowski preyed on my imagination, the things Kristina had not told me grew in my mind and I felt the lack of trust acutely. In the end, discretion, that old English vice, gave me nothing, except furtiveness, shame, and finally despair. In Jericho Lodge, Raymond sat, hour by hour, smoking his pipe, and staring beyond his typewriter into the ragged garden.

I became grateful for distractions. When a forlorn convoy of gypsies set up camp in a lay-by just outside the village, the more conservative members of Mansfield applied to me for legal advice. Mrs Boyle was especially vociferous in her complaints about vagrancy and theft, and Mr Curran spoke of his fears for public health. I explained, as I had done in the past, that it was a matter for the local authorities. I took it upon myself to raise the issue with a member of the council, though my own sympathies lay with the travellers. I liked to see their horses grazing by the roadside, and I made a point of buying the domestic items – tea-towels, shampoo and long-life batteries – their women sold from door to door. I could not help smiling at the contrast between my public and my private life.

The rhythm of the year, the unchanging routine of country life, rolled on. Once I had been comforted by the pattern of my existence, but now I was exasperated by it. I wanted to escape, and at the same time I could not leave. I would tour the village in the course of my duties, see the autumn chrysanthemums standing in their vases, and speculate about parish matters with my neighbours, but my thoughts were somewhere else.

Whenever my friends and acquaintances in Mansfield, the Stephensons possibly, or the Willetts, referred to Kristina, I became edgy and watchful. Perhaps they were hinting at something. Perhaps Raymond, Kristina and I were the victims of an elaborate social conspiracy. Perhaps everyone knew. Sometimes I was convinced that everyone was mocking me. In my more rational moments I knew that these suspicions were absurd, but still I looked for hidden meanings in the most banal passages of everyday conversation and saw my secret betrayed in the simplest glance. I was losing touch with what was real and what was not.

I could not put Kristina out of my mind. In my worst mood I imagined that Raymond had reported everything that had passed between us and that they were both toying with my feelings like the cynical, aristocratic manipulators of some eighteenth-century novel. Kristina seemed more than ever willing to perplex and tease me with an insouciance that bordered on indifference.

'Don't you care any more?' I asked her one day.

'I care,' she replied with a shrug.

I should have confronted her there and then, but I was fearful of the consequences. I was afraid to lose her, and yet the knowledge I had been given told me that she was not mine, and perhaps never had been.

[2]

It was during these difficult weeks that I saw exactly how adaptable Raymond could be. In the past, I had accused him of swallowing contradiction as the snake the rabbit, and now I watched him match the colours of his skin to the new terrain with the ease of a born survivor. My consolation was to observe my brother trapped by his own propaganda. He could masquerade in public, but once the front door closed there was no escaping the fact that his marriage was a sham. Round-faced Jane kept up the daily routine without complaint, but the home was a museum of domesticity and the children had the mute, panic-struck look of survivors from some natural disaster. Sometimes I felt that unruly Jack, no longer a puppy, was the only living thing in Jericho Lodge, barking and barking at the approach of danger like the hound in a horror story.

As the year faded and the darkness closed in, Raymond directed all his energies towards his unfinished memoirs. Whenever we met, he would pull a brown envelope out of his briefcase and show me the latest pages. 'Now this is an interesting story,' he would say. 'Fancy a sneak preview?' I would run my eye over his immaculate typing and do my best to encourage him. When he asked my advice about publication, I suggested approaching the firm that had brought out his history of the British Isles.

'Oh no, it's far too radical for those people,' he replied. 'They still want the party line. I'm telling it how it was, warts and all.'

Raymond agreed that a professional opinion would be useful and I remembered that a college friend, Alan Sinclair, worked for an American publishing conglomerate. So I wrote to him from my office, prefacing a brief description of my brother's work with a jocular disclaimer of responsibility. Sinclair replied that the idea was 'by no means impossible' and asked for a synopsis and a sample chapter.

My brother was galvanised by this outside interest. For my part, I was encouraged to hope that a modest collaboration between us could help to restore harmonious relations. We even spent an evening together at my house, discussing the shape of the outline and puzzling over the episodes he might polish up for objective consideration. I was intrigued to do this, hoping I might learn more details of his years in Berlin. I soon discovered that Raymond was more interested to fuss over possible titles.

'I found this in a dictionary of quotations,' he said. 'It's from Livy.' He cleared his throat. '"There are times, people and events on which and on whom only History can pass final judgement. The only thing that remains to be done by the individual is to report on what he saw happening and what he heard." Not bad, eh? I thought I could call my book, "Final Judgement". What do you think?'

'Sounds good,' I replied. 'There's just one snag.'

'What's that?'

'You haven't written it yet.'

'Very funny.'

He was, as it happened, in good humour. 'Listen to this,' he went on. 'This is from my early life.' He straightened his back, and held the paper out in front of him with stagey self-consciousness. '"My parents were members of the southern middle class. Anthony, my father, was a schoolteacher. He was a socialist, and he had a William Morris beard. He and my mother had flirted with Communism in the Thirties, but I was the first member of our family to take up the standard of the working-class struggle. One must remember that in those days, before the Stalin revelations, things were much simpler. We saw Communism as the answer to Fascism, and also to the uglier forms of capitalism. I joined the Communist Party on my eighteenth birthday, which was the minimum age."' He put the page down, as if closing a family Bible. 'What do you think?'

I was at a loss to answer. 'It's a good start,' I replied. 'How are you going to handle your time in Germany?'

'I'm coming to that,' he said. 'I'm coming to that.' He held up the page from which he had just read. 'Not a single typing error. When it comes to the written word I'm a real perfectionist. It's probably my communist training. I'll tear up the paper and start again if I make a mistake. It makes progress rather slow.' He studied the text critically. 'Damn,' he said. 'Here's another thing I've left out.' He crushed the paper in his hand. 'Did I ever tell you the funny story about what happened when I joined the Party?'

I shook my head. 'I don't think you liked telling funny stories when I was a kid.'

'No, I suppose I didn't. Well, it was like this. The

local branch secretary was a bus driver, Mr Jones, a rather naive sort of chap. And so he came to the door and Father opened it. You, young Julian, were all of four years old at the time. And Jones said, "Mr Whyte?" "Yes," said Father. "Congratulations, comrade, here is your party card!" And Father said, "I think you mean my son." He was terribly surprised.'

'Nice story,' I said.

'I thought you'd like it. I'll have to put that in before I send it off to your Mr Sinclair.'

Slowly it dawned on me that he was prevaricating. When, a few days later, I enquired again about his progress, he protested that before he released any part of the text there was 'a lot of nitty-gritty' he had to cross-check with friends and colleagues in Berlin. The quest for perfection was an evasion strategy beyond reproach. No one could deny he was hard at work. Whenever I came to The Lodge I could hear the sound of his typewriter clicking away in the study.

In the early days, I had seen Raymond's work on his autobiography as a blessing in disguise, a useful distraction and a guarantee of a certain privacy and freedom in my relations with Kristina. Now, however, I was dismayed to discover that Raymond's unfinished typescript was unsettling to Kristina. She did not favour a record of events over which she had no control, and he was delighted to emphasise the freedom he was finding in 'settling old scores', as he put it. From time to time, Kristina would enquire casually how much of the text I had seen, and I was relieved to be able to report that my knowledge of it was almost as patchy as hers.

I remember one Saturday towards the end of September. We were all three of us sitting at the kitchen table having tea. The children were painting with Jane next door. This was the facsimile of family life we had created. In one of the silences that fell across the conversation, Kristina asked Raymond if he had despatched his book to the publisher yet, knowing full well that he had not.

'I'm still polishing it.' He looked across the table at me for support. 'Julian says you only have one chance with these publishing wallahs.'

'No one will want to read it unless it's sensational.' She looked at me. 'Capitalists like sensation.'

My brother was wounded. 'I want to tell the truth.'

'The truth?' Her voice was strident. The veins trembled at her temples. 'You have never told the truth.'

'What do you mean?' I saw the sudden irritation I remembered from the past. 'What in God's name are you talking about?'

'You know very well what I'm talking about.' Now she was speaking in German, but I was understanding almost every word. 'You told lies to your superiors.'

'I told the truth about you.'

'You told them what suited you.'

'They knew it anyway.'

'So.' She was triumphant. 'You admit it. Whatever you say, you are still their creature.' She pointed angrily at me. 'If you were in his court, we would hear some stories.'

My brother's eyes were cold and defensive. 'I have never committed a crime, and you know that.'

'Really?' Now she was sneering. 'You are the worst kind of collaborator. You talk about obeying the law, but you don't know what justice really means.'

'Very well,' said Raymond boldly. 'What crime have I committed?'

'Perhaps you have never killed anyone, or tortured them, but you broke your trust and you created a world of fear and hatred. That is a crime.' She got up. 'I am certain that Julian knows none of these things.'

'Julian knows more than you think,' Raymond muttered, with a meaningful look in my direction.

That was my cue, but I missed it. I wanted to be alone with Kristina, and in a mood of calmness, when I addressed this question.

She, on her side, did not hear him, or chose to ignore his words. We watched her go out and close the door behind her. Raymond was smiling at me with embarrassment. He was like a boy when it came to such passions. 'Women always get so emotional,' he said, feebly. 'It will blow over. It always does.'

In the silence that followed we could hear Kristina speaking in German to Olga and Sasha next door. Her voice had an attractively soothing tone that carried no memory of her anger. I pictured her reassuring her children with words of love. Lately they had become like refugees in their parents' house. Sometimes, when I asked Raymond what Olga and Sasha made of our behaviour, it was as though for a moment a sense of reality returned. His habitual reply was that children – 'nippers' was the word he used – were incredibly resilient and took everything in their stride. I, for my part, had become distant from them, and I think it was my sadness at this new estrangement that provoked a sudden belligerence.

'Why do you always refuse to admit weakness and disappointment?' I asked suddenly. 'Why do you persist in pretending that nothing's wrong?'

Raymond did not reply for a moment. Then he said, 'That is how we were trained. We were taught to believe that everything was for the better, regardless.'

'It does you no favours,' I said. 'Not when all you have to report is various kinds of failure.'

'Sometimes you're such a moraliser,' he replied, and I saw that my remarks had found their target. 'It's easy to see things in terms of success and failure, black and white, good and bad, but you know perfectly well that real life is not like that. Things in Germany were much more complex than you give them credit for.'

'Kristina would not agree with that.'

'That's her opinion, and she's entitled to it. I must say I don't think it helps to get too involved in personalities. I'd rather analyse structures and systems.'

I pointed at the folder that contained the pages of his autobiography. 'You can look at it any way you want, Raymond, but the fact remains that if you want to succeed with this book of yours you will have to face up to what Kristina calls the truth one day, and you might as well practise on me.'

He shuffled the pages. 'You know what the problem is,' he said. 'It's not so much facing up to what I may or may not have done, it's understanding who I was.'

'What do you mean?'

'The thing is that I know what I did, but I can't understand why I did it. It is like meeting a man you once knew and being told, quite inexplicably, that you are no longer on speaking terms. I find I'm not really in sympathy with the person I was then. Perhaps this is why I find it so difficult to take my narrative beyond the earliest years.'

'If you cannot be friends with young Raymond,' I said, 'how will you make peace with those people who knew him then?'

'It's a fair question,' he said numbly.

'You talk about setting the record straight, but nothing you say to me suggests that you really want to do this.'

I looked across at him in the shadows of the late afternoon. In my experience, as people grow older they come to terms with themselves and acquire a certain authenticity. My brother was not like that. He was like an unfinished jigsaw, a random display of characteristics, scattered in front of me. I could quite believe it when he said that he didn't know himself. This writing was his way of coming to terms with whoever he was. I felt sorry for him.

'Do you think you understand Kristina?' he asked, after another long pause.

'No, not really,' I replied. 'I wish I did, but I don't.' I looked at my brother in the evening light. 'She is angry about something I don't understand.'

'So you still haven't asked her about young Walter, then?'

'No, I haven't.' I felt defensive about this. I had told myself I should not prevaricate as Raymond did, and yet I had still not found the opportunity or even the resolve.

'Perhaps you should exercise your courtroom skills on her for a change.'

'I'm not sure that it would make much difference. You see, Raymond, I've come to the conclusion that no one knows her. That's her power over both of us.' I heard myself becoming pompous and dogmatic. 'It is always the enigma that fascinates.'

'You have deluded yourself with the thought that you could somehow possess her, but she will always slip away.'

'Perhaps she will leave you just when you least expect it, and just when I least expect it, too. I'm sure she'll continue to surprise us.'

He looked at me in silence for a moment. 'You can accuse me of failure,' he said, 'but I have always known how to keep my wife.'

Raymond got up from the table and went out of the room. I heard his footsteps fade down the passageway, and caught the forced cheerfulness of his whistle, and I found myself wishing, not for the first time, that he had never come to Mansfield.

[3]

My work as a coroner often takes me into areas of heartbreak, and occasionally my court will witness some shock-horror revelation whose sensational impact on the routine exercise of the law I have, in the past, rather enjoyed. However, when a routine inquest I was holding became, quite unexpectedly, headline news, I found myself quite dismayed by those disconcerting aspects of the case that seemed to sound a fortuitous warning.

George Robertson, fifty years old, and a father-of-two, was the owner and manager of Argosy, a small travel agency on the outskirts of Brighton. He had done well in the Eighties, well enough to move to a farmhouse in the Sussex countryside. When the recession came, his customers had deserted him, his business declined, and he had been forced to take a second mortgage to keep afloat. Matters had taken a turn for the worse when he had failed to keep up with his payments. But when he had placed the house on the market he'd discovered that it was now valued at less than its purchase price during the boom and he was faced with imminent bankruptcy.

Early in the morning of the August bank holiday, traditionally a busy season for travel agents, George

Robertson had hanged himself from a beam in his garage. He had been discovered by his wife, Marjorie, when she went to get the car for the daily run to the shops. There was no note, but it was clear from the hour at which Mr Robertson chose to take his life that he intended his wife to find him.

In a case of this sort, I always try, where possible, to dispatch the distressing police and medical evidence with a minimum of fuss at the beginning of the proceedings. The family of the deceased naturally dread the recital of the cause of death, and there was nothing in the papers before me that suggested anything contentious. While the statutory authorities made their report, I took the opportunity of observing the newly widowed Mrs Robertson, a well-composed, smartly-dressed woman in her forties, I guessed. She was sitting with her two teenage sons, but I noticed that they were slightly apart from her, a fact I put down to teenage awkwardness. The older of the two boys was subdued; the younger visibly upset. He was comforted by his brother. Their mother sat staring ahead in what I assumed to be a trance of grief.

In her evidence to the court, Mrs Robertson, who worked in a secretarial capacity at the university, spoke at some length about her husband's money worries. He had, she said, always been anxious about the mortgage on the house, and when the business began to fail, he had become obsessed by the possibility of repossession by the bank. In answer to my question about their circumstances, she replied, in words that struck me as slightly odd, 'My husband was incapable of enjoying the good things of life. He was always worrying about money. That's what killed him.'

None of this was especially unusual, but there was

something about the behaviour of the Robertson family, and the absence of other family members, that made me curious. In court, the coroner is king. When the case had been completed, and before I began my summing up, I paused. Looking at Mrs Robertson and her two sons, I asked if they wished to add anything further.

To my amazement, the elder boy stood up. He seemed slightly stunned by what he had done, and for a moment looked about the courtroom almost wildly. His mother said, 'James!', but he did not sit down.

I invited the young man to take the witness-stand. He was wearing his school blazer and a badly-knotted school tie, and his face had the flushed seriousness of the adolescent. He was surprisingly calm. I spoke quietly, as I always do, looking him in the eye. I asked him to tell me whatever he wanted without anxiety.

'You've not heard the whole truth, sir,' he began. 'I mean what Mum's just said might be true, but there's something else.' He glanced at his mother, hesitated briefly, and then spoke hurriedly in a low voice, as if taking me into his confidence. 'You see, my father believed that my mother was having an affair with a colleague at work, a man called Ken. I heard him challenge Mum about it, and so did my brother. In Mum's desk at home we found an envelope full of letters and presents from Ken, silly things like chocolate hearts and stuffed animals. I am sure Dad saw them, too. There were love poems, letters, and cards. About a month ago my dad went up to where Mum works at the university and accused Ken of sexually harassing Mum. He had a big argument with them, and Mum admitted she was seeing Ken.'

I glanced at Mrs Robertson as her son was speaking.

She was showing no emotion. When the boy mentioned the affair with the man called Ken she shook her head slightly, and looked down.

'After that,' the boy went on, 'Dad came home and he was very depressed. I'm sure that what Dad did was connected with what was happening between Mum and Ken.' There was a pause, then he said, 'I'm sorry, Mum,' and began to cry.

I waited for the boy to collect himself, and asked if he had anything else to add. He shook his head. Then I invited Mrs Robertson to take the witness-stand again.

'You have heard what your son has just said?'

She nodded.

'Why didn't you mention any of this when you gave your evidence?'

She was very cool, almost disdainful. 'It didn't seem either important or relevant.'

'You don't think the state of your marriage to your husband might have been a contributory factor in his decision to take his own life?'

'It might have been,' she said. 'I've already told you that what mattered to him was money.'

'Do you recognise the description of your marriage we've just heard?'

Mrs Robertson faced me steadily. 'I think the marriage would probably have come to an end eventually. The feeling had gone on my side and George, I mean my husband, knew that.'

'Do you wish to comment on your son's remarks about your colleague?'

She looked at me with a panicky expression that touched me against my will. 'Do I have to?'

I replied that she did not, and after some further

questions to corroborate her son's testimony I let her go. I watched her return to her seat, as stiffly composed as before, and sit down next to, but apart from, her sons. I shuffled my papers. My mind was in a spin. For a moment I doubted that I could marshal my thoughts coherently.

Speaking slowly, I drew attention to the state of George Robertson's business and what I called 'the gathering storm' of his financial worries. I made a special point of commending the dead man's son for his candour. 'From what we have heard,' I went on, 'there is no doubt that this marriage had been corroding to a point where it was going to break down. Mrs Robertson had developed a relationship with someone called Ken, and it was obviously a very close friendship indeed, and provided something that Mrs Robertson needed. George Robertson did not know exactly what was happening, but presumed his wife had found another man, and the effect on him was devastating. Everything in his life seemed to be facing ruin,' I concluded, 'and we must assume that he had lost the will to live.' I paused, looked around the court, and recorded a verdict of suicide.

I watched the court break up, and saw the witnesses filing out, as if from church. There was a buzz of talk. In the corridor outside, I could see Harvey, the reporter from the local paper, waiting to ask Mrs Robertson some supplementary questions. I wondered if the press would bother to track down her lover, and what the man called Ken would turn out to be like. So often, in my experience, such figures proved a disappointment. My thoughts turned yet again to the shadowy figure of Walter Krokowski. Who was he, exactly? What did his relationship with Kristina amount to? What did he look like? I realised, then, that I was almost ready, as Raymond had suggested, to arraign Kristina in my own particular court-of-law and begin a cross-examination.

[4]

The Robertson inquest was splashed across the front page of the local newspaper and then picked up, in a modest way, by the national press. For a few days, I became something of a celebrity in Mansfield, where the case was widely discussed, especially by those who had known George Robertson personally, or done business with him. One or two more perceptive souls asked me how I had known that there was more to the story of his suicide than met the eye. I replied, as I always do, that sometimes in court a sixth sense tells you that there's another question to ask. To myself, I admitted that it was Kristina's presence in my life that made me alert to such matters. It was Kristina whose story demanded that extra question, and I exercised much thought in deciding when to make my move.

One evening, at the beginning of October, Kristina and I were in a roadside motel some distance from Mansfield, a dingy, bungalow-style establishment with a disco and an American cocktail bar. Beyond the louvres, autumn rain resounded like applause in the guttering.

We had made love, but without conviction, and were lying under the blankets listening to the rain, not speaking. At length, Kristina said she had to go back. She would telephone Raymond. To give her some privacy, I went into the bathroom, a squalid cubbyhole with a prison-camp shower, and splashed water on my face. She put the phone down as I came back into the room.

'Why does he never ask where I am?'

'He is afraid.'

'What is his fear?'

'He does not want to provoke you.'

She shook her head in a petulant gesture. 'Oh, how I would like to be provoked!' Then, lapsing into German in words I could not mistake, she added bitterly, 'I am treated like a servant not a wife.'

'How do I treat you?' I could not prevent my question and I regretted it at once.

'Sometimes you treat me like a whore.'

I felt my resolve threatened. 'Please, Kristina. Don't say that.'

'Are you going to say you love me?'

'You know I love you.' I tried to remain steady. 'But you do not love me as I would like. You have fascinated me, as you have fascinated my brother, but you do not love me.'

She looked at me sadly. 'When you speak like that I'm glad there was no baby.'

I went towards her. I wanted to comfort her, but my pain made the move seem desperate.

'Don't.'

She ran into the bathroom and locked the door. I heard her crying and then the sound of taps and water running in the basin.

I sat down and switched on the television. A local news bulletin was reporting a fatal car crash. No doubt I would hear more before the night was out, and I found the prospect of doing my duty in the service of the Crown oddly soothing. After a few minutes I heard the bathroom door open and felt Kristina's hand on my head.

'I am not myself today.' She gestured vaguely at the bed. 'You see, it is the emotion.'

I wanted to say that it was the absence of the emotion, but instead I said, 'You need someone you can trust, I think.' I put my hand over hers. 'I wish you could confide in me.'

'Julian, Julian . . .' When she spoke my name in that peculiar intonation she had, I experienced an intimacy I dared not rely on. We sat in silence together for some moments. 'You are very good to me,' she said finally, as if summoning up an admission of remorse or perhaps a formula for reconciliation. 'I think you do not understand how good.'

'I do understand,' I said. 'But I know I am not Walter Krokowski.'

Kristina stepped back. There was a long pause between us. The rain continued to patter in the background.

'He told you?'

I nodded.

'I'm glad.'

I was also relieved to have brought the subject into the open. I felt almost light-headed. 'He said you are still in love with Krokowski.' Now I turned to face her. 'I have to ask you. Is that true?'

'We always love those we have loved.' She looked away towards the door. Her raincoat was hanging on the hook, still wet from the weather outside. 'Yes, I am still in love with him.' She came towards me and took my hand. 'Only a little, of course.'

I was about to comment that I did not entirely believe this, when she put her arms around me and held me in an embrace that seemed to say she was pleased we were talking at last.

'Who is he?'

'Walter Krokowski?' When she spoke his name it

sounded different, the name of a conductor or a math-
ematician. 'He is a very special man.'

'Raymond said you had an affair.'

'We fell in love,' she said, simply. 'It was after Sasha
was born. I lost my affection for Raymond and when I
met Walter I could not stop myself. For some years I had
put my lustful feelings aside, but with him I could not
stop myself.' She smiled at the memory. 'He was so open
and free. He had vitality. And unlike Raymond, he had
an easy conscience.'

'How did Raymond react?'

'He could see that I loved Walter, and he was very
jealous. He wanted to be what Walter was, and of course
he never could be.'

'And what was Walter?'

'He was – he is – a poet,' she said. 'He was so different
from Raymond.'

'How different?'

'An honest man.'

I had so many questions to ask, but I knew from
experience that Kristina would not respond to interrogation. I had to go slowly. 'Where is he now?'

A look of great sadness came into her face. 'I don't
know,' she said. 'I had a letter a few weeks ago, but there
was no address.'

'What did he say?'

'He said he would never forget me.' She shrugged.
'How can I reply if I do not know where he is?'

'Does no one know?'

'I have written to my friends in Berlin asking about
him but there is no reply.'

'Isn't he in Berlin?'

She looked at me hard. 'No, he is not in Berlin,' she
said. There was something about my question that made

her decisive. She completed her dressing in a manner that was both organised and businesslike. I suggested, with reluctance, that it was time to go home.

'Home?' Her voice was more melancholy than ever. 'That is not my home.'

I had often heard her speak disparagingly of Jericho Lodge in the past, but today, when she uttered these words, I saw my hopes for the future broken like a cherished ornament. She was not happy here, and never would be. The time would come when she would be gone, and perhaps this time would come sooner rather than later.

'Would you go back to Germany to find him?' I asked, voicing my fears.

There was another silence between us. 'I loved Walter,' she said, opening the door, 'but I know now that I shall probably never see him again.'

I did not reply, and followed her to the parking bay outside. There was something in the way she hurried back to her car that made her seem more remote and unreachable than ever. On that occasion, as on many previous moments of departure, I watched her open the driver's door, waiting for her farewell wave. But she never looked back.

I sat in my own car and watched the tail-lights of the Mini flare as she braked to turn into the main road. Once, I had thought I could get close to Kristina through the mystery of sex, and then I had thought I could be intimate with her through a peculiar amendment in her marriage to Raymond, but now I had unwillingly to acknowledge that I was failing all round. I had reached that point at which, in the past, the women in my life had packed their bags and left. At least, this time, I was already alone. As I reflected on our conversation I heard my brother proudly telling me that he had always known how to hold on to his wife and I found myself returning in my mind to Krokowski's unexplained absence like a restless sleeper trapped on a relentless treadmill of thought.

[5]

Ever since Raymond had first uttered his name I had been troubled by Walter Krokowski. Now I became – there is no other word for it – obsessed. He was my rival, my enemy. I wanted to know all about him, yet at the same time I dared not let Kristina see that. I could refer to him from time to time, in the hope of titbits, but my real source had to be Raymond. I lost no time in relating to my brother the conversation in the motel.

'Were you jealous?' I asked, putting my own feelings into words for the first time.

'Yes,' said Raymond thoughtfully, 'there was a time when I was very jealous of Walter Krokowski.' He smiled. 'But not in the sense you are using the word, Julian.'

'What do you mean?'

'I mean I was jealous because he seemed to have the system worked out. Mine was the jealousy of the operator not the lover.'

'Kristina tells me he was a poet,' I prompted.

'An experimental poet,' corrected Raymond. 'A very bad, experimental poet.' Krokowski, he reported, was a member of the *avant-garde*. 'Prenzlauer Berg.' He laughed sarcastically. 'A ghetto for dilettantes.' He described graffiti-scarred apartment buildings, gutted by war and neglect, occupied by what he called 'the flotsam and jetsam of East Berlin'. In this dissident community, Krokowski's short stories and poems became quite famous for their coded critique of the regime.

'Before the Stasi got to him, he'd been trained as a printer,' said Raymond. 'Even when he'd been dismissed from the printing press, he could still produce a samizdat version of his work in some bombed-out cellar.'

'Any good?'

'When I knew him – we were briefly friends, you see – he was into what he called "an alternative aesthetic". Some people said it was adolescent, and others said it was agitprop. Its heart was in the right place, but it was basically crap,' said Raymond, smiling. 'Krokowski's most celebrated poem was called "das Nichts", "Nothingness", which gives you some idea. If he hadn't been such a lively, energetic figure I doubt if anyone would have paid much attention.'

'How did you come across him?'

'He was a taxi-driver. I used to ride in his cab. I was able to get him things from West Berlin, books and newspapers.' He paused, as if weighing up what to say next. 'But that's not the point, is it?' He looked at me. 'The point is that Kristina fell in love with him.'

I did not show my hurt at these words. 'When was this?'

'After my son was born.' He made a calculation. 'Nineteen eighty-five, or was it eighty-six? I forget.'

'But it didn't last? She came back to you?'

There was a pause. We could hear an ambulance siren in the distance, a faint reminder of the world of emergencies.

'Krokowski was arrested for crimes against the state. He was put in prison. Then we left Berlin.'

'Another good reason to come home,' I said.

174

He smiled. 'Exactly.'

'Where is Krokowski now?'

'I have no idea.' He gestured vaguely and unconvincingly. 'He could be anywhere.'

A scheme was forming in my mind as he spoke. 'If you want to do justice to your memoirs,' I said, 'you should track him down and find out what he's up to now.'

Raymond laughed. 'Don't be ridiculous.' He looked down, polishing his glasses on his tie. 'Krokowski has nothing to say to me.'

'If you don't talk to him, then at the very least', I said, 'you should go back to Berlin, and investigate your own experience with the benefit of hindsight.'

The conversation lapsed at this point, with my brother once again saying that he had no interest in returning to Germany. He had come here to get away from Berlin, he said. He had no desire to put the clock back. I, of course, was eager to find a reason to get him to go there, and to go with him. I wanted to trace Krokowski's whereabouts, perhaps even to see him, and if I could to persuade him that Kristina was happy in England and would never come back. At this early stage, before I knew what I knew later, I had convinced myself that my claim on Kristina was the stronger.

I don't now understand why I ever suggested that we travel to Germany – in retrospect the idea seems absurd, ridiculous – but nevertheless, a few days after this conversation, Raymond appeared at my house just as I was leaving for work one morning. He was excited and out of breath. 'I've had an idea,' he said.

I stood my briefcase on the roof of the car like a sentinel. 'What's that?'

'I'll take your advice. I will go back to Berlin.' He saw

my surprise. 'I'll go back for a long week-end.' He stepped towards me, confidential. There was a drop on his nose. 'I'd like you to come with me.' Raymond began to elaborate the scheme, pulling from his anorak pocket a railway and ferry timetable. I was impatient to get to the office, but in a matter of moments he showed how, without difficulty, we could be in Berlin by Saturday morning and, leaving on Sunday evening, return to Mansfield the next day. 'If we take the boat it won't cost much,' he said. 'Think of the train ride. It will be worth it for that alone.' His breath was foggy in the morning, and in his anorak and reading glasses he looked like a superannuated train-spotter.

I was late for work. 'I'll think about it,' I said, and suggested we discuss it further in the evening. I did not want to seem too eager, but when I came home I was pleased to find that Raymond had pushed a ticket through my letter-box.

'What exactly do you propose to do in Berlin?' I asked, when I telephoned to discuss the trip.

'There is so much,' he replied. 'People, places. It will be a trip down memory lane.' I could hear him warming to his theme. 'There's a lot of information open to the public now that wasn't available before. I promise you won't be disappointed.'

I was intrigued. 'Are you proposing to look at the files?' Here would be an opportunity to investigate the Stasi at first hand. Under Kristina's tutelage, my German was now passably good, and I would have no trouble navigating around the city.

'I don't rule anything out,' he replied. 'You can be my witness.'

I was happy to accept his invitation. 'You may need a good lawyer,' I joked.

'Attaboy,' he said. I sensed his old zest again. As our departure date drew closer, however, his anxiety returned. On more than one occasion he asked if I was familiar with the legal procedures of the European Community. When I asked him what his worry was, he brushed aside my question with an impatient wave of the hand. 'At the very least, old boy, I want to show you my side of the story.'

As I drove to the station next morning I wondered what this story would turn out to be. Our plan was to take the boat-train to Harwich, cross the North Sea to Hamburg, and then take the express to Berlin. On the first leg of the journey we would go to London Victoria and then on to Liverpool Street station. I found Raymond in the railbar. It was barely ten o'clock, but he had a glass of whisky in front of him on the counter and I guessed it was not his first. I asked if he had his ticket and his passport.

'In this new Europe of ours, sonny boy, you won't need a passport.' He tapped his breast-pocket. 'Old habits die hard.' He drained his glass. 'Let's go.' As he picked up his suitcase I saw with dismay how unsteady he was.

The train was on time. We found a No Smoking section and settled down with our books and newspapers. Raymond fell asleep. I was glad. We had a long journey ahead, and plenty of time to talk. I turned to my book, a study of post-war Germany recommended by the critics. The train rattled through the Sussex countryside. Autumn bonfires dotted across the landscape were like a battle scene. As we pulled into Victoria station, my brother opened his eyes. He frowned at the cover of my book. 'That fellow got it all wrong,' he said. 'He doesn't know Germany the way I know Germany.'

'I have to begin somewhere,' I replied, hoping to avoid an argument so early in the trip.

'You could start with your old brother,' he said, and he meant it. He was determined to impress his change of heart upon me.

We crossed London by taxi. Raymond complained about the cost but I told him not to worry. I was taking charge, as I had anticipated. I remembered Liverpool Street from childhood as a smoky, echoing, catacomb. Now it was a bright white concourse with shopping arcades and electronic information. The boat-train was waiting. The carriages were not full. Our fellow passengers divided into young backpackers and groups of elderly couples on bargain-breaks. We found our reservations and dumped our bags. Raymond announced that he could use a drink. I demurred.

'Come on, Julian. We're on holiday. What can I get you?'

I settled for a beer. 'Take care now.'

Raymond said something I could not hear and disappeared through the automatic doors. I had always known he was a drinker, but now I sensed his desperation.

The train was racing through the fields of Essex when he reappeared. I guessed he had been tippling alone at the bar with other solitary travellers.

'There we are.' He dumped the bottles on the table. 'Bingo,' he said, cracking the seal on a miniature whisky.

'You should go steady.' I watched him pour a second miniature into a plastic beaker. 'We've a way to go.'

'Precisely,' he said. 'If it wasn't for this stuff I'd die of boredom.' He raised his cup. 'Cheers.'

'Cheers.'

'I used to do this trip in the Sixties. You won't remember. I came over quite often. I had Maureen's

178

family to worry about then. Such things don't seem to matter when you're young. I knew I had to rebuild my life once my marriage broke up, and being in Germany was an interesting challenge. People like me are a bridge between two worlds, aren't they?'

Raymond had been holding forth to total strangers in this way for years. I agreed, neutrally. I knew he wasn't interested in my opinions.

'When I first arrived I lived in a tiny furnished room. It was nine square metres, I remember. What did I care? Looking back, it was quite a leap in the dark, but that's not how it seemed at the time. I was on top of the world. Those were the days.'

'Were they?'

'So we thought. The world was changing, it seemed. How wrong we were.'

The train echoed his thoughts. How-wrong-we-were. How-wrong-we-were. I looked out of the window at a line of traffic queuing at a level-crossing and felt that momentary collision of unconnected lives.

Raymond put down his glass. 'Socialism was doomed, like the railways. All it could do was modernise and try to be something it wasn't. Social democracy, for instance. Look at these trains now. They're trains, of course, but they're trying to be aeroplanes. That's socialism now, a train that wanted to fly.'

We rushed on through East Anglia. The cloud was low and here and there flocks of seagulls swooping across the hedgerows announced the approaching coastline. Raymond fell asleep again. I tried to read my book and then began to doze, too. We reached Harwich docks in time for the afternoon crossing.

It was not high season, but there was quite a crowd of foot passengers gathered in the departure lounge. I went to the cafeteria and bought a couple of black coffees. When the moment of embarkation came I noticed that Raymond had a little panic as we went through customs. I steered him towards the ferry. As we drew near the gangway, a woman with a clipboard approached us.

'Excuse me,' she began, 'I am conducting a survey and I wonder if—'

'Oh, why don't you bugger off,' said my brother, pushing past her roughly.

I apologised as well as I could and hurried after him. 'I won't come if you're going to behave like that,' I said.

'Suit yourself,' he replied truculently.

I judged it wise to avoid a scene, and we went down into the belly of the ship to find our cabin, not speaking. I stowed my bag and went back up on deck, paying no attention to Raymond.

After a few minutes, he appeared at my side, as I had expected. 'I'm sorry, frater,' he said. 'I just hate checkpoints.' When I did not answer, Raymond continued in the same confessional vein. 'I've seen too many people arrested at places like these. I once saw a man taken off a train at the Ostbahnhof. As long as I live I'll never forget the look on his face.'

We stood by the stern and watched cars and trucks clanking and rolling on board. Then the moorings were cast off. The ferry gave a long shuddering hoot and began to thrash away from the wharf. We steamed slowly past Harwich towards the open sea. I said I hoped the sea would be calm, and it was. Beyond the fluttering pennant, the coast receded into a blurred pencil line. A party of young Germans in puffa jackets and hiking-boots crowded next to us, shoving and arguing. Raymond stepped aside with an expression of distaste. He explained to me that these were teenage Ossis returning from a school trip. 'I feel out of touch,' he said. 'The sound of German makes me sick.'

'You are right to make this trip,' I said to encourage him.

Raymond stared despondently over the rail. He had the bearing of one who wanted to throw himself into the anonymous waters of the deep. 'Do you think so?'

'You have to make friends with that old self of yours,' I said with a smile. 'Remember?'

'To be frank, brother, I have my doubts.' He gave me a pathetic look. 'Perhaps we could just stop over for a day or two in Hamburg.' His eyes were full of defeat. 'No one need know.'

'Don't be silly,' I said. 'You'll be fine once we get there.'

'I wish I had your optimism,' he said darkly, and went off alone down the companionway towards the recreation area.

I stayed on deck, following the progress of the ship. I was enjoying my break from the office routine. The light faded and the stars came out. On the horizon, lights sparkled in the shipping lanes. The ferry blazed through the water like a floating hotel. From time to time one or two passengers would join me at the rail, but the air was nipping and no one stayed for long.

I lingered, only half aware of the cold. My thoughts turned to Kristina. She was probably in bed now, sur-rounded by her favourite magazines, the radio tuned to rock 'n' roll. I remembered the physical sensation of her body next to mine, the touch and scent of her skin. We had explored each other so deeply, but my knowledge of her had become purely physical. In the beginning, I had wanted to possess her, and to take her away, and yet now

I had to face the fact that it was she who possessed me, but not in any way that gave lasting satisfaction and besides there was little I could do now to escape.

Eventually I went below to look for my cabin. On the lower decks there were all kinds of duty-free shops and distractions, two restaurants, and several bars. Some of the passengers had retired to their cabins, but many were still making the most of the entertainment. The air was close and headachy, with the smell of fried food. I was surprised to find that Raymond was not in our cabin, and I guessed he would be in one of the bars. I felt it was my duty to suggest he get a few hours' rest and went to look for him.

The nearest bar was almost deserted. 'Try the upper deck,' said the barman, stowing glasses. 'You get a good crowd up there.' A group of young men in blazers, members of a sports club, was singing rowdy songs and horsing about. Others were playing cards or sleeping. Raymond was nowhere to be seen. I felt a stab of alarm. I had heard stories of people throwing themselves overboard at night. 'There's always the casino bar,' said the purser, who was flirting with a young woman in uniform.

I followed his directions towards the stern. At this time of the year, in the low season, the ferry was offering duty-free bonanzas to bargain hunters. There was a slightly feverish atmosphere. The Mayflower casino bar was where the partygoers had congregated. Situated at the stern, just above the ship's wake, it was part night-club, part disco and part gaming-room. There was a wall of slot machines, low lighting, and one or two couples dancing slowly. I found Raymond sitting at the blackjack table sandwiched between a bald man with a spotted bow-tie and a middle-aged woman in a shell suit.

'Thank God you're here,' he said, as if he had been

expecting my arrival. 'Lend me fifty quid, won't you? I've slipped a bit.'

I judged it best to comply. I gave him three twenties, and watched him play. He was quite drunk and betting rashly. In a few minutes he had lost his chips and turned to me again. 'Please Julian. A couple of good bets and I'll be all square.'

I shook my head. 'How have you been paying for this?'

'I put it on my credit card.' He waved at the cashier's desk. 'They've been very understanding.'

'How much have you spent?'

'About a thousand, maybe more. I reached my credit card limit just before you came.'

'A thousand pounds!'

He saw my dismay. 'I know. I'm a fool. I don't know what came over me. I wanted to win so badly. I had this idea that I'd buy Kristina this fantastic present, a jewel or a ring or something, and then it would be all right between us again. Not all right all right, if you see what I mean, but better anyway.' He looked at me in desperation. 'You won't tell her, will you?'

I shook my head. To tell Kristina would only heap trouble on us both. 'A thousand pounds, Ray – you don't have a thousand pounds. You barely have one hundred. That's why we're on this boat. To save money.'

'I know, I know.'

'This is where you fold,' I said firmly, escorting him away from the table. The croupier watched us with indifferent eyes. The man in the spotted bow-tie said, 'Luck be a lady tonight,' and laughed. I led my brother away through the crowd of partygoers. No one paid much attention.

'You should rest,' I said.

'I want some air,' he said, gripping my arm.

I steered him upstairs on to the deck. The sky was cloudy. The stars had gone. The ferry was rolling slightly in a heavier sea. Raymond shook his head in despair. 'Kristina's always worrying about our finances.' He gripped my arm with a sudden fierceness. 'What can I do?'

'I'll sort this out.' I had seen my opportunity. 'I'll speak to my bank manager.' Raymond began to thank me, but I cut him short. 'Promise me something?'

'Of course, of course.'

I looked down into the dark water. 'If Krokowski—' I stopped, hesitating.

'Yes?'

'If you ever were to find out where Krokowski happened to be, you'd tell me, wouldn't you?'

'Of course I would, frater. I can't stand the fellow. Never could.'

'And if', I went on, pressing my advantage, 'you were to make such a discovery, you'd not tell Kristina, would you?'

'No, no I wouldn't. Oh God!'

The ferry lurched into a wave, shuddered, and ploughed on in a burst of spray. Raymond began to be sick over the side. The sea was not rough, but with his drinking he was vulnerable to the motion of the ship. When he had finished, and had wiped the traces off his coat as well as he could, he came to where I was standing, slightly apart in the lee of a lifeboat. The light was coming up. Germany was on the horizon. His face was streaked with sweat and blotchy with alcohol.

'Do we have to go to Berlin?' he asked pathetically. 'I'm really not sure I can handle it, you know.'

'No,' I said, suddenly decisive. I felt as though I, too, was coming to my senses. Our mission was ill-conceived.

My hopes, my plans were absurd. It was better to let sleeping dogs lie. We should go home and make our lives normal. I was getting myself into the kind of crazy state that had killed George Robertson. Kristina did not love me. Nothing I could say or do would change that. It was an illusion to suppose that I would ever find Krokowski. I should devote my energies to being a good uncle, brother and brother-in-law. 'No, we don't have to go. I'll take you back.'

There were tears in his eyes. 'Thank you Julian.'

When the ferry docked in Hamburg we never even set foot in the new Germany. I negotiated an immediate return with the ship's authorities, and we stayed on board. Raymond sat in the bar, a lost soul staring into space. Tourist buses with wheezing brakes took the foot passengers into the town centre; a blackened church spire and a television mast. I paced the deck, looking down with detachment on the transactions of Hamburg harbour. There were trucks with Russian markings turning on the wharf and nut-faced men with high cheekbones at the wheel. I saw the convoys stretching into the dusty heart of central Asia and remembered from school the poem that spoke of those 'who take the Golden Road to Samarkand'. There would be trade and traffic in many directions for years to come, and everything would be exchanged several times over. On all sides there had to be a reckoning.

In a few hours our vessel was once again manoeuvring into the stream and steering towards the mouth of the Elbe. Ahead, there was a hint of wind and brightness, the open sea, pitching and dancing. Tugs and lighters chugged down the canal from the interior. On either side there were low green fields dotted with red-roofed houses. Soon, we were cruising, like a surreal travel advertisement, through the tranquil countryside of northern Germany.

'The truth is,' I said, as we watched the serene passage of the ferry through the landscape, 'you're never going to write your autobiography. You're never going to do any of the things you say you're going to do, Raymond. Why not be honest with yourself, and just enjoy your retirement?'

'Is that what you think?'

'It's my advice,' I said. 'But I have been around long enough to know that people often ignore what's best for them.'

'You're probably right. I should put my feet up and make the most of my leisure.' He prodded me with good humour. 'You've changed your tune, frater.'

'Perhaps I'm coming round to your way of seeing things,' I said.

Soon, we were turning away from the nondescript, disappointing shores of Europe and heading back across the North Sea. Now Raymond lay on his bunk and slept, snoring peacefully. I stayed beside him and read *A Tale of Two Cities*, a cheap edition I had found in the newsagent among the thrillers and romances. When, finally, I went up on deck the coastline of East Anglia was on the horizon.

'Home is where the heart is,' said a familiar voice behind me. Raymond had shaved and changed his shirt. When he looked me in the eye I saw defiance battling with remorse. He was like an old actor putting on a good show in a play he knows is doomed to close. When the ship had berthed I watched him cross the footbridge on to dry land. His steps were slow and his head was down. Without an audience he was just an old man in an anorak and frayed trousers, a defeated soldier returning from an unhappy war.

In the London train he fixed his gaze on the Fens and did not speak. The mood for both of us was introspective. 'East Prussia is rather like this,' he said, after a while.

I sensed he was still fussing about Kristina. 'We made the right decision,' I said. 'Don't worry.'

'You know what she can be like.' He smiled weakly. 'She will accuse me of running away.'

'When she hears you were unwell she'll understand.'

'Unwell.' He laughed, as if I had given his show an unexpectedly good review. 'I suppose that's one way of putting it.'

'We all have our phrases,' I said. 'A well-chosen euphemism will smooth the roughest story.' I looked out of the window. The suburbs of London were closing in. Our unhappy excursion was drawing to a close.

'My children will visit a Germany that I will never know,' he said, apropos of nothing. 'And their children will see a society united again. It will take two generations.' He sighed. 'We did our best, but we have a lot to answer for.'   .

'Would our friend Walter Krokowski say you had a lot to answer for?'

He looked at me oddly. 'You just can't leave him alone, can you?'

'A little learning is a dangerous thing,' I replied. 'No doubt if I had the full story I would lose interest.'

Raymond acknowledged my observation with a silent inclination of his head, and then looked out of the window. 'I suppose you realise', he said, not turning back, 'how much she still loves him?'

The mood between us shifted abruptly. In just one

sentence my brother had introduced a threat into the conversation, a threat that made my mind spin and my heart turn over. 'No,' I said quietly. 'No, I don't.'

The train plunged into a tunnel on the approach to Liverpool Street. The lights flickered and went out. For a moment, I remembered those detective stories in which the murderer kills his victim in a darkened train. Then the lights came on and, almost at a walking pace, we pulled into the platform with crushing brakes.

[6]

When we reached Mansfield, Raymond invited me to come with him to Jericho Lodge and with some misgivings I accepted. We found Kristina alone in the kitchen, making supper for the children. She did not hear us come in. There was rock music on the radio, turned up loud, and she was dancing as she worked. She was wearing a track-suit and her hair was pulled back in a ponytail. When she turned and saw us she broke off in embarrassment and surprise. There were dark rings under her eyes, but she was still beautiful, and I realised with sorrow how much less I was seeing her now. My brother did not speak, but sat down at the table, ghostly with exhaustion.

Kristina switched off the radio. 'I'll explain,' I said softly. 'He's very tired.'

She gave an indifferent nod and went next door to find Olga and Sasha. I heard her say, 'Papa ist nach Hause gekommen', and I guessed the kids were watching a video.

'I think I'll go and have a bit of shut-eye,' said

Raymond. He put his hand on my shoulder as he went out. 'Thanks, Julian. You saved my life.'

'Don't be silly,' I said.

I sat in the kitchen with a whisky and soda and watched a game show on television while Kristina fed the children. She ignored me as she had ignored Raymond. After their meal, Olga and Sasha were allowed to solicit a goodnight kiss and went upstairs to bed. Once Kristina had tucked them up she reappeared downstairs in a better mood.

'I was not expecting you so soon,' she said.

'Raymond could not cope,' I began.

'He may look innocent,' she said, 'but he causes pain.' She came towards me, and put her arms around me. 'You are always so reasonable,' she said.

'Shall I tell you what happened?'

She shook her head. 'I don't want to talk about it now.' She seemed tired and distracted. 'Take me to California,' she murmured.

Under her track-suit she was naked. We made love on the sofa, there and then, without a thought for anyone. The fire heaved and sighed in the grate. I was released from care and when she cried out to me I did not even bother to put my hand over her mouth as I had in the past. I assumed Raymond was asleep but I was not concerned. I was certain we would not be disturbed, and we weren't.

I suppose we must have slept for a while. When I opened my eyes, the fire was low and cooling into ash, but still giving warmth. We held each other, not speaking.

'If we could live like this . . .' I said.

'Darling,' she murmured, in that way of hers which

189

despite our intimacy always seemed so remote and non-committal. She stirred in my arms. 'So tell me now. What happened?'

'He got drunk. He became quite ill. He told me he could not face going back.'

'There is too much unfinished business for him in Berlin,' she said.

I had a momentary vision of empty tram-tracks, military check-points, and the grey Wall, snagged with wire, snaking between the backs of houses.

'Did you want him to face that business?'

'I want him in your court.' Her eyes were unforgiving. 'I want you to ask him how many he hurt, and ask him how.'

A log slipped in the hearth and there was a sudden flare of flame. I knew I had to take advantage of this moment. 'Why was Krokowski arrested?'

'What does Raymond say?'

'He said something about crimes against the state. He did not go into the details.' Even then, I could not bring myself to put my suspicions into words. Kristina must have sensed my reticence. She gave a sarcastic laugh. 'How surprising.'

'I don't understand.'

Kristina's scorn was uncontained. 'Raymond was responsible, of course. Walter was planning to take a holiday in Bulgaria, and he was suddenly accused of planning to flee the country. That's a crime. When they searched his taxi he was found to have all this illegal literature. That's another crime. He was sentenced to two years. Raymond was the one who arranged everything.'

I was sceptical. 'Can you prove that?'

'I don't need to,' she said. 'It happens to be true.'

'What's Raymond's line?'

'Raymond denies it all, of course, but no one believes him. Everything he says is lies. Lies and half-truths. Innuendo. Rumour. He does not know right and wrong.'

'He always tells me he loves you,' I said. 'Isn't it possible that he did these terrible things for love?'

'If I can't believe anything he says, how can I believe him when he says he loves me?'

It was a desolate question, and I could not answer. 'Where is Krokowski now?'

A look of great sadness came into her face. 'I've told you,' she said. 'I don't know. He went into the West after he was released.'

'Is he in Germany?'

'Some say he went to India.' Kristina gave a shivering yawn. 'I have tried to find him, but he has disappeared.'

'What would you do if you found him?'

'What would I do?' She looked at me and my heart turned over. 'I would start to live again.'

'What about Raymond?' I was wondering out loud, but secretly I was talking about myself. I was not prepared for her answer.

'He will die,' she said, with sudden finality, and then she laughed. 'Isn't that sad?'

That was when Death stepped into the conversation, like a neighbour who has dropped in for the evening. I am, as I have said, familiar with his presence, and I discovered, to my surprise, that my thoughts did not so much turn to Raymond's death as to Krokowski's. As I lay there, sensing the rhythm of Kristina's breathing next to mine, it occurred to me that perhaps if Krokowski did not exist she could be taught to focus on me as the true object of her affections.

I felt weary but restless, and as much as I wanted to

share these disturbing reflections I wanted also to be alone. My mind was full of violent contradictions. I needed time. I got to my feet, and stretched with a yawn. Then I made a brief farewell and hurried out into the darkness, grateful for the solitude. There was sadness in our parting. I think perhaps we both knew that we would never again experience such intimacy.

I drove home through the lanes of Mansfield. There was a half moon just above the horizon, and the shadow of the Downs loomed above the village like a silvery wall. When I reached home I was in for a shock.

I parked the car in the garage and went to the front door. To my surprise it was not locked, and in my exhausted state I thought that perhaps I had neglected to lock it. The minute I stepped inside, I understood. Books, clothes, papers, crockery: the house was in chaos. I hurried from room to room. The burglars had been hasty and none too discriminating. They had taken the television, the video, my camera, and all the silver, but had missed some valuable eighteenth-century prints. I felt that obscure sense of violation that comes with a break-in, but I was not overwhelmed. For some reason, they had tipped coal from the grate on to the rug in the sitting-room, but there was no other gratuitous mess. No defecation. No vandalism. Should I call the police? I decided to wait for morning. I made up my bed with clean sheets and fell into a deep sleep.

With first light, I placed my call, and discovered with satisfaction that the case was to be handled by Sergeant Kenny, one of the most popular detectives at the police station. He was round before nine o'clock, shaking his head over the aftermath of the burglary, and promising to do what he could. We both knew that it was a vain hope. I had often gossiped with him about the rising crime rate, and we had always concluded our conversations on the subject with remarks to the effect that the only answer was a good insurance policy. He sat at my kitchen table and made a sympathetic inventory of my losses. 'Let's put it all down, Mr Whyte,' he said, cheerfully. 'We may as well take them for all we can.'

I was glad to notice that Kenny did not automatically blame the local gypsies, as I knew my neighbours would. After he had gone, I spent the day tidying up, and putting my personal effects into order. I took the opportunity to lay my accounts on the desk. I had always taken a pride in my financial prudence, but now I realised that my reserves of capital were exhausted. If I was to settle Raymond's debts, as I had promised, I would have to raise a loan.

On Monday I was in my office first thing. I opened the post, dictated some replies, and made an appointment to see my bank manager. Then I rang my brother. 'I'll need your account number,' I said. 'I shall raise the money directly, then you can send a cheque to the credit card people. We shall never refer to this again.' When he began to express gratitude, I cut him short. 'You don't have to thank me,' I said. 'Let's just add it to the list of things we don't discuss.' I was late for my appointment.

I have known my bank manager, Terry Alton, for several years and we have a certain mutual respect. We both hold positions in the community. My interview with him hovered on the edge of awkwardness. It was not a pleasant experience to have to lie to a fellow professional.

Alton's desk was empty, as if he had read somewhere that an empty desk is a sign of power. He gave me coffee from the percolator and then his secretary brought in my file. 'I see you have the beginnings of an overdraft.' He smiled, a professional smile, a doctor diagnosing a disease. 'This is not like you, Julian.'

In the same position I would have said Mr Whyte, but I let it go. 'I have been doing things to the house,' I lied. I was inwardly relieved that I had paid for those hotel rooms with cash.

Alton brightened, as if inspired by a vision of emulsion and double-glazing. 'Ah, improvement.'

I was amused to think of Kristina in such a category. 'I have these costs under control.' I hesitated. 'It's not just my overdraft. I need a loan.'

'More improvements? A loft conversion, perhaps?'

'Alas, no.' As succinctly as possible, I explained my brother's predicament. I painted a picture of an old man inexperienced in the ways of the West. I admitted my embarrassment. One does not like to ask a bank to settle a gambling debt. I volunteered to monitor Raymond's future expenditure.

Alton listened. I could see from his there-but-for-the grace-of-God expression that he felt sorry for me. 'How much do you need?'

'Two thousand.' Like all gamblers, Raymond had underestimated his losses.

Alton raised an eyebrow but said nothing. He was tapping figures into his calculator and for a moment I imagined he would tell me how much of a loft conversion that would buy. 'We would prefer you to repay the interest on a monthly basis,' he said. He pulled out some forms. 'Just sign your name. I will be happy to complete the details.' He handed me his fountain pen, like a diplomat at a summit meeting. 'No problem, Julian.' He was having an imaginary dialogue. 'You are an old and valued customer of this bank.' He rose from the desk, shook my hand and opened the door in a well-practised move. 'We are here to help. Call me any time. Regards to your wife.'

It was a slip, but something about it made me challenge him. 'I'm not married,' I said. 'At least, not yet.'

'How silly of me,' he replied. 'You know how it is. These phrases we all come up with. I beg your pardon.'

The door closed behind me, and with it the awkwardness. As I walked out along the seafront, I puzzled in my mind. Surely he knew I was single? He had just lent me a large sum of money. Did that give him the right to insult me? To threaten? Did he want to tell me that, actually, he knew about Kristina? I felt the satisfaction of a new source of funds quite overshadowed by these worrying reflections, and it was in a mood of some anxiety that I made my way to the Grand Hotel. I had arranged to meet Raymond for coffee there to give him the news of my meeting with Alton.

The hotel was like a wedding cake in the sunshine, a preposterous confection. I stepped inside with confidence. In the past, meeting Kristina, I would skulk through such lobbies, but today I was carefree, at ease. I strolled into the lounge. A party of Japanese tourists was posing for photographs next to a mountain of identical suitcases. Raymond was already there, and as I sat down the waiter arrived with the coffee. For some moments we occupied ourselves with arranging the cups. I was pleased to see that we were sitting apart from the other guests and had a measure of privacy.

'You'll be glad to hear,' I began, 'that the bank is only too happy to oblige.' I took out my wallet and handed him the cheque. 'This should put you firmly in the black.'

He took the cheque and slipped it into his pocket. I

could see his sense of shame fighting with his gratitude and relief. 'Thank you, Julian.' He gave a wan smile. 'Now I really am in your debt.'

'You're family,' I said. 'That's all there is to it.' Then I laughed, mostly to myself. 'You never know when I may not want to ask for something in return.'

'Whatever you want,' he said grandly. 'There's nothing I'd refuse you.'

'Nothing?'

He smiled again, with that familiar mixture of bravado and embarrassment. 'Well, almost nothing.'

Again, I had the sense of Death hovering on the edge of the conversation, and in the odd way of these things, Raymond seemed to know my thoughts. Speaking of obligations, he said, perhaps I should help him draft a new will. I said that it might be rather improper, and suggested he speak to one of my colleagues.

'That's what I like about you,' said Raymond. 'Your properness.'

I laughed, and our conversation became light and inconsequential. I looked across the hotel lobby and saw the old Roman Catholic priest sitting alone with a pot of tea and the *Tablet*. I have always been an agnostic, but I had the oddest sensation of being overheard by a higher power.

[7]

I was learning to be solitary again. Now that summer was over and darkness was closing in, Olga and Sasha were no longer allowed the freedom of the village and I found myself missing them. Kristina herself became increasingly remote; our furtive meetings ceased. Somehow there always seemed to be an excuse. I was disappointed, but worse than that, I was bitter. My irrational heart told me that Kristina's behaviour was my brother's fault. When I allowed myself to dream about the future, I watched the lie he was living become a worry, then a trauma, then a pain, and finally a malignant cancer. Sometimes, when I pictured myself standing at his graveside expressing my grief with Roman dignity, I could still persuade myself I could be free to live with Kristina. I was still under her influence; I had not yet rediscovered myself. I could sit for an hour at a time reading and re-reading the simplest thing. I was lost.

We put the clocks back. Autumn gales stripped the leaves off the trees. At night, the temperature fell close to zero. Darkness and solitude went together. I listened to Wagner and Bach, and watched the rain sweeping across the valley from the Channel. Looking out of the window, I would watch the raindrops racing down the glass and wager myself against Raymond, and against Krokowski. He was the unseen presence who shaped our lives, yet I was powerless to do anything about it. I could feel my obsession turning to hatred.

I had a call from Susan. We had not spoken since her last visit and a trace of mutual embarrassment lingered in our conversation. I noticed, too, how much of my life was being taken up with Raymond and Kristina. I was in danger of losing touch with friends. Susan's call was a reminder of the wider but distant world.

'I think I should come and see you,' she said. 'You don't sound yourself.'

I had hardly spoken. I repeated that I was fine, but when she insisted, I did not try to dissuade her. Inwardly, I was grateful. She would come on Saturday, for the day. We left the arrangements vague, as we had done before, and I found myself wondering if it would be appropriate to suggest she stayed the night. I did not tell Raymond or Kristina about Susan's visit, and I could not stop fretting. I slept badly and my dreams were disturbed with dark, nameless figures. I had known dread before and now dread was returning.

When I woke, unrefreshed, on Saturday, the silent October morning was like burnished copper and time itself seemed suspended in the stillness. There was a heavy dew, but the sun was burning through the mist and the leaves were brassy-gold. The year's end was approaching, but there was life in nature, a last glorious fanfare. I stood in the quiet of the morning at the back of my house, cupping a mug of coffee in my hand, and listened to the familiar sounds of the country.

I drove out of the village by the back route and climbed to the top of the Downs, grinding slowly through the layers of mist. At the top, it was suddenly clear and blue. I pulled into the car-park and hurried up the ramparts to get a view of the countryside. The river was a ribbon of silver. Behind me, the fields were ploughed. In the tree line there were rooks croaking. I took another paracetamol for my headache.

At the railway station I bought a newspaper, and sat with it in the corner of the waiting-room, hoping to remain anonymous and unobserved. The headlines carried news about a government meeting in Maastricht, Arab-Israeli peace negotiations, Tory party politics and the Princess of Wales. In the obituary columns, I noted with interest that the creator of *Star Trek* had died, aged seventy.

Susan's train arrived. As she came hurrying towards me, I noticed how well she was looking. She had cut her hair short and was as full of talk as ever. She had a glow about her that I hadn't seen in years. I hugged her like a sister, relieved to be with someone who knew me so well.

'What's the matter, Julian?' she said with her customary directness, as we walked to the car. 'You look terrible.'

'Do I?' I murmured. 'I've probably been working too hard,' I added defensively. 'You know how it is.'

'I don't want to hear about your work,' she said. 'I want to hear about you.'

I confessed I was feeling rather cut off, and asked what she had been up to since our last meeting.

She gave a knowing laugh. 'That seems ages ago.'

I wondered at her merriment. 'A lifetime,' I murmured sadly, and invited her, as usual, to tell me her news. The display of candour was part of our ritual, but I think that secretly we both feared what the other would report. As we pulled out of the station, Susan announced that she had just returned from a long week-end in Venice.

I thought of Terry Alton and my overdraft, and I laughed. 'Venice is rather out of my reach these days.'

'What's come over you, Julian? Don't I remember long week-ends in Paris and Amsterdam?'

'That was in the old days,' I said. She did not respond, and I knew that she was inviting further enquiry. 'So, tell me. What's up?'

'I think I've met someone.'

'In Venice?'

She smiled. 'You could say we made contact in Venice.'

'Not a fling?'

'It just might be serious.'

'Might be? That sounds rather provisional.'

'I'm nervous,' she said. 'I don't want to make any more mistakes.'

I pulled into a parking space beyond the pier. 'Was I a mistake?'

'Don't be stupid.'

'Who is he?'

We sat in the car staring out to sea. The weather had turned and the horizon was blurred with rain. I watched the sea-birds scavenging viciously along the tide-line. I was aware that Susan was speaking and I was only half hearing.

'He's so different from the others,' she was saying. 'He's a doctor.' She took my hand, rather sweetly. 'He seems strange to me, and yet quite familiar. Is that odd?'

'What's his name?'

'He's called David.' She paused, caressing my hand. 'Dr David Holmes.'

'Where did you meet?'

'He collects rare books,' she said. 'He came to the library with a query about a first edition. Then he asked me out. We sort of clicked right away.'

'I think you are in love,' I said.

The windows of the car were steaming up. I traced a triangle on the glass, and then a heart. Susan reached across and added an arrow. The scent of her body close to mine reminded me of old times.

'What about you?'

'It's been a difficult month,' I said. I described the non-trip to Berlin, but could not bring myself to mention Krokowski.

'You need help, Julian,' she said, squeezing my hand. 'You don't realise it, but you're in a bad way.'

I suggested we have lunch in the country. I drove out past the marina along the coast road towards Newhaven. After a few miles we turned inland and found the restaurant, a converted chapel lost in a leafy part of the

Downs. The owner and his wife are friends of mine and they had saved us a good table.

Slowly, as we talked, I simply could not stop myself, Krokowski came into the conversation. Susan sat still and listened, rarely interrupting. I heard my voice as if I was a stranger, and I heard my obsession put into words in a way I had not known before. I realised as I spoke that Kristina could never love me as I had loved her. Finally, I had finished. 'Well?'

'You feel betrayed, don't you?'

'I suppose so,' I said, acknowledging how well she knew me. 'That's life.'

She took my hand. 'Poor baby.'

'It's so peculiar,' I said, 'to think you've found some-one, and then to discover that they are not really available.'

'You didn't find her,' she said. 'I think you invented her.'

'Whatever I did,' I replied, 'it felt real enough at the time. You always said I was out of touch with myself. Now I feel painfully exposed to all parts of myself.'

'What does she say?'

'She says different things at different times. She is not constant.'

'Do you still love her?'

I saw her eyes move this way and that assessing my reaction. 'I thought I did,' I said. 'I thought I could not live a minute without her.' I shook my head. 'Now she seems so alien.'

'You've never admitted that before, have you?'

I shook my head. 'No, I haven't.' I sighed. 'It's hard.'

A look of great practicality came over Susan's face. 'You're the one who should be having the fling,' she said.

'With you,' I replied. I was only half-joking.

'Silly boy,' she said.

We finished our lunch and took coffee in the lounge. Then we drove back to Brighton. The short day was drawing to a close, and there were lights winking out to sea in the shipping lanes.

'What shall I do?' I said.

'Be indifferent. Fold your tents. Head on. Boats against the stream and all that. You've done it before.'

'It's not so easy now. When I'm alone I can still persuade myself I am in love. The worst of it is the secrecy. You're the only one I can talk to.'

'Perhaps you should let the secret out. You might feel better.' She fiddled with the car radio, skimming over the airwaves. Nothing seemed to please her and she snapped it off. 'You should definitely tell her it's over as far as you're concerned.'

'She knows that already.' A wave of exasperation swept over me. 'My problem is not with Kristina, really, it's with this man I've never met.' I stared ahead, into the twilight. 'He's got under my skin and I don't seem to be able to get rid of him.' I looked at Susan with a wild candour. 'I've never met the man and yet I want to kill him.'

She gave a nervous laugh. 'You don't mean that.'

'I do.'

Susan was shocked. I could tell that she was looking at me as though she did not know me any more. Quite abruptly, she suggested we get out and go for a walk to clear our heads. We parked the car again and strolled along the front. Only a few months ago Kristina and I had been here, holding hands, full of hope and excitement. How happy and carefree that day seemed now.

The sea had been like glass then, now the waves were churned by autumn gales.

'I feel so trapped,' I said, speaking my thoughts.

'Get out. Take a break. Go to Italy.'

'Come with me.'

'I'm sorry, I can't.'

She put her arms round me and we kissed. I wanted her back, but she was no longer available and besides, she knew I was confused in my heart. She drew away and we began to walk, aimlessly, arm in arm. We reached the aquarium. It was gloomy and cavernous and it suited our mood. The phosphorescent bubbling of the water was almost hypnotic and the fish and seahorses moved like creatures in a dream.

Our sad outing was coming to an end. We came into the gift shop and Susan went to look for the Ladies. Once, I would have bought presents for Kristina and the children, but now, regretting my failure with Susan, I found myself buying her a silly memento. When she returned, I asked her to stay but I knew it was in vain. She said she had to catch her train.

'When are you seeing him?'

'Tonight.'

We walked up the hill to the station. 'Here,' I said, handing over my gift. I had bought her a glass hedgehog. 'A souvenir.'

'You're so sweet,' she said and kissed me. 'I don't think you know that.'

The train was standing at the platform. The station was damp and funereal, a cathedral of despair. I walked Susan to the empty carriage.

'Take care,' she hugged me, and then turned to leave, blowing me a parting kiss.

I walked out of the station, through the shadows, not looking back, and found my car standing alone in the darkened streets.

[8]

Children have short memories. Once Kristina's behaviour made it clear that Uncle Julian was simply Daddy's brother, nothing more, nor less, I found myself slowly restored to my previous relationship. Hallowe'en was approaching. The children's drawings were all witches and broomsticks. A luminous green skeleton and a pair of bloody hands appeared in the window of the village shop and one day, on my way back from the office, I stopped and bought five pumpkins. Sitting at the kitchen table we made pumpkin skulls together, spooning the wet vegetable matter into a mixing bowl. Then we put candles in the skulls and turned out the lights. The glimmering yellow faces were like gargoyles. Sasha perfected a banshee wail. We were at the frontier of a demon world of magic and the supernatural, and for a moment I was fearful of the spirits we might summon up. When Olga asked me if I believed in ghosts I did not know how to answer. In my rational way, I had always scorned such superstitions.

'I've never seen a ghost,' I said, 'but some people have.'

Olga was squeezing a mess of orange pulp and seeds through her fingers. 'Do you become a ghost when you die?'

I had often puzzled over this question, but my experience with the dead provided contradictory evidence and even now I was no nearer to an answer. 'No one knows what happens when you die,' I said.

'Daddy says you go to a place called Heaven,' said Olga. 'Is Heaven a nice place?'

'Heaven is—' I stopped.

Kristina was standing in the doorway, smiling. 'What is Heaven?'

'Oh, I don't know.' Her intrusion was unwelcome. 'A stupid medieval fantasy.' I got up from the kitchen table. Under the watchful eyes of the children, I felt awkward with Kristina, unsure of the exact terms of our relationship. I heard myself making an excuse and leaving in a hurry. She followed me to the door.

'You can stay if you like,' she said. 'Raymond is not coming back until later.'

Kristina still wanted to exercise her power over me but she was appealing to a part of me that had been thoroughly humiliated. I did not want to stay. I did not want to turn the clock back. I wanted to forget. Still, I could not stop myself embracing her as we stood in the darkness. 'I must go,' I said.

'You are angry with me?'

I shook my head. I had already directed my bitterness towards my brother and Krokowski and, besides, it is not in my nature to admit such things. I explained that I hoped we could return to the life we had enjoyed when she and Raymond had first come to Mansfield. Kristina responded by asking me to help her with Hallowe'en. Raymond was not reliable, she said, and if Olga and Sasha were to go trick or treating as they wanted, another adult about the place would be helpful. This was a role I would enjoy and I agreed with pleasure.

On Hallowe'en itself, the office closed late. There had

been an extra load of coroner's paperwork to clear, and I like to end the week with a clean desk. Finally we were done. We sat with our ties off in the conference room surrounded by the debris of the day while the Spanish cleaners hoovered the corridor. One or two of the younger people in the office were going to a party, and to my surprise I found myself invited to join them. 'It'll be a laugh,' said one. I replied, with a yawn, that I had to go home. 'My sister-in-law needs help with her kids,' I said.

No one in my office, apart from the receptionist, had ever spoken to Kristina, but my colleagues would ask from time to time how she was getting on, neutral questions that I could handle with ease. I liked the formality of 'sister-in-law'. It was a label that discouraged further enquiry. As I drove back to Mansfield through the dark, it seemed an apt choice of vocabulary: near in blood, yet formal and distant.

Raymond greeted me at the door. I saw at once that he had been drinking. He was jolly but belligerent. There was something in his mood that made me fearful. I saw my raindrops chasing each other down the windowpane. 'When I was a boy, Julian, there was none of this Hallowe'en nonsense. When I was a boy, it was Guy Fawkes Night.' He lurched towards me with watery eyes. 'Penny for the guy! Penny for the guy! Remember?'

I explained that there would be plenty of opportunity to celebrate Guy Fawkes Night as well, and steered him towards the kitchen.

'Glad to hear it.' He poured me a glass of wine from a box. 'This trick or treat nonsense. Everything's American now – language, food, entertainment, everything. Talk about Big Brother. It's a one-party state run by Uncle Sam.'

The door-bell rang. Outside in the darkness a party of perhaps twenty children was whooping and chanting 'Trick or treat! Trick or treat!' Raymond, in full cry, went to answer. I could not stop him. I heard the voice of the teacher introducing herself. Then I heard Raymond's voice raised as he launched into another tirade against American cultural imperialism. The teacher, Mrs Harris, tried to appease him, but in vain. Now he was demanding to know what had happened to the good old English customs from the good old days. Then Mrs Harris remonstrated with him, and all hell broke loose. He became abusive. Some of the children, who had been silent during this scene, began to cry. I called out to Kristina, who was upstairs getting Olga and Sasha dressed up, and hurried to the front door. Apologising to Mrs Harris, a motherly woman in a shapeless raincoat, quite unprepared for this onslaught, I took Raymond aside with the suggestion that he should come back to the kitchen. Kristina arrived in a fluster. 'I'm sorry, Mrs Harris, the children will be down in a minute. I'd ask you to come in, but I don't think it's a good idea tonight.'

Olga and Sasha arrived before Raymond could do further harm. Wrapped in sheets, they burst into the hallway in excitement, oblivious to their father's mood. Olga had a witch's hat. Sasha, wearing an ogre mask, was making his banshee wail. The awkwardness passed. Kristina apologised again to Mrs Harris, kissed her children goodbye and watched them join their friends.

Raymond followed me out of the hall, muttering to himself, angry and ashamed. 'I'm a bit drunk tonight,' he said. 'I'm sorry.' He steadied himself against the door frame. 'I'm really very, very sorry. Don't know what happened.' He went next door into the lounge and I heard him switch on a jazz compilation tape. Kristina came back into the kitchen. She turned off the lights and we sat by candlelight. I closed the door. I did not want Raymond to disturb us.

'That was embarrassing,' I said.

'I hate him,' she said.

I was silent for a moment. 'He seems very far away.'

'And he hates me. He does not show it to you, perhaps, but he does.' The jazz came to us faintly through the door. 'We have nothing to say to each other.'

'You can't live like this,' I said, suddenly. In my heart I knew I had to challenge her. 'What are you going to do?'

'If I knew the answer I would give it to you.'

'Sometimes you find answers to questions by asking other questions.'

'I don't want to think about it.' She became suddenly withdrawn. 'This is not a night for such things.' I noticed that the music had stopped. 'He's probably asleep,' said Kristina. 'This happens most nights now.' She got up. 'Raymond?' As I watched her stride into the sitting-room, I feared another scene. 'Raymond?'

I waited for his slurred reply. There would be an explosion, then shouting, and finally an uneasy truce. But there was no reply and no explosion. I heard Kristina's voice in the darkness. 'Raymond? Are you there?' She came back, much calmer. 'He must have gone out,' she said.

I felt a momentary twitch of anxiety. 'Should I go and look for him?'

'He'll come back. He always does.' She took a bottle of vodka from the fridge. 'Have a drink.' She poured us both a measure and I was happy to feel the Polish spirit burn within. 'Who is this Guy Fawkes?' she asked.

I explained as well as I could. 'The children will have a great time. I always used to love fireworks.' Something stirred in my memory and I began to talk about my own childhood. I remembered the sounds and smells of Kent in the autumn. I remembered the burning leaves, and the mixing of woodsmoke and fog. I remembered the sausages on sticks my mother used to prepare for the other boys in my scout group. It seemed a distant time, and yet when I began to talk about it, I could see those days so clearly. I realised, as I spoke, that part of the pleasure I get from living in Mansfield comes from remaining in touch with those half-forgotten years.

As I explained to Kristina, the 5th of November has a special significance in these parts, and when October comes, firewood, boxes and old doors begin to pile up in the open space by the village pond. Slowly the pyre takes shape. Mr Curran generally takes it upon himself to organise a collection for fireworks, a fund that's boosted by a raffle at the church fête. As far back as anyone can recall, boy scouts have toured the village singing 'Remember, remember, the fifth of November . . .'

On the night itself, many local families hold parties, wine-and-cheese affairs, as a curtain-raiser to the main event. I've done this myself in my time. As a matter of fact, Susan and I did it together one year, a rather successful evening, I recollect. It's one of those moments in the annual cycle when the village comes together, and it's always been this way. There are old people in their eighties who can remember being taken to see the fireworks when they were children.

After the business with Mrs Harris and the embarrassment of Raymond's behaviour, which, needless to say, was all over the village in forty minutes, I was anxious to celebrate this occasion in my own way. I wanted to get back to my old life, my tranquil routine. So I was delighted to receive a number of invitations – from the vicar, from my doctor – to join various cocktail parties. While I had been caught up with Kristina, I had lost touch with this circle. Tonight, I was properly alone and single again, mixing with my neighbours as I had in the old days.

I was reminded, as I stood in Charles Stephenson's cosy sitting-room with a glass of punch, that I am not without status in the village. Michael Watkins came over to consult me about a copyright question that had arisen at the library. Joe Vaughan invited me to speak to his NUJ branch dinner. Colonel Matthews muttered that he had a family problem he wanted my advice on 'in the strictest confidence', and asked me to call on him one evening at my convenience.

I had become so preoccupied with Raymond and his troubles that I had also forgotten how the women of Mansfield wanted to marry me off. It was more or less a public matter of regret that 'nice Julian Whyte' (I was always 'nice') should be without a partner. 'A good wife would be the making of you,' these women would say.

I had put up with this, in the days before Raymond's arrival in the village, with good humour. 'No one will have me,' I'd reply, only half-joking. From time to time, the hostesses of the parish would contrive a blind date, pairing me with an attractive divorcee. The results of these harmless social experiments were often comic or embarrassing, but I had accepted that they were usually done from the best of intentions.

Tonight, I enjoyed myself. I began to relax, to chat. I accepted a glass of mulled wine, and then another. My hostess, Alice, an amusing woman in her fifties, compli- mented me on my good health. She was eager to introduce me to the guests I did not know. I found, as usual, that people were eager to ask about the bizarre experiences of the coroner's life. On this occasion, perhaps because of my recent appearance in the newspapers, I found myself challenged by an earnest young student about another verdict I had given, a verdict that had also received some coverage in the local paper. A young woman had died of an asthma attack after the ambulance failed to arrive. I had been reported as saying that 'dying of asthma is a natural death', but the family had been pressing for a judicial review. Now this young man was challenging me on this point.

'People like to use the coroner's court to air their grievances because there are no court costs involved,' I said.

'Isn't that a rather cynical attitude?'

I explained, patiently, that it was realistic. 'The problem with this job is that the public expect too much. We don't have the jurisdiction, and we often don't have the resources. Yet the public still expect us to expose undetected homicides and uncover official negligence.'

The young man was not appeased. 'You're an officer of the Crown, Mr Whyte, don't we have a right to expect a measure of effectiveness?'

'Unfortunately, in the real world', I said, 'it's not that simple. If the coroner resists playing the hero he's always accused by the family of the deceased of complicity in a cover-up. And if he does ask awkward questions, the authorities brand him a troublemaker. It's a no-win situation.'

Miss Edwards, who had been listening on the edge of the circle, turned to my interlocutor. 'You see, young man, what an excellent public servant we have in Mr Whyte.' I turned away in self-deprecation, but she pursued me. 'I have to say,' she added, lowering her voice, 'that I cannot say the same for your unfortunate brother.'

'Raymond is a very unhappy man,' I said.

'A number of people here', she murmured, gesturing vaguely, 'feel rather worried about him. Did you hear what he said to Mrs Harris?'

'I was there,' I said. 'There was nothing I could do.' I had hoped that perhaps the episode might have been overlooked, but now I saw at once that my brother's reputation was a lost cause. 'I will have to speak to him,' I added.

'You must, you must.'

I sensed that Miss Edwards, a Christian Socialist spinster, was about to deliver one of her little homilies about responsibilities within the community, but I was rescued by my hostess. 'You're looking well tonight, Julian,' she said, interrupting. 'How's life?'

This was, conventionally, an invitation to speak of one's heart, and in recent weeks I had been afraid to do this, or to admit my feelings. Tonight, I felt almost blithe, and no longer burdened by uncertainties. I answered, easily, that life was not as bad as it might be.

Alice Stephenson took me aside, as if to speak of an intimate matter. 'That brother of yours is letting the side down,' she said. 'You'll have to do something, Julian. We can't have this sort of behaviour in Mansfield.'

'Drink up,' said our host, before I could give my reply. 'We mustn't miss the fireworks.'

The church clock was chiming eight as we crowded up to the ropes to watch the display. I kept close to the Stephensons' party, not wishing to bump into Raymond and Kristina. I did not even scan the crowd for them.

The sky was clear. The rockets made a brief, glorious new heaven, shooting up towards the stars. Men in donkey-jackets moved around in the darkness setting off the display. The cold November air carried the pleasant tang of gunpowder. Everyone said it was a perfect night for it. Several people said, Hello, nice to see you. There was no sign of my brother or his family.

When the fireworks were over, a small boy, escorted by his father, was handed a flaming torch and invited to light the bonfire. Petrol had been poured to prime the fire. A sheet of flame rose in the air with a sickening whump. A cheer went up. The fire caught hold rapidly and people ran forward to add their contributions. The Guy in his hat and mask sat crazily on the top in the flaming shadows. Someone had attached a Labour Party rosette to his lapel.

It was then that I spotted Raymond and the family. They were standing slightly apart, pale and silent, watching the events from the side. One or two people I knew came near them but did not stop. Mrs Jacobs, who runs the estate agency in the High Street came up to me and said, with an odd jerk of her head, 'That brother of yours is a funny one.'

'I beg your pardon.'

'That business with Mrs Harris and the children. I don't like the sound of that at all. Is he still a fellow traveller?'

'You'll have to ask him,' I replied. I had said this often enough in the past, half joking, but now there was a reason to avoid this question. I was alarmed how defensive I felt about Raymond.

Someone else said, 'Any more trouble from that brother of yours and we'll be burning him at the stake next year.'

The laughter that greeted this suggestion was disturbing to me. I looked across the open space. In the lurid light of the bonfire I saw Kristina lift her hand and give me a faint, despairing wave, an appeal as much as a greeting.

I waved back, a trifle self-consciously. I did not move to join them immediately. My attention was distracted by Mrs Evans, a retired civil servant, who wanted some advice about her pension rights. She had been speaking at some length, almost tediously, when all at once she brought her remarks to an abrupt close and hurried off.

I turned. My brother was standing behind me. If he had been carrying a scythe and lantern he could not have seemed more menacing. Kristina and the children were approaching through the dark. Their expressions were frightened and painful, as if they had just had a row. I felt sorry for them.

'Hi,' said Raymond, quite awkward. I kissed Kristina, a brother-in-law's kiss. The children were quiet. The Guy Fawkes' festivities were going on all round, but Raymond was not in a good mood. We were an oasis of embarrassment and silence. I did not know what to say. I saw that Raymond was carrying an Oddbins bag.

'Going to a party?' I said, forcing jocularity into my voice.

He shook his head. It was as if he had been waiting for my question. Suddenly decisive, he stepped under the rope that kept the crowd at bay and ran unsteadily towards the bonfire. He stood staring at the blaze, and for a wild moment I thought he was going to do something really stupid. Around us, some of the spectators were pointing, but before any of the organisers could reach him he had lifted the Oddbins bag high into the air over his head and tipped the contents into the flames. One or two sheets of paper fluttered upwards like flaming birds.

I shook my head, but I said nothing. I did not intervene. I just watched my brother destroying his past and wished I could as easily wipe away the anxieties of the present – and the near future – but the truth was that I had nothing but apprehension in all directions.

He came back. 'My memories, my notes, my auto-biography,' he said. 'That was my life that went up in flames, every shameful moment of it.' He stared at me. 'Blame yourself, if you like, Julian. It's done now. Come on, Kristina.'

He grabbed the children and stalked off into the darkness. Kristina, looking back at me briefly, followed him like a lost child.

The Oddbins bag lay at my feet. There was a single sheet left inside. I picked it up, automatically scanning the heavy sentences for Krokowski's name, but once again I found him tantalisingly absent.

[9]

I waited for Kristina to call me, but she didn't. I expected Raymond to make contact, but he was silent. Several people, notably Mr Watkins, who continued to relish introducing 'Staatssicherheitsdienst' into the conversation, pointed out that neither my brother nor his wife were as active in the village as they had been. It was as though they were retreating to the security of Jericho Lodge. Only I knew how provisional that refuge might turn out to be.

Then, perhaps two weeks after Guy Fawkes night, I came home one evening to find the Mini parked outside my driveway and Kristina sitting inside, alone. I saw at once that she had been crying, but she shook her head when I asked what the matter was and followed me into the house without a word. As I was fixing drinks for both of us, scotch and water for me, a glass of white wine for her, she handed me an envelope. The moment I saw the German stamps I knew whose letter lay inside.

'May I?'

Kristina nodded, and her eyes were shining. I held Krokowski's pages in my hand and felt like a voyeur or an eavesdropper. He had a fine gothic script, but I was embarrassed to look for words I might understand. It was as though I had come into a room and found him naked. Now I wished more than ever that I had completed the trip to Berlin, but it was too late for regrets.

'What is it about him?' I asked. 'What is it that he says to you?'

She pointed at the letter in my hand. 'If you could read that you would see that he is a philosopher, an artist.'

'What am I?'

'You are a lawyer.'

I have always been proud of my calling, but on her lips my job sounded cold and mercenary. 'And a public servant,' I protested.

'Why do you always pretend that you are neutral?'

'I suppose it's in my nature,' I said quietly.

Kristina took the letter back. She had made her point. 'He says he is coming to England.'

'To Mansfield?'

'Where else would he go?'

I shook my head in dismay. 'When's he arriving?'

'He does not say.' Kristina's excitement had given her cheeks colour again. 'Soon.'

I was puzzled. When I had found her here waiting for

me, she had been crying. Yet this was exactly the news she had been longing for ever since she had come to Mansfield. I asked her why she'd been crying. She looked at me with tears in her eyes again. 'I am so happy,' she said. 'I thought I would never see him again.' She spun round like a girl. 'I could dance for joy.'

On impulse, I went to my CD collection, found the All-Time Greatest Hits we had made love to in the summer and slipped the disc into the machine. Kristina kicked her shoes off and we began to dance, slightly apart.

'What does he say in the letter?'

'He wants me to go home with him to Berlin.'

'Do you still love him?'

Kristina sighed and looked down. 'Of course.' She took my hand and moved for a moment to the music.

Then I asked a more calculating question. 'Does he know about – about us?'

She looked at me steadily. 'No. Why should he?'

Kristina had always claimed to be a good liar and in the past we had joked about her economy with the truth. Once, her lies had been told for my benefit. Now I was afraid that I was the victim. I held her close as we danced. 'I cannot imagine it here without you,' I said. 'Please Kristina. You must stay.'

'I haven't decided what I shall do. Perhaps he does not come, after all.'

Her words gave me an absurd rush of optimism. There was, there might be, something to keep her here. I held her closer in my arms and she did not resist. She pressed her lips against my cheek. 'You will like him,' she said. She must have seen the doubtful look in my eyes. 'He is very special.'

'Every time you kiss me I'm still not certain that you love me,' I murmured, karaoke-style, 'every time you hold me I'm still not certain that you care.'

Kristina laughed and lifted her arms in ecstatic movement. Our dancing figures threw tall primitive shadows against the crowded walls of my living-room and, as the music quickened, I echoed that question to which I already knew the answer, 'Do you speak the same words to someone else when I'm not there?'

Kristina was not really listening. 'I want you to be friends,' she said, pursuing her own thoughts. 'I just want you to be friends.'

'I am your friend,' I said, obtusely. 'You know that.'

'Not me,' she replied. 'Walter.'

'Oh,' I said. 'Him.'

'Is that possible?'

For a moment I did not answer. The voice of Elvis Presley faded and the song ended. In the silence between the tracks I said, 'Walter Krokowski will be very welcome in Mansfield.'

WINTER

[I]

They say that a sad tale's best for winter. A week passed, and then another, but Krokowski did not come. Sometimes, I would park my car high up on the Downs and look out across the Channel with the unspecific expectation of a garrison commander. The drab winter clouds pressed low to the fold of the coastline and I was joined in my fancy by centuries of ghostly watchers, waiting for the enemy. Perhaps he would never come. The thought left me oddly dissatisfied. He had become too much part of my secret demonology. I did not, of course, anticipate the consequences of his appearance. Sometimes, when I sit by the fire now, turning over the events of these dark months on my own, pondering the powder-train of cause and effect that resulted in my brother's death, I can only wonder at the strange workings of Fate.

In the days following Guy Fawkes night, I had kept my distance from Jericho Lodge. I was content to feel shut in by the season's torpor and to leave my brother and his wife to their own devices. Then one afternoon I bumped into Kristina in the village shop. For the benefit of Leslie and Shirley, standing attentively behind the counter, we rehearsed a pantomime of gossip. I helped Kristina outside with her shopping.

'You're such a stranger now,' she said.

I was dismayed to admit how little my heart was touched by her comment. 'I've been busy,' I replied.

'Busy, busy . . .' She was scornful. 'I don't believe it.'

'Any news?'

She knew what I was referring to, and shook her head. 'No news.'

Inwardly elated, I offered to carry her bags to the car. When Olga and Sasha saw me approaching they began to jump up and down in excitement. Wearily, Kristina told them to be quiet.

A winter gale was buffeting the south coast. I held the door while Kristina eased herself behind the steering-wheel. 'How's Raymond?'

'The same.' She started the engine and revved it hard. 'Everything's the same. Nothing changes.'

'You have changed,' I said.

She fixed me with her sweetest expression. 'I wonder if I should take that as a compliment or an accusation.'

I did not reply. I watched her drive off and returned to my own car, wondering with sadness when we would speak again.

Remembrance Day came round, and a small detachment of the British Legion, led by Michael Watkins, paraded through the village to the war memorial. The Last Post was sounded and the wreaths of poppies laid. The dead were with us, and amongst us, and it was the season of mourning.

Some evenings later, Raymond appeared at my door. I had heard Jack barking as he approached and was not taken unawares.

'Hello, frater,' he said cheerily. 'I was just passing and thought I'd pop in.' He was in excellent spirits. 'We don't seem to see you any more.'

I changed the subject. 'How's the kennel training going?'

'Slowly.' The dog was still barking. 'Shut up, Jack.' He cuffed the animal on the nose and, after much repetition, it obeyed the order to sit. 'He'll have to do better than this next week. You must congratulate me. I've been asked to join Sir Douglas Ashley's shoot.'

'Congratulations,' I said. 'I'm glad to see you've finally joined the landed gentry.'

Long before the Hallowe'en business had made Raymond something of an outsider within the narrow circle of village life, he had become quite friendly with one or two local bigwigs, easygoing landowners who didn't give a hoot for housewives' gossip. Raymond was good at getting along with these county types. Once they discovered he was a communist with a sense of humour, a Marxist with a taste for anecdote and good wine, they made him welcome and did their best, in a jovial way, to convert him to their line of thinking. I think they were fascinated by his story, and they prided themselves on being broadminded towards a fellow sportsman, whatever his affiliations.

When winter came, their idea of relaxation was an all-day shoot with an early dinner at a county hotel, followed by a bottle of port and a rubber of bridge. Sometimes, when I had questioned him, he would say that these country squires were, after their fashion, not so different from party apparatchiks. In the GDR, the conversation had been about the make of the car and the texture of the suit. Now the topics were the choice of shotgun and the pedigree of the horse.

'People are people,' my brother would say, 'whatever their politics.'

Raymond liked their conviction, their directness and their lack of pretension. They were what he called 'straight'. Of course, he would add, he found their attitude to women and racial minorities fairly objectionable, and yet, he was forced to concede in the spirit of fairness that in their private lives they often treated their wives and dependants with consideration and generosity. My brother was always the most flexible of ideologues, and he preferred to try to find the best in people.

He was also tickled pink to have penetrated the inner circle of the shires. He was amused and amusing, and he played his part as 'Red Ray' – his nickname – to the full. 'Here comes old Reds,' the guns would say, and my brother would be expected to come up with some preposterous remark, as they saw it, about US imperialism or Third World politics. They would happily argue about this all day. He became, so to speak, their court jester.

In this genial fraternity, Sir Douglas Ashley sat, so to speak, at the head of the table, a county grandee, a Justice of the Peace, and a mainstay of the local Tory Party who might have stepped from the pages of Jane Austen.

'Not bad, eh?' Raymond could not conceal his pride. 'You can't get much higher than old Ashley.' He was preening. 'I really have been accepted now.'

'You're a Rowley-Whyte,' I said, teasingly. 'They think you're one of them.'

I watched him depart into the night, with the dog leaping at his heels. I hesitated on the step, wondering if I should call Kristina and attempt some kind of *rapprochement*, but deep down I knew there was nothing to be done. I had to accept that there was now a gulf between us that could not be bridged.

I got up early to go to work. My dispute with the local undertakers had worsened and my day presented only the prospect of more protracted negotiations. I reflected gloomily on the obligations of the public servant: there would be no escaping my desk this week-end.

The morning of the Ashley shoot itself was clear and bright, as sharp as a knife. I was still in my dressing-gown, browsing through the obituaries and postponing my week-end chores, when Raymond appeared on my doorstep. He was dressed for a day in the field, and flourished a brand-new hip flask.

'Good to be out and about on a morning like this,' he said.

I complained that I had to go to the office.

'You work too hard.' He was pleased to flaunt his leisure, and perhaps to observe that his wife no longer played a part in my routine. 'Well, I must be on my way. Fancy a bird or two this evening?'

I replied that I would welcome a brace of pheasant. I wished him luck, and he trudged off. Jack was bouncing about in the back of the Volkswagen, barking madly. Raymond seemed happier than he had for weeks. I wondered if he and I, at least, had not perhaps turned a corner.

I spent the morning dictating letters, enjoying the deserted calm of the week-end office. At one point I broke off and almost without thinking rang Susan's number in London, but she was out and I was reluctant to talk to her answerphone. I was afraid what I might say when I began to speak, and nervous of having my words overheard by someone else. It was safer to say nothing.

I finished with my desk in the early afternoon and drove home, pausing at the supermarket to buy one or two items for my supper. There are times when I prefer to eat simply. After tea, I sat and read the newspapers and listened to a new compilation of operatic highlights, including my favourites, *Vissi D'Arte* and *Una Furtiva Lacrima*. I had Christmas cards to write. The fire blazed and the room was cosy. Later, I saw there was a screening of *The Killing Fields* on television. I would open a bottle of wine, watch the movie, and go to bed late. Such are the pleasures of life in the country.

At about four-thirty, with the light fading fast, I went outside. It was cold now, and a wind was getting up. Low cloud was sweeping in from the Channel, promising rain. I checked the greenhouse and made sure the garage door was locked. I gathered up an armful of logs and went back inside. If the weather was about to take a turn for the worse, I did not wish to have to venture out again.

The phone rang. I hoped it might be Susan, but it was the police. The body of a tramp had been found in a lay-by on the A23. The old boy was known to the authorities and foul play was not suspected. I gave my usual instructions, and went back to my fireside. I had, as it happened, spent that very morning dictating letters about certain irregularities in undertaking procedures, but I did not want to go into that just then. I would deal with the paperwork on Monday. It is a fact of my job that in bad winter weather, blood-pressure worsens, and the rates of heart attack, suicide and industrial accident go up.

It was quite dark now. As I drew the curtains, I noticed the first rain driving against the glass. I imagined that if Raymond was going to bring me any game it would be tomorrow. I was just starting on my Christmas cards, listing the local dignitaries whom I should not on any account forget, when there was a violent banging on the back door.

I put my pen down and went to investigate. It was Raymond. He was wild-looking, soaked with rain, and with streaks of blood on his sweater. He was empty-handed.

'No luck?' I said, attempting a note of normality.

He did not reply at once. He threw his hat down. 'Bloody awful luck.' There was brandy on his breath. 'Bloody awful, bloody luck.'

'What's the matter?'

'Can you believe it?' He was pacing up and down in considerable agitation. 'I think I've just seen Krokowski.'

As calmly as I could I asked him to describe what had happened. Raymond shook the water out of his hair, and smoothed himself in the hall mirror. He had been driving home from the shoot. As he came into the village he had passed a man in the road. He was carrying a bag, and had his back to the traffic, but Raymond believed he had recognised Krokowski's blond hair and long leather coat. He'd driven on for a mile or two, debating in his mind, then turned the car and come back for a second look. But now the road was empty and whoever it was had disappeared. 'He could easily have slipped into a side street, or taken refuge somewhere from the rain.' He hadn't pursued his search. 'If it was Krokowski, I didn't want him to see me.'

I invited Raymond to come and sit down, and we went into the sitting-room. The music was still playing and the fire had settled in the grate. My brother filled the room like a dirty beast. Outside, the wind was getting up and rattling the glass. Suddenly, everything seemed threatened and precarious.

'Are you sure it was him?'

He shook his head. 'If I was sure ... Well, who knows?' He was helpless and uncertain. 'It's funny. All day I had a shotgun in my hand and I felt so strong. Now ... now I know how weak I am.'

'No you're not,' I said, cheerfully boosting his spirits. 'You're Mr Adaptable. You can handle this.'

'I suppose it was inevitable that once those Stasi archives were opened the fellow would pop up here one day. He was bound to go and look at his file once it was available to the public.'

I saw how shattered he was, and how dependent on

227

my support. 'Do you remember saying that if you ever found out where Krokowski was you'd tell me before you told Kristina?'

'I remember all right. That's why I'm here.' A new decisiveness came into his manner. 'I'm not going to tell Kristina, no, of course I'm not.'

'Good,' I said.

There was a flash and then, after several seconds, a rumble of thunder. The rain was lashing at the window. Up here, on the hillside, when the winds began to blow, the house sometimes felt like a vessel on the high seas.

I made up my mind. 'I'm going to look for him.'

'What shall I do?'

I stood up. 'Go home. Say nothing.' I went to the door. 'If I find him, I'll bring him here. If I don't, I'll phone you.'

'You're very good to me,' he said.

Outside, the storm was coming closer. I had this urge to be out in it. 'I'll be back as soon as I can. Make sure you've gone before I get back. If it is our friend Krokowski, we don't want you meeting him unawares.'

He waved his gun cheerfully, 'I'm not sure I could be answerable for my behaviour . . .'

'You go home now,' I said, wondering if he was fit to drive. 'I'll deal with this.'

I ran out to the car. The rain was hard and cold, and lightning flickered in the clouds massed above the trees. I switched on the engine and bumped and splashed down to the main road. I turned towards Jericho Lodge, driving slowly, looking to left and right. The lights of local mansions glimmered through storm-tossed trees and in the full beam of the headlights I checked a roll-call of driveways; Normanhurst, The Cedars, Three Oaks, Manor Farm.

The road was empty and, so far as I could determine, the young man was not sheltering at any bus-stop. I circled round and began to cruise back towards the village. When I reached the crossroads by the church hall, I turned up in the direction of the Downs, driving slowly as before. In my determination to find Krokowski, I became oblivious to the passage of time. I was almost at the top of the hill before I realised I was straying too far and once again swung round, turning down the slope towards the village. The rain was sweeping across the valley before me, and when the lightning broke through the darkness the trees along the roadside flickered in the ghostly light of the storm.

As I returned to the village I saw a figure hurrying down the side of the road. I slowed down, and pulled up alongside, lowering the passenger window. I recognised a local boy whose name I did not know. He was soaking wet, and when I asked him if he had passed a young man in a long leather coat, he looked at me suspiciously. I explained that I was expecting a visitor who had gone astray. The boy could not help. He had seen no one. He was anxious to be out of the weather, but I was pre-occupied with my quest and did not offer him a lift. I accelerated back to the High Street once more.

I was about to set off down the London road when it struck me that if it had been Krokowski he would not be getting himself soaked to the skin for no reason. He would have taken shelter until the weather lifted. Perhaps he would have gone to the pub. I parked outside The Royal Oak and went inside.

It was early evening, and the bar was quiet. No one paid any attention to me as I lifted the latch and came in. Two regulars were playing darts. A boy and a girl in skin-tight denim were lounging sexily against the snooker table, whispering and laughing together. The girl had her arms round her boyfriend, pressing his body against her with a billiard cue. Barbara, tall and statuesque and heavily made up, was at her customary station behind the saloon bar, engrossed in the crossword.

'Evening, Mr Whyte. What brings you here on a night like this?'

'I was looking for someone,' I said, ordering a pint of bitter. Without reference to my brother or his wife, I explained that I was expecting a foreign visitor who might have got lost.

Barbara put a hand on my arm. She nodded in the direction of the snug bar round the corner. 'There's a young chap by the fire in there,' she said. 'On his own. I thought he must be one of those gay boys from Hamburg.'

'An old family friend,' I said, with a smile.

'How wrong can you be,' said Barbara, handing over the change.

I took my drink and strolled through the bar. There was a young man in a leather coat sitting alone by the fire. For a moment, I watched him unobserved. He was handsome, with swept-back blond hair, wide blue eyes, and the strong physical presence of someone who takes exercise. His clothes were well worn but not scruffy and there was a traveller's rucksack on the floor beside him. He was hunched over a paperback with a student's intensity. I was convinced that my intuition was correct. This was a young man with whom you might share your deepest thoughts and feelings. This was a person whom you might never forget. I wondered at the complicated process that had brought him here, speculating in my mind at his likely response to my challenge.

I walked up and sat next to him by the fireside.

He nodded. I smiled. 'Hello,' I said. 'You are Walter Krokowski, I believe.'

[2]

I took him home. My offer was calculating but his response was instinctive. I had smiled. I had spoken his name. That was enough. He was cold and homeless in a foreign land. 'Who are you?' he asked. As I started the car, I mentioned my brother's name, and he shifted uneasily. 'Don't worry,' I said. 'I will look after you.'

I turned the car with a triumphant flourish and circled round the village, swooping with a bump over the bridge by the pond, braking at the corner by the parish church, speeding towards The Royal Oak, then swinging back past the Texaco garage towards the High Street. I wanted to be sure that Raymond was safely back at Jericho Lodge. The rain flashed in the headlights and beyond the metronomic beat of the windscreen wipers there were boughs tossing in the high wind. The car crunched over twigs and branches and, fearing the fall of a tree, I accelerated through the darkness as much as I dared. We did not speak. I was stimulated and alert. I was in control. When I guessed that the coast was clear, I turned towards my cottage. 'Now we are going home,' I said.

The driveway was empty. Raymond had gone. I escorted Krokowski in through the back door. He did not seem to notice that the lights were on, or that the fire was lit, and he did not comment on his surroundings. To make a diversion I stirred the fire and offered him a drink. He accepted, and I saw that he was shivering. I opened a bottle of wine, while my strange guest sat close to the fire, warming himself at the flame.

Krokowski was weary and travel-stained. There was stubble on his chin. When he removed his coat, I saw that he was dressed entirely in black, black jeans, black T-shirt, black sweater. He was obviously fit. His blond hair was parted in the centre and he had the sun-tanned skin of the traveller. He was heavy-eyed, with the look of one who reads late at night. I could see why Kristina might find him attractive. When I came back into the room with the wine and two glasses he stood up and made a little bow.

'Walter,' he said, speaking with the German pronunciation.

'Julian.'

We shook hands. His grip was firm, and his eyes searched deep into mine. I handed him a glass. 'Cheers,' I said, inwardly saluting my good fortune. Here he was, my rival, my enemy, sitting before me in my house, in my power. Apart from Barbara, no one knew he was here. I recognised that I did not have long. If I delayed, he would become restless and wary. Whatever my move it had to be made quickly and decisively. That was for tomorrow. Tonight at least I could give him food and drink and make him welcome, as I had once promised Kristina.

'Tell me about yourself,' I said, after I had given him a supper of omelettes and green salad, and we were sitting with the fruit and cheese.

Krokowski's accent was heavy but his English was quite good. He explained that until recently he had been back-packing in India. He had loved a woman and had been separated from her on a trumped-up charge. I sensed that he had told this story to strangers on many occasions.

'That was my brother's wife, of course,' I interrupted, to remind him who I was. 'Kristina.'

At the mention of her name, Krokowski frowned. At first, he went on, he had believed that she had been part of the conspiracy against him, and had wanted nothing to do with her. Now he knew that such a suspicion was false. Needless to say, I betrayed nothing but the most scrupulous interest in what he had to say. I had to win his confidence and establish a trust between us.

'So you see,' he said, at length, with a tiny, self-satisfied smile, 'I am – how do you say? – das Opfer.'

I took down the dictionary Kristina had given me. 'A victim,' I said. 'A scape-goat.'

'Yes,' he repeated, savouring the description. 'A victim.'

Krokowski looked across at me in the firelight and began to unburden himself. He had much on his mind. He had been in pain for so long. He had been in prison, and then in exile. He had been tormented by his love for a woman he had believed to be faithless. Now, at last, he had decided to confront his accuser. He had come looking for Kristina of course, but he had also come to challenge Raymond.

'You are his brother,' he said, more than once. 'This is so strange.'

'He is much older,' I replied, leading him on. 'We did not know each other for many years. When I was growing up, I was like an only child.'

'I have sisters,' he said, 'but I am the only son.'

He had been born in 1957, the year of Sputnik. Often, as he spoke, he would laugh at happy memories, and against my will I found there was a rough, attractive freshness to his disposition that was rather winning. He had grown up in Köpenick, on the edge of Berlin. His father's family were artisans, boat-builders, whose livelihood had been taken over by the state.

'My father is a genius with wood,' he said. 'He can make it come alive. He taught me how to love nature.'

His mother, the daughter of a Protestant minister, had devoted herself to raising her family, making extra money by giving piano lessons. She loved music and poetry and had encouraged her son's literary activities.

'I had seen what the regime did to my father's business,' said Krokowski. 'There was no way I could be a conformist.'

He had trained as a printer, in the knowledge that he wished to express himself outside the law, and had moved to Prenzlauer Berg in the late 1970s. When he had lost his job at the printing press, forced out for his political activities, he'd become a taxi-driver, circulating his poems and short stories in his spare time.

'I had a magazine,' he told me, 'and I had many admirers.' He laughed aloud. 'Sometimes I think that everyone had a poem they wanted me to print.'

At this time, he had tried to get into the university, but with his record he found it impossible to get a place. So he'd hung around on the fringes, giving readings in basements, mixing with students and academics, and occasionally taking them in his taxi.

'That was how you met Kristina?' I said.

'Ja, ja.' He had taken her to the apartment on Karl Marx Allee. He had been playing Czech jazz music and they'd got talking. He had no idea that she was married, still less that she could be living with an Englishman. She had taken his number and had often called him for driving work after that.

I asked him what Raymond's reaction had been, but

he seemed unable to answer this. He had known little about Kristina's marriage, and on the few occasions he had given rides to Raymond, he had been discreet. Kristina herself had been vague about her husband's attitude, he said. She had seemed happy, even eager, to have an affair, and by Krokowski's account, had made all the running.

'You know, my love for her became—' He picked up the dictionary on the table to find the word he wanted, ' – an obsession.'

'That is the nature of love,' I said, making a grand entrance into the theatre of seriousness. 'How did Raymond find out?'

'Think,' he replied, speaking with sudden authority. 'The Stasi were everywhere. Wherever you looked – Stasi. Every church had Stasi, every farm, every factory, every hospital, every school. Everyone in the university was spying. It was only a matter of time before Kristina's husband, whoever he was, would know. I am too open about my life. I am not good at keeping secrets.' He shook his head. 'I am not a lucky man.'

'You were lucky with Kristina,' I said.

As I listened to him I acknowledged to myself how upset I was to have lost Kristina. Perhaps I had channelled too much of my disappointment into my obsession and my loathing for Krokowski. I had been passive for too long. It was time to take charge and make something happen.

Krokowski told me that his luck was short-lived. The Stasi came for him early one morning. He was arrested, charged with subversion, *Staatsfeindliche Aktivitaten*, activities against the state, brought to trial, and imprisoned. I asked him what these activities had been.

'They searched my taxi,' said Krokowski. 'In the back

they found many bundles of illegal literature, Biermann songs, dissident leaflets and so on. It was a great surprise to me. I knew at once that it was Rowley-Whyte who must have put them there. No one else had the opportunity to get these papers from the West.'

'A few papers? That doesn't sound too serious.'

'On its own, that is not so bad, but then they accused me of trying to escape the country also. That is a crime, Republikflucht.'

'Was this true?'

'It was a false charge, naturlich. I was going for a holiday in Bulgaria. Remember, we could not travel in Europe. Everyone wanted to go to the seaside in Bulgaria. They said they had evidence that I was planning to escape through Yugoslavia.' Krokowski's expression was affronted at the memory. 'That was a lie. Now I have visited the Gauck-behorde and seen the victims' files, I know who it was that arranged that story.'

I watched Krokowski as he spoke. He was angry, as he had a right to be, but he was also cool and detached, and perhaps a little naive. He had suffered and had known bitterness, but his concern was to establish the truth. He described his fate quite clinically and theoretically, as if it were pre-ordained. He seemed to see himself as part of an historical process. He was very much a child of the GDR. The more he talked, the more I felt he was someone I could manipulate. My instinct had been correct. I was well advised to ask him into my home.

'I would like to help you,' I said, pouring another glass of wine. 'You deserve help.'

'I think I have been foolish to come,' he said. 'It is a crazy thing to do. But I have to see Kristina. Perhaps—' He was shy. 'Perhaps she still loves me.' He flashed his confident smile. 'You know, I think she does.'

'And if she does,' I asked, unable to stop myself, 'what then?'

'I will say these words to her husband,' he replied, rehearsing a prepared statement. 'I will say that what you have done is a terrible thing, but I forgive you. Now you must let your wife follow her heart.' He grinned foolishly. 'Then I will take her back to Germany.'

'Back to Germany.' As I heard myself repeat his words I knew that I was alarmed. 'What if she does not want to go back? After all, she has made a new home now.'

'She says she hates it here,' he broke in fiercely. 'She does not love him. She will come with me. I am sure of it.'

He was so transparent. He wore his emotions so clearly on his sleeve. I, who am used to seeing extremes in my courtroom, could read him as if the letters were written up six feet tall. He began, in a broken way, to tell me about their affair. He was painfully frank about his desires. 'She wants my child,' he said. 'And I want hers.'

'When you were . . . ?' I gestured awkwardly. 'I mean, how did you see each other?'

'I had my taxi.' He smiled at the memory. 'We used to drive around for hours on end, talking, and singing songs. And then occasionally we would stop in some quiet place and make love.' When he laughed, his face became illuminated with pleasure. 'We went to my apartment, but that was more difficult.' The memories were returning. 'When we had the money we went to hotels.'

I did not want to hear this, but I had to know more. 'How long did this go on?'

'Until the Stasi came.'

He had been arrested, tried, and imprisoned. 'I remember sitting in my cell one day after the trial was

237

over. All of a sudden I heard this cry, and I looked around, and then I realised that it was me who was crying.'

The West Germans had purchased his freedom, as they had so many other political prisoners. He had planned to make a new life with Kristina, if he could, but when, finally, he reached West Berlin during April 1989, he had become depressed and unable to act. He had stayed in his apartment, and stared at the wall, afraid to go out.

'Once you have been in prison, you see the world differently. In your mind, you are always in a cell. I was paralysed in my feelings about Kristina. I could not decide what she had done, or not done. I started to travel. I wanted to put everything behind me. I went to the East and ended up in Bombay. Then one of her letters arrived.'

I concealed my dismay as well as I could. 'Her letters?'

'There's a network. She had sent me many letters.' A look of pain came into his eyes. 'At first they didn't reach me, but in the end I saw them.'

I leaned across and slowly re-filled his glass. 'What did she say?'

'She said how unhappy she was. But she said I was free to do as I wanted.'

'Did she write about Raymond?'

'A little. She wanted me to know what he had done, but at first I did not believe her. I wanted proof. She also wrote about her feelings for me.'

I could not restrain myself. 'Why did you not come here before?'

'I applied to the Gauck-behorde, but I had to wait for my application to be processed. I was in limbo. Until I had the evidence, I could not act. I had to see the files for myself. It was not until I had the papers in front of me that I knew I had to come.'

The telephone rang. I looked at my watch. Nine-thirty. I was afraid that it might be the police or the hospital. A night such as this was often the background to violent or unexplained deaths. Now that I had found him, I did not want to leave Krokowski alone and unsupervised. I excused myself and went next door to take the call. It was Raymond. We spoke guardedly, and I suggested we reconvene for a tactical discussion in the morning. 'We have much to consider,' I said, cryptically.

When I came back into the room, I found Krokowski leafing without embarrassment through the papers on my desk. 'You are a policeman,' he remarked, turning round.

'I am a lawyer.' I consulted the dictionary. 'Ein Anwalt.' I watched him consider this. I could see that he feared a trick. Perhaps my invitation was a devious English way of putting him under house arrest.

'You are my guest,' I reassured him. 'Stay as long as you wish.' I gestured grandly. 'My house is your house.'

'I want to see Kristina.' He helped himself to the wine. The alcohol had brought the faintest colour to his cheeks. 'Above all, that is why I am here.'

I was not displeased to hear the note of extremism in his voice. The uncommitted are hard to manipulate and the passionate are always vulnerable to a person of my temperament. When I made my moves I could be reasonably certain of Krokowski's response. 'How can I help you?' I asked, as if I was at his disposal.

Just as I had hoped, Krokowski responded with utter frankness. 'I want to see Kristina alone. I will persuade her to come back. Then—' He hesitated. 'Then I will have my interview with her husband.' He gestured at his

239

rucksack. 'I will show him the file. I will confront him. Then I will forgive him.'

'If that is your plan,' I replied, 'let me advise you to see my brother first. If Raymond knows you are here, and if he suspects that you have spoken to his wife . . .' I hesitated. 'Well, who knows what might not happen?' I watched him digest what I was saying and then made my next move. 'If you were to see him first, then you would be free to take Kristina away at once.' I smiled at him like a conspirator. 'I will be glad to help you.' I developed my plot. 'I could easily arrange for Kristina to come here after you have seen Raymond. That's how you stay in control of the situation.'

He was sceptical. 'You won't tell your brother?'

I shook my head. 'No.'

He was puzzled. 'Don't you talk to your brother? How can I trust you?'

'My brother and I – how can I put this? – we aren't close.'

'But he is living here.'

'That was his choice, not mine. He is older. We are on different sides of the fence, as we say. You must trust me. I am used to giving out justice,' I said, with happy inspiration, 'and I will see that you get justice.'

He seemed reassured by this little speech. 'I have to thank you for this.' His expression took on a look of candour. 'It is not easy to do what I am doing.'

'I understand,' I said. 'You will be safe here.'

He looked about him at the fire and the low lights and the cosy, settled air of comfort. 'It has the safe feeling, I think.'

Then I made my best move, my most cunning. 'It does,' I said. 'You must use it as a place to hide. In this way, you will have the advantage of surprise.'

240

He liked that. 'The advantage of surprise,' he repeated. 'That is good, ja!' He yawned and I took the opportunity to suggest that I show him where he could sleep. Then I escorted him upstairs to the spare room and invited him to make himself comfortable, repeating that he was welcome to stay as long as he pleased.

'I live alone,' I said. 'It is nice to have company.' I saw that he was exhausted and perhaps a little drunk. He seemed grateful at the prospect of some rest.

I closed the door on him and went downstairs. Alone in the firelight I sat staring into the embers, considering how best to exploit the opportunity that lay before me.

[3]

Krokowski was a late sleeper, I discovered. He did not appear until nearly midday, unshaven, and still dressed in black. In the light of morning, he seemed pale and bloodless, despite his sun-tan, but taller than I remembered and more imposing. He greeted me with a cautious 'Guten Morgen.' I was glad to have him safely under my roof. I wanted him under my control. I had been afraid to venture out until he was up. I did not want him surprised in my kitchen by Raymond or Kristina. While he helped himself to coffee, I explained why it was best that he stay in his room, again citing the advantages of surprise. He accepted my analysis without question. I watched him retreat upstairs, then switched on the answer-phone, and went to collect the Sunday papers.

The storm was blowing itself out. It was a perfect winter's day, bright, blustery and invigorating, a day to conquer the world. At the newsagent I observed my Sunday routine, exchanging pleasantries with Derek.

Across the street, the congregation was just coming out of Matins. The Reverend Findlater was in the porch, shaking hands with Mrs Harris and Mrs Simpson. He waved and I waved back. Shirley Crutcher was helping her old mother down the steps to the street. Watkins and a couple of cronies were heading across the cemetery and I knew from experience that they would be making a beeline for the pub. I climbed back into my car and drove quickly to The Royal Oak, ahead of the crowd. I found Barbara preparing for the Sunday onslaught, setting out little bowls of savouries along the bar, and I ordered a half of bitter.

'That young German,' I said. 'An awkward customer. Just between you and me, I think he was a little bit crazy.'

Barbara put my drink before me. 'Whatever you say, Mr Whyte. He's your friend.'

'My brother's friend,' I corrected.

'Well, that figures,' said Barbara meaningfully.

'Raymond knows nothing about it, of course.'

'You've lost me there, Mr Whyte.'

'I took our visitor back to the station and sent him on his way. I don't think he'll be troubling us again.'

'What about your poor brother?'

'In his present state of mind,' I said, 'he's better off in the dark.' I leaned closer, flattering her with my confidentiality. 'And that's the way it should stay. If you don't mind, Barbara, I think we'll keep this one to ourselves.'

'Mum's the word, Mr Whyte.' She was pleased to have my trust, and I judged that it would be many months before our secret would find its way into general circulation. When Watkins and the other members of the congregation arrived, once again we had moved on to the subject of my burglary. The word 'gypsies' slid sibilantly into the barside discussion, and I played my part as a responsible member of the community.

On my way home I made a detour past Jericho Lodge. My brother was in the driveway, clearing fallen branches. On the road, after the downpour, there were little dams of beechmast, dead leaves, and small twigs. The moment I appeared, Raymond put his load down and hurried over to the car. I guessed he had been looking out for me. I described briefly what had happened, and then asked about Kristina.

Raymond explained that she was in bed with a temperature and would probably stay there all day. I replied that it was a good thing she was out of the picture. 'How do you propose to handle this?' I asked.

I knew, as I put this question to him, that Raymond would want my advice. When he was part of a system, the Stasi network of informers, he was a weak man made strong by information and authority. Now, for all his bluster, he was hollow and unsure of himself. He had become a man without conviction.

He came straight to the point. 'How do you find him?'

I was direct, too. 'He wants to take Kristina back to Berlin.'

'For Christ's sake, she's my wife. He can't do that.'

'For what it's worth, my impression is that he'll do whatever he wants.'

'What about me?'

'You don't exactly figure in his calculations, Raymond. He blames you for his imprisonment, and though he doesn't put it like this, he has come to get even.'

I saw Raymond's indignation turn, as I had hoped, to alarm. 'What on earth am I going to do?' He looked across the paddock towards Sasha and Olga running up and down between the apple trees and I knew he was fearing for the future of his family.

'Whatever you do,' I said, piling on the pressure, 'you haven't much time.' In answer to further questioning, I said I believed I could occupy Krokowski for just one more day. After that, he would insist on seeing Kristina. I made my next move. 'Last night he said he wanted to see you first.'

'What did he mean by that?'

'He said you could not be protected from the consequences of your behaviour.'

'What did you say?'

'It's difficult for me, of course it is. But we have to recognise that what happened in Germany – what you did there – was something that has consequences.' I took a deep breath. 'You're in the wrong, Raymond.'

'I know, I know.' He stood leaning on his rake. 'I have to say, little brother, that I'm afraid to see him.'

'Surely not.'

'Oh yes.' He stooped to clear a branch off the driveway, groaning with exertion. 'If I was him, I'd want . . .' He drew back from what he was saying, then said it anyway. 'If I was him, I'd want to kill me.' He delivered this claim with a curious kind of pride, as if to assert his own importance, and straightened up.

I shook my head. 'That's not in his mind. All he talks about is reconciliation and the forces of history. You really have nothing to fear.'

'I don't believe that kind of talk. Germans are like that. They are full of abstractions and theories, and then just when you least expect it there's violence. It's like an underground river, but it always comes to the surface in the end. He must have revenge in his heart, but he's

244

disguised it. Besides, he's not going to tell you how he really feels. That's obvious.'

I was surprised, but not displeased, at the speed with which Raymond had introduced this new, darker note into the discussion. I added another incendiary detail into the conversation.

'Krokowski told me he is sure he can persuade Kristina to go back to Berlin.'

He looked at me wildly. 'What did you say to that?'

'I judged it best not to over-react.' I kicked a stick with my shoe. 'We can agree, at least, on our opposition to that idea.'

'Indeed we can,' he said, with emphasis. 'Indeed we can.'

Then I left him. I said he should think things over. He should call me later. I would tell Krokowski that he and Kristina had gone out for the day.

I watched him return to his labours, an old man with much on his mind, then I executed a three-point turn and drove straight home. Krokowski was sitting with a cup of tea and a copy of *Der Spiegel*. He seemed to accept without question my assertion that Raymond and Kristina were absent from home. He was happy to wait, he said, but he spoke in such a way that made me realise I could not keep him shut up here for much longer. 'In prison,' he said, 'you learn the meaning of patience.'

I read the newspapers, attempted to work in my study, and turned over the events of the day in my head, examining and re-examining every move for unforeseen complications. Fortunately, there had been no demands on my professional expertise. As soon as the light began to fail, I drew the curtains against passers-by. I was restless. I went upstairs and tidied my bedroom. I went into the spare room with a knock and inspected Krokowski's neat pile of belongings. On the chair by the bed, he had a Walkman and some tapes, Polish jazz, rock and roll compilations, and Bruce Springsteen. Then I came downstairs and fussed about in the kitchen. Shortly after six o'clock, Raymond telephoned. I knew at once that he'd been drinking.

'I've been thinking things over,' he said. 'I will see him.' There was a note of determination in his voice I had not heard before. 'I will see him tomorrow, and I'll have him out of Mansfield by nightfall.'

'How?' I asked.

'Wait and see,' he said mysteriously. 'Wait and see.'

I judged there was nothing to be gained by pressing him on this point, and we agreed to speak again in the morning.

[4]

When I returned to the living-room, I found Krokowski lying on the sofa. He had taken his shoes off and spoke, without getting up, of how he liked to refresh his spirits with an afternoon nap. I found his casualness irritating, and it only increased my desire to resolve the many questions posed by his irruption into our lives. He asked, boldly, who had telephoned and I judged that it was a good idea to admit that it had been my brother.

He swung his feet to the floor, ready for action. 'What did you tell him?'

I was pleased to note his agitation. 'Nothing.' I made a calming gesture. 'Remember, my friend, we have the advantage of surprise.'

'Ja, the advantage of surprise.' He stretched. 'To-morrow I shall see him when he does not expect it.'

'I will bring him to you,' I said. 'Then you can confront him.'

'That is good.'

After that conversation, Walter Krokowski's presence in my house accumulated a greater and more oppressive significance with each hour. He spoke interminably about his need to absolve Raymond's sense of guilt, but whenever he spoke of Raymond's 'crimes', his true feelings were ominously displayed.

In the hope of distracting him, I proposed that we take a meal together in a restaurant. I wanted to get him out of the house – I could not be certain that Raymond would not suddenly appear on my doorstep – and I wanted to go somewhere we would not excite attention. I suggested Indian food, and mentioned a popular spot down the coast in Hastings. When we reached our destination, winter breakers were throwing stones against the seafront and some boys in a bus-shelter were dodging in and out of the spray. The restaurant was empty. Three waiters in ruby tunics showed us to a corner table. Sitar music jangled overhead. Krokowski became increasingly voluble and self-possessed.

'You talk of the victim. What does the word "victim" mean in a country when so many millions died in the gas chambers? How do you redefine a dictionary to take account of Auschwitz and the crimes of Nazism? I am happy to accept the consequences of the Third Reich in my lifetime. Yes, happy. I have made a sacrifice and so have millions of East Germans. Good. It happens that history was against me. So be it. History teaches many lessons, but it has few pupils. Now if I want to exorcise the Stasi I will do it through debate and discussion. I shall do it with dignity, not with weapons or aggression.'

'Did you ever believe that socialism could work?'

'I wanted it to work, of course I did. The ancient dream of equality? Isn't that the best? Yes, even as a victim I have to admit a sadness. Our revolution failed. We betrayed everything that we ever promised. We emerged from the humane tradition of the Enlightenment and our poets were Heine and Büchner, and yet in the end we turned our back on humanity and poetry and became murderers. Now we are left standing at the open grave of a fixed idea. We are left again with the questions: Where are we now? Are we back where we started? Where do we go from here?'

'Do you accept that the people let you down?'

'The people?' There was an arrogance in his voice, the scornful note of the disenchanted. 'The people have always let us down. For a generation. The people and the system. I am a member of the working class and I say you cannot trust the people. All they want is blue jeans, bananas and pornography.'

'I so agree with you,' I said smoothly. 'Man is an acquisitive animal. He hunts. He explores. He has primitive desires. A system of thought that ignores this does so at its peril.'

'It's true. I am forced to recognise this, just as I am forced to recognise that so-called intellectuals like your brother behave as they do for reasons of the heart as much as for reasons of the head.'

'There is no ideology stronger than the ideology of the bedroom,' I said. It seemed a good moment to ask how the Stasi had invaded his privacy.

'The great irony of the famous Stasi', said Krokowski, 'is that most people regarded them as incredibly stupid.

248

Yet at the same time they allowed them to accumulate an amazing amount of detail about their lives.'

'My brother justifies his actions by saying that if everything is known then nothing is known.'

'I have heard that before, but I cannot accept it.' Krokowski began to explain the corrosive nature of the files. 'The Stasi was an assault on our peace of mind, on the security of the home, our Hausfriedens.' Like many others he had wanted to know the extent of the violation. Until he had been sure it was Raymond, he wanted to know who it was – what friend or neighbour or relative or colleague – had informed the Stasi that he was an enemy of socialism, and what, specifically, he had been accused of. Everything came down to the lost details of that former life. He went to the files because he wanted to discover if his suspicions about the black BMW parked outside his apartment were justified. He went to the files to confirm the identity of the concierge. He went to the files to verify that the girl he had screwed after the art gallery opening was just another ministry stooge reporting on his pillow talk. Finally, he said he knew he had to put the files behind him. 'I do not want to spend the second half of my life reading about the first half,' he said. But he acknowledged that there had been something cleansing and therapeutic about the search. He had come to understand a little more about his own life. 'We are all informers,' he observed.

I wondered aloud. 'What makes an informer?'

'Oh, many things.' When Krokowski concentrated on a thought I could see what it was about him that Kristina found so attractive. 'Weakness, blackmail, adventurism, a quest for identity. I have read somewhere that informers are the marginal men, dissenters who lack the courage to dissent, or idealists who cannot find the courage to believe, or individualists without the courage to be independent.'

I had to agree that he was describing my brother rather well. 'Raymond would claim that he was a pragmatist.'

'That is the illusion of all informers,' said Krokowski, 'that they are the realists in any situation.'

'What'll my brother say when I tell him you are here?' I broached the question that had been troubling me.

'He will find a way to make it normal in his heart.'

I recognised at once that Krokowski was absolutely right. I thought of all the weeks and months in which Raymond had painstakingly not told me the truth about his years in Berlin, and then of all the weeks and months in which he had lived adjacent to those lies and evasions, cohabiting with his former self. He had come to believe his lies, as people who lie professionally often do, and then he had learnt to forget them, at least in his conscious life. He had the collaborator's schizophrenia.

The waiter arrived with two pints of lager. Krokowski drank deeply from his glass. I saw a calmness come over him as the alcohol took effect.

'When I see your brother,' he said, 'I want you there as a witness.'

'You don't need a witness.' I dismissed his appeal with a laugh.

'I insist.'

Noncommittally, I said that we would see what happened and when the waiter appeared with the sizzling trolley we turned to our dinner. After the meal was over I asked for brandies and Krokowski took out a leather pouch and rolled himself a cigarette. He was relaxed, even expansive, and quite at ease with me. In my secret heart, it gave me enormous satisfaction to have him here, and yet oblivious to my manipulation. This was my finest hour. I was thrilled. I felt wily, powerful, even brilliant. There was an exuberance to my inner mood that I had never known. Here he was my rival, my enemy, almost literally in the palm of my hand. As I turned to drive him home through the lanes of Kent I gave the steering-wheel an extra flourish. We did not speak much until we came to the track to my house.

'You know, Julian,' he said, as we walked down the path to the front door, 'I am looking forward to meeting your brother again.' There was an arrogance in his satisfaction that was repulsive to me. 'Then we can proceed to the resolution of everything.'

I had to admire his way with absolutes. Sometimes I long to be free of compromise, to escape from my world of provisional settlements. 'I must tell you that my brother would be terrified if he knew you were here. When we have discussed you in the past, he has always said he hopes you will never find him.'

'He has no choice,' said Krokowski. 'I have to talk over my pain with my tormentor. I have to find my identity. I want to help him find his. I wish to direct the programme of his remorse. I wish to help in the healing. We were both of the east. We were both of the revolution. There is much to share.'

'I suspect—' I hesitated as I fiddled with the front door key.

'What is that?'

'I suspect he thinks you want to hurt him.'

Krokowski's arrogance was infuriating. 'I can understand this,' he replied. 'That is the obvious fear.' He stepped inside. 'But it is a false fear. If I wanted to hurt your brother, I would go to him at night and put a bullet in his heart.'

I was curious. 'You have a gun?'

251

'As a matter of fact, I do,' said Krokowski with a smile. He loped across the front room to his rucksack, rummaged inside and retrieved a plastic shopping bag. I watched with astonishment. He took out a small black pistol, pointed the barrel at the fire and squeezed the trigger. He was amused when I flinched. 'It's not loaded.' There was a click. 'Look,' he tossed it over to me, laughing, 'it's just a silly toy.' He shrugged. 'I thought I would give to the little boy, Sasha, for a present.'

I turned the weapon, a perfect replica, over in my hand. I regretted my sudden fear, and was ashamed of my suspicion. I was annoyed with myself. My reaction spoke badly of my own thoughts. 'Pure James Bond,' I said, lightly, passing the gun back. 'Sasha will love it.'

'I am sure of it.' He stretched and yawned, and put the toy back into his rucksack. 'You know how much I would like to see Kristina with her children, but I understand you are saying that first I have to see Rowley-Whyte.' He parried an imaginary sword thrust, and then dropped to the floor and assumed the lotus position. 'That is correct. Victims and informers must come to terms with each other. Only the victims have the right to decide what kind of vengeance is appropriate.'

Krokowski's confidence and his familiarity annoyed me, but I gave nothing away. My concern was simply to see him to his room. After a while, I explained that I would speak to Raymond about tomorrow's arrangements in the morning. It was getting late. Krokowski watched television, speaking with approval of the BBC. I busied myself with courtroom papers. I felt like a prison warder. Finally, close to midnight, he yawned again and stood up. The fire was almost out and he had drunk more than half a bottle of whisky. We had exchanged no more than a dozen sentences.

'Gute Nacht, Julian.' Krokowski was unsteady.

''Night, Walter. Sleep well.' I tried to sound relaxed and easy. 'Tomorrow's a big day.'

I watched him go upstairs. I heard him use the bathroom and then he was bumping about in the spare bedroom. When I heard the light go out, I rose from my desk and went to his rucksack. I took out the shopping bag and inspected the toy gun, marvelling at its authenticity. Then, reassured and intrigued, I placed it back where I had found it. I checked that the back door was securely fastened. Then I double-locked the front door, and put the key in my pocket, something I do not usually do.

[5]

Sometimes I remember my dreams, but usually my rest is not disturbed by the affairs of the day and I wake refreshed with only faint memories of the night's inventions. However, on that Monday morning, 9 December, 1991, a day I shall never forget, I awoke tired, as if my mind had been troubled during its unconscious hours. I realised at once that I had overslept. I got up quickly and, as I passed from my bedroom to the bathroom, I saw that Krokowski's door was open. There was light at the window. He was already up. 'Good morning, Walter,' I shouted, and was relieved to hear an answering call from the kitchen below. My bird had not flown.

When I came downstairs, I was in for a surprise. Krokowski had found a rusty can of oil and was cleaning his Swiss Army knife with a rag at the table, like an off-duty soldier.

'Until I am seeing your brother, I will rest here,' he remarked, not looking up, as if I had no say in the matter. I was pleased to encourage his illusion of mastery, and glad to know that he would be accounted for while I was gone.

I explained my plan. I had made an appointment to meet Raymond at my office. By some kind of subterfuge, I would bring him back to the house where I assumed, I said, that Krokowski would be ready for him. He nodded, like a soldier acknowledging orders. Yes, he would be ready for him a thousand times over.

'What about Kristina?' he asked.

How I hated the relentless efficiency of his mind. It was all I could do to keep my temper. I wanted to tell him we would come to the question of his fucking girlfriend in due course and that he should be fucking grateful for my efforts on his behalf. I wanted to tell him to fuck off back to Berlin, but of course I just smiled with a neutral, professional calmness that I have perfected over the years and said that once he'd spoken to my brother I would take him personally to Jericho Lodge. 'Kristina has not been well,' I said, playing on his fantasies. 'She may not be ready to travel.'

'I have patience,' he said.

I despised his earnest and credulous intelligence, but the failure of his understanding gave me the courage to make one last move before I left for the office. 'I expect you'd like to make the most of your surprise,' I said, casually.

'That is so.'

'May I suggest,' I went on, 'that you give my brother a little fright with that toy gun of yours.' I smiled at him. 'It's quite authentic and it will terrify the life out of him.'

I laughed. 'That would be rather amusing, don't you think?'

Krokowski joined my laughter. 'Very amusing, ja.'

'Then you can say to him whatever you like.'

'That is an excellent idea.' He stood up to shake my hand. 'A little fright.' He squeezed my hand. 'I like that.'

I finished my coffee and hurried off to work. I said I expected to bring my brother back before the morning was over.

Raymond was waiting for me. He was wearing a corduroy jacket and a knitted tie and might have been going for a job interview. He seemed keyed up and excited. We sat in the car drinking takeaway coffee while I explained that Krokowski believed him to be ignorant of his presence in Mansfield. 'He is expecting to surprise you,' I said. 'He wants me to bring you to my house on some pretext, but I don't think that would be a good idea.' I added, for emphasis, that I thought it would actually be a very bad idea.

A look of concern came into Raymond's eyes. 'Why's that?'

'Krokowski has a gun,' I said. 'A pistol.'

'What did I tell you?' There was a mixture of triumph and alarm in his voice. 'I know these Prenzlauer Berg types so well. They are like characters in Dostoevsky.'

'On closer inspection, I think it was a toy. That's what he told me, anyway.'

'I wouldn't trust him for a moment. People like Krokowski have the weirdest ideas. They believe in the philosophy of violence. At the drop of a hat, they'll talk about the purging power of blood. You have no idea what else he might have in that bag of his. Think of Baader-Meinhof.'

I agreed that it was best to be on the safe side. We decided that he and Krokowski should contrive to meet out of doors, away from the village. I suggested we go up on the Downs, overlooking Mansfield. At this time of year there'd be hardly anyone about. Raymond could take Krokowski for a walk along the top of the hill. It would be safer in the open air. 'You do understand,' I said, 'if he won't accept your arguments about going home, you may have to force him.'

He nodded. 'I understand.'

'You are willing to use violence, then?'

'I have every intention of doing whatever it takes,' he said. 'As a matter of fact, I'm preparing to give him the fright of his life. He's been wrecking everything for long enough. I'm going to have it out with him, once and for all. I've said it before. It will not be the first time I have had to fight to keep Kristina.'

I asked how she was, and he replied that her temperature was down. 'She's still in bed,' he said. We both agreed that in the circumstances it was lucky that she was not in better health. I wished him well, and went into my office, satisfied that Raymond was prepared to go to extremes.

I returned to my house at about twelve-thirty that day. 'My Music', one of my favourite radio programmes, was on at that hour, and I listened to it as I drove back to the village. I remember so many details. The weather was fine, with a few wispy clouds, and the lunchtime traffic light. On the way, I had to slow down for Kevin Carey, who was towing a car-wreck into his garage. Nevertheless, I made good time. As I drove I planned what I would say to Krokowski. I would confess that I'd been unable to deceive my brother, and had been forced, against my will, to give away his arrival here. Krokowski would be disappointed, but he would accept what I said. He would have no choice, and then I would explain the new rendezvous.

Krokowski was pacing up and down in his leather coat. He had shaved his stubble and had dressed for the occasion, like a duellist. His skin was the colour of pine and his blond hair, freshly washed, was luxuriantly swept back from his forehead. In his long coat, his black jeans, and his tall boots, he made an imposing, rather romantic, figure.

'Where is he?' he asked, nervously, as I came into the house.

I made my explanation and he was, as I had anticipated, dismayed. 'Don't worry,' I said, encouragingly. 'You can still give him that little fright we talked about.'

He smiled. 'Oh yes,' he said. 'That is something I can do.' He seemed eager to be off. Just as we left the house, he shook my hand and thanked me for all that I had done. 'You are a good man, Julian,' he said. I looked into his eyes and saw a sparkling blue sincerity, and replied that I was just acting in everyone's best interests.

The one o'clock news was on the radio as we passed through Mansfield. At the junction in the High Street, I spotted Michael Watkins coming out of the Crutchers' store. He saw me and waved. I accelerated away from the village and began the long climb up the hillside. We reached the top in no time. There were three vehicles in the car-park, but my brother's was not among them. For a moment I feared that Raymond had thought better of our plan, or lost his nerve.

'Is he here?' asked Krokowski, looking over his shoulder.

I shook my head. Just at that moment, I saw Raymond's van in my rear mirror, pulling up the slope into the car-park. Raymond hooted. I turned. 'There he is.' I got out in a hurry. Krokowski followed, more slowly. Raymond parked with some deliberation, straightening and reversing, and then he got out too.

Raymond and Krokowski came towards each other like generals after a ceasefire and shook hands. Their breath smoked around them. My brother was wearing an anorak over his jacket and tie. He had on his walking boots. He carried, as usual with him, a stick. He had become a natural part of the country scene. Krokowski looked as if he had stepped out of a loft in Prenzlauer Berg on his way to read the *Tageszeitung* in a local café.

I looked at my watch. One-fifteen. I said I had to be back in my office by two at the latest, and made my farewells, remaining scrupulously vague about my future plans. I watched them start the gentle climb to the top of the Downs. As I followed their progress, wondering how they would both fare, Krokowski turned and looked at me with a strange backward glance. I admit that if I am ever questioned about this moment in a court of law, I shall have to say that it was the last time I saw him alive.

[6]

I conducted coroner's business throughout the long afternoon, shuffling through a slim file of routine deaths: an overdose, a bad car smash, and an accidental drowning. There were sudden moments of grief on the witness-stand but I was far away, 'anderswo' as Kristina would have said. I expressed my regrets and made my summing-up in the automatic sentences of experience. When I returned to my office after tea I half expected to find a message from Raymond, but among the yellow slips on my desk there was only official business. The weeks before Christmas are often busy, but my workload that day was light and I was able to leave, on time, at about five-thirty.

It was a sharp night, with a searching wind from the sea, and I was reluctant to go home. I sat in the car overlooking the dark winter waters and read the evening paper. I was about to ring through to The Lodge, but thought better of it. I have rarely been more powerfully aware of the presence of my colleague, Death, hovering, like a chilly shadow, at the edge of my consciousness.

Finally, I switched on the ignition and went home to Mansfield. My gate was closed, just as I had left it. The house was dark and the garage shut up. There was no sign of Krokowski. As I parked the car, I heard the sound of the telephone ringing unanswered inside. I unlocked the back door in a hurry, but as I switched on the light, the ringing stopped. I stood there, out of breath, and looked about. I called out 'Walter.' There was no reply. The house was cold and deathly still. Then the phone rang again.

I grabbed the receiver. It was my brother. 'Where on earth have you been?'

'I've just got in from work,' I said. 'Where are you?'

'I'm in a phone-box.'

'Where?'

'I don't know.'

There was so much I wanted to ask, but I did not trust the telephone. 'Raymond.' My voice had authority. 'How far away are you?'

'Ten, maybe fifteen miles.'

'Do you have the van?'

'Yes.'

At my most severely official, I told him to listen

carefully and gave directions to a seaside bar just outside Newhaven. I looked at my watch. Wherever he was, I wanted to give him plenty of time. It was six twenty-five. 'I'll see you there in an hour.'

I put the phone down and went to my desk. I was watching myself in a film, experiencing the exhilaration of a script going according to plan, directing myself as the star of the show. I sat in the circle of light and quite deliberately noted the events of the day so far, a summary of times and salient details, as far as I could remember them. I knew that it was important to remain clear-headed and to make no mistakes. It is error that incriminates and punishes us.

After I had done this, I changed out of my suit into casual clothes – jeans, loose shirt, navy sweater, and sports jacket. Before I came downstairs again I glanced into Krokowski's room. It was neat and tidy, the bedroom of an indigent man who is keeping up appearances. There were a few clothes folded over a chair. By the bedside was an edition of Hölderlin and a copy of *Perfume* by Patrick Süskind. Downstairs, I noticed that he had taken his rucksack.

As I drove, I found myself wondering what had happened between Raymond and Krokowski. Perhaps Raymond had achieved what he'd intended and sent Krokowski home? I played our recent conversation in my head over and over, looking for clues, but found none. My thoughts drifted towards Kristina. Absurd though it seems to me now, at that moment I believed she would have to stay on in Mansfield, and I found myself welcoming the idea. I had a fantasy that she would come to me and admit that she had been resisting my claim, break down at last, and give herself to me as she never had before. In the darkness, then, anything seemed possible.

I reached the bar, The Admiral Benbow. I have driven heedlessly past it on the coast road many times, but have never ventured inside. Tourist pubs are not my taste. In summer I have seen daytrippers overflowing from the bars into the car-park and the scrubby garden with the children's climbing-frame, but in winter it is often deserted. Inside, I found some disaffected young men playing darts and snooker, shouting conversations with each other, watching football on satellite television, and ragging the bartender with a casual, slightly brutal, familiarity.

Raymond was sitting alone next to the jukebox with a large scotch. I ordered a pint of lager and went to join him. He looked at me with stricken eyes, unable to speak.

'You must tell me, Ray.' I put my hand on his arm. 'What happened?' I looked over my shoulder but it was an unnecessary precaution. We were nowhere near the other customers and the sound of the jukebox covered our speech. 'Where's Krokowski?'

It was a rhetorical question, but it was enough to get him started. He was frightened, lost and confused. His story, the dreadful events of the long afternoon, came out in pieces, drowned in the noise. Gradually, I put it all together into a narrative that made sense.

Nothing had gone as I had expected. After I had driven away, back to my office, he and Krokowski had set off on their walk. Against all expectation, perhaps because he had lost the benefit of surprise, Krokowski's behaviour had been utterly unthreatening. He had been full of the talk he had rehearsed with me, and had gone on at length about forgiveness and reconciliation, but he seemed to Raymond no longer the demon of his imagination. When he had got a stone in his shoe and had asked my brother to support him while he adjusted his sock, Raymond had felt that against all the odds they need no longer be adversaries. Emboldened and relieved, Raymond had expressed his regret and finally his remorse. Perhaps this was the confession he had for so long yearned to make. He offered to make amends. He would do whatever he could. He spoke of recompense. It was then that everything had gone terribly wrong.

Krokowski announced that he was taking Kristina back to Berlin and Raymond replied that he was sure she would not go. Krokowski insisted that she loved him and would certainly go with him. To clinch his argument, he produced tickets.

'Did you know that?' he said. 'He had boat tickets.'

I shook my head.

The mood of reconciliation turned sour. As they walked, they argued about Krokowski's plans. Raymond said that perhaps they should 'have it out' with Kristina once and for all. Krokowski, with characteristic self-confidence, suggested an immediate meeting. Raymond, in a panic, imagined Kristina leaving that very afternoon. He was at a loss. On the way back to the Volkswagen, he pointed down the hill to Mansfield and identified Jericho Lodge on the outskirts. He suggested to Krokowski that he might like to walk down the bridleway, a short cut. He wanted, he said, to collect his thoughts. He would meet him at the foot of the hill and then give him a lift back to the house. Krokowski, magnanimous in victory, had agreed.

When my brother returned to the car-park, he was angry, frustrated and desperate, his mind in a turmoil. He drove to the foot of the Downs and then, with time to kill, he took out Father's gun and went to shoot pigeons in the woods along the bridleway. But once he had the gun in his hands he felt strong again and found himself powerfully attracted to his original intention. He would force Krokowski into the Volkswagen, drive him to the Dover ferry, there and then, and make him leave the country. It was a wild, impractical scheme and he was just considering how best to achieve it when he caught sight of Krokowski coming towards him through the trees. Raymond was holding his gun, of course, and the next thing he saw was Krokowski taking what looked like a pistol out of his rucksack.

'I don't know what happened. It was an accident. My gun just went off. I was sure he'd kill me. I can't explain it. He's dead.'

The jukebox thundered next to us. I did not question his version of events. I simply leaned closer towards him. 'What have you done with his body?'

'I've hidden it in the bushes.' He was speaking in a rush. 'No one saw me. I'm sure of that. No one. And no one knows who he is. The people in the village never saw us together. Not even Kristina knows he was here. If any one saw him—'

'Watkins saw him,' I said, interrupting. 'Who knows who else besides . . . ?'

'We can say he went back to London. I've thought it through. Every angle. Who knows, the body might remain undiscovered for weeks?' I had seen it so often before, the crazed rationale of the killer. 'You've got to help me,' he said.

I finished my drink as coolly as possible. 'Let's go and find the body,' I said. 'You drive first. I'll follow.'

I wanted time to think.

It was a strange and lonely journey, and I have repeated it a hundred times in memory. At first we retraced the coast road and the oncoming traffic blinded my attention. Then we turned inland and took a deserted country route. All at once, we were lost in the night and there was only the full beam of Raymond's headlights in front. I was grateful for the darkness and relieved to be alone while I worked through a plan of campaign in my mind.

We reached the foot of the Downs. Raymond slowed, braked, and turned up a farm track through the trees. The branches seemed incredibly black and bare, silhouetted against the sky. Now I was nervous. So far, my actions had been within the law. We were not two miles from Mansfield. I had presided over enough inquests to know that unexpected witnesses to wrong-doing can turn up in the most unlikely places, at the most unexpected times. It was past eight o'clock on a chilly evening, but you never knew who might be out walking the dog or coming home late from an evening ramble. What had happened between the time Raymond fired the fatal shot and our arrival on the scene of the crime?

Raymond's brake-lights flared red. He stopped and plunged his vehicle into darkness. I parked close by, snapping off the high-beam with relief. Then I took a torch out of the glove compartment and joined him on the track. It was cold and overcast, and I took comfort in the furtive atmosphere of the trees and brambles along the bridleway.

'Along here,' said Raymond, speaking low.

He led the way, lighting his footsteps with my torch. I followed cautiously. This path was a popular route with ramblers. If Raymond was correct in believing he had been unobserved, then he was indeed lucky.

It was difficult to gauge the distance in the darkness, but I guessed we walked another two or three hundred yards. Raymond was moving more slowly, as if looking for something. Finally, he stopped. 'Wait here,' he whispered, and he stepped off the track into the undergrowth. I looked backwards and forwards, hoping against hope that no one would suddenly discover us. I saw the beam of the torch wavering through the bushes and was absurdly reminded of the Dong with a Luminous Nose. The light steadied and stood still. 'Julian,' he called. 'Come over here. Quick.'

I pushed through the scrub, oblivious to scratches. I was excited. I reached Raymond's side. Krokowski was lying face down in some leaves. Raymond had dragged him, after the shooting, some thirty or forty yards, and he was well hidden. Lying as he did, there was no sign of the wound that had killed him, just the unmistakable inertia of death. I have, of course, seen bodies lying in the undergrowth on countless occasions, but always as an observer.

'Give me the torch,' I commanded, and I switched it off. We stood there in the darkness. The wind was in the trees and the wood creaked around us. 'What did you do with Father's gun?' I whispered.

'It's in the van.' Raymond's teeth were chattering and I could almost smell his fear. 'Come on, Julian. You're the expert. You've got to get me out of this.'

'You shot him in cold blood, Raymond.'

'It was a mistake. I didn't mean it. I don't know how the gun went off. It was an accident.' He gripped my arm. 'You're the coroner round here. You can say it was an accident if you want to. For Christ's sake, Julian, you're my brother, aren't you?'

'It's a conflict of interest, Ray. I'd have to turn the case over to my deputy.'

'Oh my God. What am I going to do?'

He had spoken for both of us. I tried to think clearly,

as I knew I must. Entry and exit wounds do not lie. Any forensic pathologist worth his salt would know how this man had been killed. 'I can't say it was an accident.'

Raymond started to scrabble pathetically at the earth with his bare hands. 'You must help me hide the body.' He was on his knees in desperation. 'We'll bury him here and now. Come on, frater.'

I stood there looking down at him. 'Bodies have an awkward way of turning up when you least want them to. Dogs or foxes will find him in no time.'

It was bitterly cold. We were both shivering. 'This is a nightmare,' said Raymond. 'When am I going to wake up?'

He started to sob hysterically. We were alone and still undisturbed. Now I was in a quandary. I had exaggerated the difficulty of hiding the body. My mind was working. There were measures that one could take. I had come to love my brother. He was old and pathetic and I had treated him badly. I would do one good thing for him. I would show him how I loved him. I would even help him keep Kristina. I looked up and saw that the clouds had cleared. The stars were crowding brightly overhead, and I had the oddest sense of being scrutinised from above. I stared into the black infinity of the heavens and found the strength I needed.

'Stay here,' I said. Together, we would commit the perfect crime.

[7]

I knew exactly what I had to do. For years, I had studied killers' mistakes. Now I would show them how it was done. I would conduct a murder master-class. I drove

266

home as if nothing had happened. I knew from experience that it is abnormal behaviour that betrays people. I even paused for twenty minutes to drink a half of Guinness at The Royal Oak, chatting with Barbara and two other regulars to establish my alibi. Then I drove through the village and parked on the dirt road outside my house.

I hurried indoors, rehearsing my agenda for the last time. In the kitchen I collected a large black rubbish bag and went upstairs to my bedroom. Here, I changed into a track-suit, and placed a spare set of tidy clothes in a British Airways bag. I moved across the landing to the spare room. Krokowski was a methodical person and most of his things were folded away. There was so little, really. It took me no time at all to bundle his personal effects into the black bag and to carry it, together with my British Airways hold-all, down into the hallway. There, I switched on all the lights, as if I was at home, and made a couple of telephone calls to strengthen my alibi. Then I left the receiver casually off the hook to deflect incoming messages, and put a CD into the player, turning up the volume for the benefit of any passers-by. Finally, I collected a carving knife, a bottle of household bleach and a second rubbish bag from the kitchen, and then a shovel, a hacksaw, a tarpaulin, some rope, gloves and a pair of pliers from the garden-shed, and took all these items out to the car, dark and silent in the lane under the starlight.

I have to confess that the experience of eradicating all traces of Krokowski from Mansfield had a profoundly stimulating effect on me. My mind was eager and alert. This was a moment I had thought about in the abstract for many years and now here I was executing it in meticulous detail. I noted, as I drove back to find

Raymond, that it was now nine-thirty. Fortunately, my duties allow me to come and go as I please at strange times of the day and night, and my unorthodox movements would pass unremarked. Nevertheless, I was anxious to have the job over and done with and to be back home at a reasonable hour.

When I reached the spot where I'd left Raymond I had been away for just over forty-five minutes. I found him pacing up and down under a tree. He was shivering with cold and fear. I suggested he warm up in my car. If he saw anyone approach down the track he should warn me. I would take care of everything else. I prefer to work alone. Besides, I did not want to share the responsibility. I wanted my brother completely in my debt. So I posted him on guard at the entrance to the bridleway and set off into the bushes.

I pulled on my gardening gloves, picked up the rubbish bag, with the bottle of bleach, the hacksaw, the tarpaulin, the knife, the pliers and the shovel, and went to find the body. For a moment, with a surge of panic, I thought it had crawled away into the undergrowth. Then I found him, face down in the leaves as before. I stood looking at the sprawled figure, the strange immobility of death, and wondered what I would find when I rolled him over. I soon discovered that Krokowski had taken the blast full force in the chest. The terrible wound was jagged and deep and matted with blood and dirt and leaves, and his guts were spilling. His face, in contrast, was almost unmarked. The eyes were glazed and staring and white in the starlight. I bent over and pressed the lids down in an involuntary gesture of respect.

I knew I had first to strip the body. Krokowski's limbs had begun to stiffen with rigor mortis, but my task was not impossible. I took off his shoes and socks and thrust them into the black bag. Then I unbuckled his belt and pulled off his black jeans, taking care that nothing should fall from the pockets. I speculated that perhaps he would have black knickers, but in fact he was wearing a pair of dirty white underpants. I stripped these off, noting the wormy penis and the sagging, lifeless balls. The upper body was unpleasant work, but I had the knife for that, cutting the black T-shirt away, and ripping through the heavy stitching on the sleeves of his coat. At length I had completed my task and his clothes were in the bag. I was warm with exertion and fully absorbed in my plan. Krokowski lay naked on the ground, unearthly white in the darkness with the terrible shotgun wound a hideous black crater in his chest. Now I had to take out his teeth.

I was fairly certain that if, as an anonymous corpse, he was ever uncovered, it would be difficult to trace him through GDR dental records, but I was taking no chances. In anticipation of what I had to do, I knew that a dead body does not bleed, but the business of extracting his teeth with a pair of garden pliers was extremely unpleasant. I started with the upper quadrants, working from incisors, to canines, to pre-molars and at last to molars. The molars, in particular, I found to be most recalcitrant, and in two cases I contented myself with simply smashing out the fillings. A skull is anonymous; it's the fillings that incriminate. After each extraction, I paused and dropped the tooth into the bag with the clothes, like a fisherman with his catch. When the upper jaw was clear I turned my attention to the lower quadrants, gripping Krokowski's head between my knees and wrenching, as before, from incisor, to canine, to pre-molar and finally to molar. When I had finished I was shaking with the effort and also, if I am honest, with the nature of what I had just done. There remained one further mutilation to perform. I had to slice off his fingerprints and cut off his hands at the wrists.

I have attended many autopsies and I was familiar with the surgical details of the deed. I knew where to place my hacksaw, and where bone and gristle were weakest. In what seemed like no time at all, I was tossing first the left hand and then the right into the bag with the clothes and the bloody teeth. Lying on the ground, without his hands, and with blood smeared across his face, and his chest wound oozing its juices like oil in the darkness, Krokowski was no better than a piece of meat. The sooner I had him buried the better.

With my hands still clad in my regular gardening gloves, I cleared a space near the bushes, away from any track that I could see. I carefully piled dead leaves and branches to one side. I marked out a space approximately six feet by two and then I laid out the tarpaulin, on which to heap the earth. I wanted to leave no trace behind. So far I prided myself on my thoroughness. Then I took up my shovel and began to dig.

The ground was hard and sticky with clay. There were roots and flinty stones. The shovel jarred and jolted in my hand. The labour was heavy and exhausting but I worked without pause, driven by the fear and drama of the situation. As I worked I had these bizarre fantasies, as if I was on some mind-enhancing drug. I saw the murderers I had read about standing at the graveside declaiming to each other from 'The Tell-Tale Heart'. I saw the corpses I had inspected circling the body of Krokowski in a *danse macabre*. I saw the eviscerated cadavers of the autopsy room filing into my court trailing snakes of intestine beneath green surgical gowns.

At one point, my fearsome reverie was interrupted by

Raymond, hurrying up the bridleway. 'There were three people on the road,' he said, whispering hoarsely.

'Where?'

'They've gone.'

'Did they see you?'

'I don't think so.' He was wild-looking and no doubt I was too.

'What are you doing here? Get back to your post.'

'How are you getting on?'

'Raymond, for God's sake, get back to the car.'

I had become so absorbed in my task that I had almost forgotten the outside world. I set to my digging with renewed vigour. I was soaked with sweat and breathing hard. I am happy to garden and go for walks but I am not used to violent exercise. There were blisters forming on my hands and the beginnings of real, excruciating pain in my shoulders and thighs. I could not turn back. I found myself singing traditional hymns – 'Praise my soul, the King of Heaven'; 'Eternal Father, strong to save . . . For those in peril on the sea' – under my breath, to accompany my labours. After thirty, perhaps forty, minutes with my spade I had created a hole, a grave, of about one foot deep. I pressed on. Eighteen inches, two feet. The work was getting harder. I measured the depth. The hole was over three feet deep. If I was to dig much deeper I would be climbing in and out like a traditional grave-digger. The deeper I dug, the chalkier and flintier the grave became. Soon I would need a pick. I had been working for over an hour when I stood up to my waist in the pit I had created and marked the space taken by the body. I decided I had done enough.

Now I trussed Krokowski's body with the rope. Rigor mortis was advancing rapidly. I tied his arms behind his back to simulate a gangland execution, dragged his naked, mutilated corpse to the edge and pushed its deadweight into the pit. He lay there on his back, with his blind, grey face as still as a mask. The fine blond hair was caked with mud and I regretted the mess I had made of his mouth. I tried to wipe the blood and dirt away with some leaves without much success. Then I knelt by the hole and spoke those words I had heard often enough in the course of my duties. 'We therefore commit his body to the ground: earth to earth, ashes to ashes, dust to dust: in sure and certain hope of the Resurrection to eternal life.'

Then I stepped back and emptied my bottle of bleach over the carcass in the hope that it would neutralise the stench of decomposition. The liquid splashed on to his white skin in a silver arc, and the smell of disinfectant rose up from the pit. I began shovelling back the earth and clay, jumping on it to pack it tight around the body and between the limbs, as if I was planting a tree. Layer after layer I shovelled in, and after each layer I paused to pack it down hard. At first the body yielded beneath the earth, but then the torso became covered and the earth above it was firmer too, and there was no movement as the weight of the earth piled up. When I had shovelled most of the earth back, I looked about me and found a large stone to lay over the hole to deter foxes and badgers. Then I covered that with more earth until, finally, I was done. I scooped the last grains and lumps of earth and clay on to the grave, as I must now call it, and folded away the tarpaulin like a nurse folding the bedclothes of a deceased patient. Then I dug the roots of the brambles back into the soil in the hope that they would grow again in spring. Finally, as a kind of benediction, I scattered leaves across the slight mound of earth that marked

Krokowski's last resting place, and pulled a rotten branch across to disguise where it was. With luck, the body would never be found.

I looked at my watch. It was eleven-twenty. I took off my gloves and dropped them, with the pliers and the knife, into the black bag with Krokowski's hands, teeth and clothes. Back at the car I stripped off my track-suit and my boots and put them into the bag as well and sealed it up. I reached for my British Airways bag and pulled on a clean shirt, a tidy pair of trousers, a sweater, and some polished brown shoes. I straightened my hair as best as I could in the rear-view mirror and tossed the black bag with all the incriminating material on to the back seat with the bag containing Krokowski's clothes. I also checked that his rucksack was safely on board.

As I backed my car down the path to the corner, I felt an extraordinary sensation of fulfilment. I was almost light-hearted and quite refreshed. I found Raymond sitting in his Volkswagen, a limp, broken scarecrow.

'All done,' I said.

'Now what?'

'Go home,' I said. 'Take a bath. Leave your gun in the van. Clean it tomorrow as if you'd been out after rabbits.' I instructed him never to speak of what we had done, and if he called me at the office to use a public telephone. I was taking every precaution.

'What about Kristina?'

'What about her? Krokowski's dead.' I looked back down the path. 'Dead and buried.' I slammed the car door. 'Now we can get back to normal.'

[8]

I attempted normality. I went home and had a bath and a drink. I played *Das Lied Von Der Erde* but I could not listen. I rubbed antiseptic cream on to my hands and dressed my blisters. I felt fit and tired and in remarkably good spirits. The truth is that I was rejuvenated by what I had done. I felt redeemed by my crime. I had dedicated myself to a good cause. My brother had made his appeal to me and I had stood by him. I felt pleased with my foresight and my courage. I had proved that despite everything I could still love him. Now, once and for all, he was in my debt.

I slept like a child, waking to feel an agreeable stiffness in my arms and legs. I had not dreamed. My sleep had been uninterrupted. Nevertheless, I woke early. I had set the bedside radio for seven o'clock. There were still several vital matters to which I had to attend. Perhaps the most difficult of these was my next conversation with Kristina. I knew she was expecting Krokowski, but I did not know, and nor did Raymond, what plans she might have already made. Krokowski had come with ferry tickets in his pocket, but I did not know if these were to have been a surprise for Kristina. Without arousing suspicion, and without giving anything away, I had somehow to determine the extent of Kristina's familiarity with Krokowski's plans.

Finally I got out of bed. I had a shock when I looked at myself in the bathroom mirror. My face was scratched down one side. In my rush through the undergrowth I must have caught a bramble. There it was: the un-expected clue, the indelible mistake. I scrutinised the broken skin like a plastic surgeon. The wounds were on the surface and would heal soon. I could contrive a cover story about slipping in my garden. Everyone knew my horticultural proclivities.

Now I had to set my house in order. By the light of day, I searched every room for further evidence of Krokowski's brief visit. He had been alone in the house. I had to check for give-away signs. A close inspection revealed another book, *Illuminations* by Walter Benjamin, a pack of playing cards, a tube of German toothpaste in the bathroom, and a couple of cassette tapes next to my CD player.

I threw everything away. There remained only Krokowski's rucksack, lying where I had left it last night in the corner of the kitchen. I picked it up and tipped the contents on to the table. There was a woolly hat, a map of the South-East, the Stasi file, some fruit, a bar of chocolate, and then finally the toy gun clattered on to the table. I pressed the trigger. Click. And again. Click. I was playing an adult version of the games children play, and I had survived. I ran my fingers over the scratch on my face. 'I slipped in the garden,' I said out loud. 'I slipped and fell into a bramble patch. Silly, isn't it?'

I put everything, but not the toy gun, back into the rucksack and concealed it in the cupboard under the stairs. As I performed this task, I understood why murderers got caught. There would always be one thing they could not let go of, a memento, or a photograph, or a letter. It was always a sentimental attachment that would trap them. I told myself I would not be like other men. I would throw the rucksack into the sea, or I would bury it in my garden, but first I had some serious evidence to destroy. At some point in the course of the day I had to drive my car with the black bags to the municipal dump, and I judged I would be wise to do that after dark. And then I had to speak to Kristina. I could not forever postpone that conversation.

I was getting late for work. I washed my hands again, applied sticking plaster to my cuts, and made my face presentable. I checked the house one more time, collected my briefcase, and went out to my car, the picture of a rural commuter. Further down the lane I could hear my neighbour manoeuvring his vehicle for the daily dash to the railway station. I considered my own car with a suspicious eye. There were traces of mud and chalk on the tyres but nothing more serious. Country cars are always dirty. The black bags with the evidence of the night's work were on the back seat, under a blanket, hardly visible to the passer-by. In the country, people use their cars for all sorts of transport. So I drove to work in a reasonably relaxed frame of mind, and made a point of collecting a takeaway cappuccino from the corner café as usual. I varied my schedule in only one way: I parked in the multi-storey car-park. At this delicate moment I did not want the complication of having my car stolen by joy-riders. It is the outside chance that one must fear. I have often observed that one should never confuse the impossible with the unexpected.

After lunch, a sandwich and a can of Diet Coke, I sat in my office and watched the light go down. We were approaching mid-December and the winter solstice was drawing near. It was dark by four and at five-ish I took a call from Raymond. I was pleased to find he was in a public telephone-box, as I had instructed.

'Everything okay?' His voice was edgy, as if he half-expected me to hand him over to the authorities.

'No problems,' I said. 'How are you doing?'

'I didn't sleep. I feel terrible. What happened, Julian?'

I ignored his question. 'You'll be fine,' I said, chiefly to convince myself. 'Take a sleeping pill and go to bed. How's Kristina?'

'I don't know where she is,' he said.

'Is that why you rang?' I was alarmed but I did not want Raymond to know it. 'Where are the children?'

'Downstairs,' he replied. 'Her car's gone.'

I said that there was probably a simple explanation, and rang off in a hurry. I left the office at once. I had to find Kristina, and find her quickly. I retrieved the car from the multi-storey car-park and drove as swiftly as I dared to the municipal dump. I passed another car on the way in, but otherwise the place was deserted. As I pulled up, a flock of scavenging seagulls stirred, and settled lazily near some smouldering rubbish further off. Smoke from several small fires drifted on a desolate wind. Moving quickly, not wanting to be observed, I opened the back door of the car. I took out the two black bags and hurled them into the darkness. Two bags of clothes without labels. A pair of bloody pliers. A carving knife. A mouthful of teeth. Two severed hands. In the event of discovery, it offered little to the investigator. I felt as secure about this as I could. It was the end of a life. It was nothing.

I drove away from the tip and found the nearest petrol station. There was a Christmas tree in the forecourt with electric decorations, and the proprietor had stencilled Seasons Greetings across the glass by the cash-desk. In my anxious state I was noticing everything, and watching everywhere for suspicious reactions. I took the vehicle through the automatic car-wash and felt cleansed. Then I filled the tank with premium unleaded and paid for the car-wash and the petrol in cash. I wanted to leave no evidence of my movements that day. Then I hurried on home.

My first thought, the moment I saw the lights shining through the trees, was the bizarre notion that Krokowski had risen from the dead and had come to haunt me. Then I guessed that it was Kristina. Perhaps she had already searched the place and found Krokowski's rucksack. I came in, hurried and breathless, and there was Kristina to meet me, smiling concern.

'What is the matter with you?'

'What do you mean?'

'You look as though you had seen a ghost.'

'I don't know what you are talking about,' I said, coldly. 'What are you doing here?'

'Something has happened to Walter,' she said. 'I know it.'

'I don't understand.'

'He was supposed to come, but he is not here. Something has happened.'

'When was he supposed to come?'

'In his letter he said he would be here in a few days. Now three weeks have passed, and still he is not here.'

'You could write to him,' I said.

I wanted her to experience my sympathy, but I did not try to put my arm around her. I knew she would rebuff that gesture. I sat next to her on the sofa that Krokowski himself had sat on, and with careful questions reassured myself that she knew nothing of his visit, nothing at all. As we talked, I thought of the mound of earth by the bushes on the bridleway to the Downs. If everything went according to plan, Krokowski would lie there for ever, undisturbed. I wondered how many millions of such bodies there were, lost in the earth, without a memorial. It was not such a bad fate. Most of us live ordinary, unremembered lives and those who are remembered often pay a high price for immortality. I have come to the conclusion that ordinariness is all. In my own life I have found that contentment and routine go hand in hand.

'What am I going to do?' Kristina's voice was low and defeated. 'He made me a promise.'

'A promise?'

'He would come, and then he would take me back to Berlin.'

'Of course he will come,' I said glibly. 'I am sure of it.'

'I know he will not. I cannot say why, but I know I will never see him again.'

She began to cry and there was nothing I could do or say to comfort her.

[9]

I do not believe in ghosts, but I have to confess that in the days after his killing I was haunted by Krokowski's presence in my house. He had stayed with me for only two nights and I had eradicated all traces of his visit, burying his rucksack in the bonfire at the bottom of my garden. Yet whenever I turned I sensed his shadow and whenever I heard a noise in another room I had to stop myself calling out his name.

Christmas was approaching. After Mother died, I would while away the season of good cheer in solitary, even melancholy, isolation. This year, with a family to share the holiday, I should have been looking forward to a Christmas get-together. There seemed small prospect of this now. I took myself to Evensong on Sunday and sang carols with a sad heart. In the porch I shook Findlater by the hand. 'Murder or suicide?' he asked. We chuckled together and I murmured something about old age. 'Ah, memento mori,' he replied.

I went shopping for presents – malt whisky and Monte Cristo cigars for Raymond, expensive toys for Olga and Sasha, lingerie and Chanel No. 5 for Kristina. I wrapped my purchases at home, tagging them 'with love', but I felt hollow inside. I accepted invitations to seasonal cocktail parties and whenever anyone asked me what I was doing for Christmas I'd reply, 'Oh, I'll be joining Raymond and the family at The Lodge. It should be fun.'

But I did not see Raymond, and I did not see Kristina. A day passed, and then another, and then a third. As the next week-end approached I began to fear for Raymond's state of mind. He and I were linked in crime. If, for any reason, he was apprehended, he would not withstand even the mildest interrogation. He would get life imprisonment and I would be utterly disgraced. I entertained a thousand dreadful scenarios. I was afraid that Raymond might become sufficiently depressed to make a confession. In my worst moments, I imagined him walking into a police station and giving himself up, or breaking down and telling Kristina the whole story.

On Friday, after a week of silence, I resolved to wait until morning and then pay an informal visit to find out what was going on. I sat in my front room, watching television and drinking. Once, at about ten o'clock, the phone rang. When I answered, there was no reply, and then the line went dead. Normally I would have thought little of such a trivial incident. Such things happen. In my nervous state, it turned my nerves another degree.

At nine o'clock on Saturday morning, I picked up the

telephone and rang Jericho Lodge. When there was no reply, I found that I was getting ready for the day with more alacrity than usual. I had to assume that my brother and his wife had set out early for their Saturday shop. If the house was empty, then so much the better. I would leave a note and hope that we could meet up during the week-end.

As I left the house I remember noting with satisfaction how bright and shiny the Volvo still looked in the winter sunshine. Its cleanness gave me confidence. Perhaps the worst was at last behind me. Outside the trees were bare and the sky was frosty grey. I was bundled up in my overcoat. Just before I left the house, and for no reason that I can think of now, I went back into the kitchen and took Krokowski's toy pistol out of the drawer where I'd hidden it. I stuck it in my coat pocket. I would do what he had intended and give it to Sasha.

In a few minutes I was turning into the driveway of Jericho Lodge, past the ominous cypress trees, crunching over the gravel by the sundial. There was no sign of my brother's Volkswagen, confirmation that he and Kristina had gone shopping, and I felt reassured by this sign of normality. I could leave a note, and depart. We could arrange to meet and talk later on. At least I would have made contact.

I knew that if they'd gone shopping the front door would be locked. I walked round the side of the house, peering into the kitchen window as I did so. There were plates and food on the table, as if someone had recently finished a meal. As I came round the back, I noticed that something was different. For a moment, I could not place it, and then I saw that the garage door was shut. In all the months that Raymond had lived at Jericho Lodge he had never closed this door. Kristina, indeed, had berated him for his casualness, but he had insisted on the safety of the countryside. As I went towards it the smell of exhaust fumes caught my senses and then I saw the gas seeping like an evil weed under the door of the garage.

I ran to the door. It appeared to be locked from the inside. I cannot remember if I called out. I put my ear to the keyhole. Inside, I could hear the distinctive sound of a Volkswagen engine purring in neutral. I tried the handle. It was locked. I pressed my eye to a crack in the wood. There was darkness within. My eyes began to water from the fumes. Then I did call out, and began to bang on the door. But there was no movement, only the relentless throb of the motor.

In the course of my coroner's duties I have visited such scenes on many occasions, but never in all these years have I been in the position of first-at-the-scene. I found it hard to remain calm.

I ran back to the house. The back door was, as I had expected, open. As I went in I called out in a panic. 'Raymond.' No answer. 'Kristina.' Silence. 'Olga, Sasha.' Not a word. 'Raymond' again. There was a deathly silence, and for a moment I dreaded what I might find in the house as well as the garage. I stood there. In the silence, I could hear the old Volkswagen throbbing behind me, like an ominous motorboat heard across a distance of dark water.

I told myself I had to deal with the garage. I knew the correct procedure for this. I went upstairs to look for a towel. I moved with caution. I did not know what I would find. Perhaps Raymond had killed his family. As I reached the landing I saw that what seemed like a burglary was, on closer inspection, a hasty departure. Clothes and toys were strewn everywhere. Cupboards and drawers gaped open. There was a trail of bags and suitcases. Coat-hangers and bits of dry-cleaning were scattered in the bedroom. There was the desolation of empty rooms.

I picked up a towel in the bathroom and soaked it in cold water, then I hurried back downstairs to the garage. The door was locked fast. I found a screwdriver and levered the door open, splintering the wood. The light flooded in. The Volkswagen's engine was still running and the garage was thick with fumes. I wrapped the towel round my head, like an Arab, covering nose and mouth, and went to the driver's door.

My brother lay as if he were asleep on the front seat. His face was cherry pink from inhaling the carbon monoxide, and he was wearing a suit. He might have been resting after a dinner party. There were photographs of Mother and Father, Kristina and the children, arrayed on the dashboard in front of him. I switched off the ignition and a great calm came to the garage. Then I hurried back into the sunlight and took gulps of cold winter air. Gradually, the fumes dispersed. I opened the doors of my brother's van to assist the process. Then I sat in my own car, staring into the middle distance.

My brother was dead. Amid the many conflicting thoughts that came to me then, there was one great realisation. Raymond had taken the truth about Walter Krokowski to the grave. I was free.

Then I cried, and I cannot say if these were tears of regret or shame or relief. Slowly, I recomposed myself. After several minutes, most of the gas in the garage had dispersed into the winter air. From where I sat there was no evidence of death, just a clapped-out Volkswagen parked in a family garage. Raymond's body, sprawled on the front seat, was hidden to the casual eye. That is the way with Death. He can be melodramatic, but generally he is discreet. I went back into the house and conducted a long, thorough search, trying not to disturb the evidence.

Kristina had gone. That much was clear. No doubt detective work in the future would locate her whereabouts, somewhere in Germany. At this point it was hard to tell if she had stormed out after an argument, or if Raymond had come home to find her missing. The remains of a solitary meal in the kitchen, an empty bottle of red wine and a bottle of vodka suggested that Raymond had spent his last hours alone. The portable phone was near to hand, and so was his address book. I guessed that it was he who had called last night, before hanging up. I could determine that without difficulty. The telephone company would have the call logged.

My chief concern, of course, was to discover if Raymond had left a note. His desk was an untidy heap of writing, some of it in German, but nothing that was, so far as I could determine, suggestive of Krokowski's visit. I put the German pages in my pocket with the toy gun. I decided that it was better to be safe than sorry.

Then I took a clean sheet from the laundry cupboard and went downstairs to the van. It was very still in the garage. The engine, cooling, was creaking in the cold. There was a faint tang of exhaust in the air, but nothing more than a hint. Raymond lay on the seat. I forced myself to rummage through his pockets. I found nothing. An autopsy would no doubt establish quantities of alcohol in his blood. I shook out the sheet and draped it over his body. I hoped he had died without too much pain. I stood there in silence for a moment. I wanted to say something, a prayer or a line of poetry, but the words would not come. Then I turned and went outside. It was time to hand the matter over to the authorities.

[10]

I was alone again. At times, in those days after my brother died, I experienced a loneliness that was actually comforting. I had explored the outside world, and had found only pain and loss and death. Now I knew instinctively where to take refuge. It was safer within. And yet, when I returned to myself, I found that something had changed. I could no longer simply immerse myself in the satisfying procedures of death. I was different. I was divided. I had felt the pulse of originality in my veins. I had discovered risk. I had participated in a terrible crime. The urge to tell someone about it was overpowering and it was only with the greatest difficulty that I resisted calling Susan in London.

I found myself doing things I had never done before. One evening I toasted my luck in vodka, called a minicab, and ordered the driver to Hove. I felt my heart explode with lust and power. I picked up a prostitute on the front. She was young and dirty. We had sex in a room smelling of Vaseline and talcum powder. I came home and washed in a hurry and when I saw myself in the bathroom mirror I saw the face of a stranger trapped between excitement and self-disgust. I finished the bottle of Stolichnaya and watched a James Bond film on television. It was Christmas Eve.

Throughout those days, in the run-up to the holiday, the scandal of my brother's death had rocked the village in a series of seismic tremors as more and more details of his death emerged. I did what I could to keep my counsel, saying with dignity that I could not discuss the case. I was the object of gloating sympathy and, in some quarters, disapproval. Mansfield had always been 'a nice quiet village' and I was blamed for upsetting what the village called the applecart. Derek, the newsagent, kept me up-to-date with successive waves of rumour, exaggeration piled upon exaggeration.

Everyone agreed that my brother was a spy, as they had always suspected. Kristina was a double-agent, of course. She had been recalled by her masters in Berlin, some said Moscow. At least one, perhaps two, suspicious Germans – according to others, Russians – had been sighted in The Royal Oak. Strangely enough, my connection to these mysterious agents, as it was reported by the regulars in the pub, was not considered significant, though their appearance in the village was generally held to be decisive. Informed opinion was agreed on one thing: Raymond had not committed suicide, he had been murdered.

Christmas Day came not a moment too soon. To my relief, no further work could be done on the Rowley-Whyte case until the New Year. Good Dr Stephenson and his wife came to my rescue, inviting me to Christmas dinner on the strict understanding that we should not talk shop. It was Dr Stephenson who had pronounced Raymond dead and supervised the removal of the body to the morgue.

Charles is a tall, athletic, much trusted figure in our little society and Alice, his bouncy, energetic wife, is a universal favourite. When I crossed their threshold and submitted to the family ritual of a kiss beneath the mistletoe, I felt as though I had stepped into an enchanted cave. There was warmth and light and laughter and good company. We pulled crackers, put on paper hats, and played charades. For a moment I remembered the high anticipation of Raymond's arrival, just over a year ago, and was sad. Charles saw that I was having a blue moment and made me perform 'Like A Virgin', to general merriment.

As I said goodbye, Alice took me aside. 'After the inquest's over, Julian, you should take a holiday. Go ski-ing.'

I smiled. 'The universal panacea.'

Susan had telephoned that morning to wish me Happy Christmas. She told me she was getting married. I would be getting an invitation shortly. I offered my congratulations, but I was empty inside. Susan heard my sadness and suggested I take a ski-ing holiday. When I protested that I could not ski, she said it was easy to learn. There were glamorous young women on hand to give lessons. I was not in the mood to talk. 'I'll call you in the New Year,' I said. 'After the inquest.' Susan offered to come down, 'for moral support', but that was the last thing I wanted. I was afraid what I might confess. I knew I had to go through the inquest on my own.

And so I did. As next-of-kin, I was obliged to hand the case to my deputy, Nigel Parker. He is my senior in years, a former policeman, as reliable as a car that starts in any weather, and devoid of imagination. As soon as my brother's death was reported and it was known that Parker would be the coroner of record, he made his loyalties clear, telling me on more than one occasion how sorry he was for me, but never uttering a word about the deceased. I knew that with careful briefing I could trust him to concentrate on the matter in front of him and not to play to the gallery with ill-founded speculation, as some coroners do when they have a case that is making a bit of a splash. The police had accumulated a certain amount of evidence, but, with luck, I hoped we would be able to conclude matters without fuss in the course of an afternoon.

Ever since Raymond's body had been taken to the morgue, the local constabulary had made creditable efforts to trace Kristina and the children. Her Mini had been found in Brighton, not far from the station. A ticket-inspector had volunteered that he had seen a woman of Kristina's description boarding the London train on Friday afternoon, but after that the trail went cold. There was a sighting of a tall blonde on the Dover-Calais ferry that I was inclined to discount. The German police were happy to assist but came up with little information. Kristina's few remaining relatives in Germany denied all knowledge of her whereabouts. The police did not press for facts. Kristina was, after all, not under any suspicion. I was forced to accept that she had simply disappeared. Since no one involved in the investigation knew that Krokowski had been coming to see her, no one made inquiries about any attempt she might have made to trace him in Berlin. That was my secret, and I did my best to pooh-pooh the stories about Russians and Germans in Mansfield. When I thought about Kristina I felt empty and depressed. In my darker, self-centred moods I even felt betrayed by her departure. Occasionally, I wondered what had happened to Jack, the dog, and imagined that he had been taken in somewhere as a stray.

Whatever the gossip said, the authorities – the police, the doctor, the pathologist – were agreed on one thing: my brother had committed suicide, asphyxiating himself in his car. There was no doubt that it was premeditated. He had taken good care to ensure that his plans would not fail. He had prepared himself for the deed by a session of heavy drinking.

And so, at the beginning of January, in the first session of the New Year, and barely a month since Krokowski's visit, I found myself in the unusual position of sitting in the public part of my coroner's court waiting to be called as the principal witness. The room was crowded. Raymond was, after all, quite a figure in his own right and the case had attracted local press attention.

I found it odd to stand in the witness-box and give evidence. Parker behaved as I hoped he would: going by the book, as if he had usurped my place and was himself in the spotlight. I painted a black picture of my brother's situation – the gambling debts, the difficulties of his marriage, the adjustment to a new and unfamiliar way of life, and the anxiety about his past.

'Would you say,' said my faithful deputy, 'that Mr Rowley-Whyte was under a lot of pressure?'

'I would.'

'Had he ever spoken of taking his own life?'

'When he was depressed, he spoke of his life as a mistake.'

'In your judgement, had he been depressed?'

'Lately, yes.'

A verdict of suicide while the balance of the mind was disturbed was reached in the space of two-and-a-half hours. Outside the courtroom, I expressed my 'profound sadness' to Harvey and the other local reporters, and drove home.

My statement was insincere. I left the inquest feeling light and easy. I was free to dispose of my brother's body. Once that was done I could restore the status quo, and this made me glad in a way that was hard to define. The New Year seemed replete with possibility.

I chose cremation. An anonymous, municipal ceremony appropriate, I thought, to the departure of a lifelong communist. About a week later, the ashes arrived in a copper-coloured, plastic urn, delivered to my house in a box, like a takeaway meal. I put my brother's remains on the kitchen table. I was expecting a visit from Mr Barker, the landlord of Jericho Lodge, and had other things on my mind.

Barker arrived on time, as glum and pernickety as I remembered. His gloomy manner was contradicted by a chestnut toupee and it was all I could do not to smile. We agreed to the termination of the lease and I produced the documents for his signature.

'Not a happy house,' he said, as he gathered up the papers. He looked at me oddly. 'People say the strangest things.'

'Local gossip,' I replied, lightly. I hoped he was referring to the fact that notoriety might depress the sale price. 'I'd advise you to retain a London agent,' I said. 'Vacant possession is always attractive. To a metropolitan family, the property will seem most desirable.'

'I suppose it could be a nice family house,' he said. 'My wife won't have children,' he added abruptly. 'Sometimes I wish she'd bugger off like . . . like whatshername.'

'Kristina.'

'Exactly.' He stood up. 'They say the market will pick up in the spring.'

'Things always improve in the spring,' I said.

'Vacant possession, eh?' He seemed encouraged, repeating his watchword two or three times. 'Vacant possession.' We shook hands and he left.

I went out into the garden for a breath of air. The sky

was lead-grey with the promise of snow. Already there were daffodil shoots peeping through the yellow grass. Next year I would plant daffodils on Krokowski's grave.

I went indoors again, pulled on my anorak and my walking boots, and collected Raymond's ashes from the kitchen table. As I coasted in the car down to the village the snow was coming down, hard and blinding, and beginning to settle.

I drove past the turn to Jericho Lodge. I will always avoid that road for as long as I live. I reached the foot of the Downs and parked the car by the signpost to the bridleway. In the half-light of dusk, the snow was like blossom on the branches and thickening underfoot by the minute.

When I reached the shallow mound among the bushes I hesitated for a moment, looking around like a man about to expose himself. I was alone. I tipped my brother's ashes over Krokowski's grave and watched the snow falling on to the grey dust and the rotting leaves with my usual detachment. A few moments later I was back in my car, listening to the radio, a concert on Radio Three. As I like to say, when asked about my work, life and death go on.

I still have Krokowski's toy gun. I have become quite attached to it. Occasionally, when country life seems unbearable, I speculate about getting a real one with real ammunition. I often think about Kristina. One day, perhaps, I will take a ride in the Channel Tunnel and go looking for her. For the moment, I have my work and my place in the village. On fine evenings, after work, I stroll in the cemetery and I'm planning to place a memorial plaque to my brother there, once things are a little quieter. I keep myself to myself perhaps rather more than I used to and I ignore the gossip. My routine has changed slightly. I avoid the village store and The Royal Oak now, and I shop in Brighton, where I can pass unrecognised. Like many of my neighbours, I have always preferred to lead an everyday sort of life.